HEADSHOTS ONLY

A ZOMBIE ANTHOLOGY

COMING SOON FROM OPEN CASKET PRESS

BIGFOOT TALES
ZOMBIE BUFFET
CREATURE FEATURE
DEAD CHRISTMAS
WARRIORS OF THE APOCALYPSE: BOOK 1

HEADSHOTS ONLY

ISBN Softcover ISBN 13: 978-1-61199-026-3 ISBN 10: 1-611990-26-2
All stories contained in this book have been published with permission from the authors All rights reserved.

Open Casket Press is an imprint of Living Dead Press. ww.livingdeadpress.com

For more info on obtaining additional copies of this book, contact:
www.opencasketpress.com

Cover art drawn by Chris Gevenois
Coloring by Doug Spencer

HEADSHOTS ONLY
A ZOMBIE ANTHOLOGY

EDITED BY
ANTHONY GIANGREGORIO

Table of Contents

REMAINS IN THE VEHICLE

REBECCA SNOW

"Are we there yet?" Dotty shouted from the confines of her safety seat.

The lights in her heels blinked every time she stomped her foot on the back of her brother's second row seat. Tom leaned forward and groped for the lever underneath him, but the bench sat as far forward as the rails would allow. Dotty kicked again.

Tom twisted sideways in his seatbelt to look his sister in the eye. He glared for a full twenty seconds before she stuck her tongue out and rolled her eyes. He tapped his mother's shoulder as she pulled a wad of cash from her purse.

"Yes, dear. We're here," Shelley Turner said from the front passenger seat to her three children. They were buckled in behind her as the minivan pulled off the highway and took the road leading to their destination. Her husband Doug was driving.

"Mom," Tom said. "Dotty's kicking me."

"Dotty leave your brother alone." She handed her husband some folded bills.

"I am not," Dotty said.

Shelley swiveled her neck and lowered her sunglasses so they perched like a hungry vulture on her nose. "If you kids don't behave, I'll have your father turn around and drive home. No safari park today and no dessert for a week."

At her words, the chaos transformed into the kind of silent stillness you only find in a sensory deprivation tank.

Shelley eased around to face the windshield and smiled. "Good," she said pushing her glasses back up to the bridge of her nose. "Now that you're quiet, I'll read the rules." She cleared her throat and squinted at the painted placard next to the razor wire topped entrance gate. "Rule number one. Keep windows and doors closed at all times. Rule number two. Do not exit your vehicle at any time." She turned the rearview mirror so she could see all three of her children. "Are we getting this?"

Tom and Dotty nodded. Jamie, the middle child, sat with his chin resting in his hand and stared through the glass at the steel-reinforced guard shack.

"Jamie?"

The boy slid a lazy gaze toward his mother.

"Are we clear?"

Jamie nodded before returning his attention to the Kevlar uniform adorning the armed sentry. His father skimmed a stack of papers before signing on the bottom line.

"What do they say?" Shelley asked, leering over his shoulder.

"Just standard stuff, I'm sure." He passed the clipboard back to the unsmiling man. "They're just trying to avoid lawsuits."

"Okay," Shelley continued. "Rule number three. Stay on the paved path at all times." She patted her husband's arm. "Rule number four. Do not feed the zombies." She wiggled her fingers at the man handing a map and change to Doug Turner. "Yoo-hoo." She tapped her manicured nails against the window ledge. "Officer."

"Yes, ma'am?" the man asked, his voice a deep growl. The guard rolled back on his heels and craned his neck to the side as she draped herself over her husband.

"Why can't we feed the zombies?" she asked.

Tom huffed in the back seat and dropped his forehead into the palm of his hand.

"Feed the zombies…feed the zombies," Dotty chanted.

"Ma'am," the man said. "Have you read the first two rules?"

"Yes, sir." She nodded up at him with a bright smile plastered on her painted lips.

"Can you tell me how you'd manage to feed them if you followed the first two rules?" He smiled back at her with a tight grin and a raised eyebrow.

She tilted her face to the sign and read the rules again to herself. Her mouth dropped open before she placed her fingertips over her mouth and squealed, "Oh! I'm such a ninny. How could I have missed that?"

"Happens to us all sometimes," the guard said as he flipped through the signed pages.

"Feed the zombies…feed the zombies," Dotty said.

"Not today," Shelley said.

The little girl let out an ear-piercing shriek. Doug cringed as he raised the window. The security officer shrugged and waved them through the first gate.

"Dotty, dear, they're not hungry today," Shelley told her youngest child. "I have an idea," she added, trying to quell the little girl's tooth-rattling cries. "Why don't we play 'I Spy?' I'll start." Her head flew from side to side as she searched for something to describe. "I spy with my little eye something that begins with the letter S."

"Stupid," Tom said. "I'm almost eighteen. Don't make me play."

"Sorry, Tom, you got it wrong. Guess I'll give another clue. I spy with my little eye, something black and white."

Tom looked at the back of his mother's head and sneered. The screeching from the far back seat simmered to a sniveling whimper.

"Is it the five miles per hour sign?" Jamie mumbled into the side of his palm and

Shelley clapped.

"One point for Jamie." She pointed to him with a lacquered red nail. "Your turn."

The car pulled through a second security fence. Jamie pressed his nose against the window, steaming a circle around his face. He wiped the condensation with his sleeve and peered into the dim woods. In the gloom, movement caught his eye

"Mom, do zombies avoid sunlight?" Jamie asked.

"No, dork. That's vampires." Tom snorted.

"No, I don't think so," Shelley said. "At least, they didn't when I was a girl." She flipped down the visor and opened the makeup mirror. "Go on, it's still your turn."

"I think I saw something move." Jamie strained his eyes to see into the darkness.

"I wanna feed 'em," Dotty hiccupped.

"Jamie, take your turn or your sister will blow a gasket," Shelley said. She ran a tube of blood-red lipstick over her mouth and smacked her lips together.

Jamie slouched against the dull, blue upholstery. "I spy with my little eye, something that begins with S."

"S-s-s-ky!" Dotty shouted.

"Shhh," Shelley said. "Use your inside voice."

"Sky," Dotty repeated in a forced whisper.

Jamie shook his head. "I spy something dark."

"Dark S," Doug mumbled. "Dark S. I don't see any sangria here." He nudged his wife with his elbow and threw her a wicked grin.

"Swerve!" Shelley yelled, grabbing the dashboard with both hands and pressing herself into her seat. "Doug!"

"Huh? How do you see a…" Doug looked back to the road as the car plunged into a huge pothole.

Dotty yelped as the back tires fell into the fissure and she bounced against her restraints. Her cry started low and grew into a high-pitched wail. She barked again as the car climbed out of the hole.

"Are we all okay?" Doug asked. His fingers squeezed the wheel as his tanned knuckles turned white.

"Just shut up and drive," Shelley said as her teeth scraped off the fresh lipstick.

"See what you made him do?" Tom punched his younger brother's arm.

Jamie tried to smack him back, but Tom caught the smaller boy's thin arm and squeezed. Jamie opened his mouth to shout, but Tom released his grip and jerked around to stare out the window.

Jamie rubbed his arm and returned his gaze to the passing scenery. Aside from the sniveling girl in the car seat, the minivan's occupants were silent.

"I thought we were going to see some dead guys," Tom said after five minutes had passed. "This place sucks."

"I saw something," Jamie gasped, pressing a finger to the window.

Tom unfastened his seatbelt and scrambled over his brother. "Where?" he asked as his eyes darted around the thinning treeline.

"Over there." Jamie pointed to a shadow bent over a writhing form.

"Cool," Tom breathed, his voice hushed in reverence. "I think it's feeding."

"Feed the zombies…feed the zombies," Dotty sang.

"I wonder what it's eating," Shelley mused. She lowered her sunglasses to get a better look. "Honey, can you drive closer, so we can see?"

"Anything for you, sweetcakes," Doug said with a smile.

He turned the wheel and drove over and through a few scraggly bushes. Branches scraped against the battered paint job and squealed down the metal sides of the vehicle. The feeding corpse ignored the rumbling engine.

"I think it's eating a deer," Tom said.

Shelley turned her phone sideways and snapped a few pictures of the gorging corpse.

"Can't be," his father said, lowering his window and pointing. "Those aren't hooves."

At the sound of the man's voice, the animated cadaver's head emerged from its meal.

"Look, it sees us," Shelley said. "You'd better roll up the window, dear."

Doug pressed a button on his armrest and the glass slowly rose as the creature took its first step toward the minivan. A strand of intestines unraveled from the creature's belly as the dead man shuffled closer.

"Feed the zombie…feed the zombie," Dotty cried.

"He's already eaten," Shelley said. "See?" She pointed at the bloody mess on the ground. "You don't want him to get sick, do you?"

"No sick zombies…no feed zombies." Dotty's bottom lip jutted like a diving platform above her chin. She shook her blonde curls.

The dead man pressed his decaying face against the driver's window and chewed the nub of its own black tongue.

"I wish we could hear the moaning better," Jamie said. "My teacher said it's a feeding call." He moved to a better position on his seat, sliding over a foot.

"We could if your mother had let me keep the window down."

"Oh, Doug. You don't want him to fall apart on the upholstery, do you?" Shelley threw back her head and laughed. "I've heard that rotting flesh is a killer to remove."

A line of dark blood trailed the dead man's ruined hand as it slid down the window.

"Dad?" Jamie asked. "What happened to all the zombies?"

"Well, son, they died." Doug shifted into reverse and returned the minivan to the paved road.

"But they can't die." Tom crawled over his brother and dropped onto the worn patch of velour Jamie had deserted. "They're already dead."

"Well, if you want the technical term, they were put down." Doug gestured to a legless woman pulling herself through a muddy ditch.

"Why didn't they put these ones down?" Jamie asked. He watched the pathetic dead woman's fingers sink into the dark brown goo.

"The brochure said they're studying them in a free range atmosphere to raise public awareness." Doug slowed down so he could pull the folded map from his shirt pocket, and ran his finger down a long paragraph. "It says here that they're the last of their kind and that the facility is providing a unique family experience by offering the opportunity of zombie encounters in a safe environment."

"So they didn't kill these disease ridden corpses because they're endangered?" Tom snorted a wry laugh. "The endangered dead…coming to a theater near you."

Doug tossed the map to Shelley and resumed their forward crawl.

"Find where we are," Doug said to his wife. "I don't want to get lost."

She shook open the map and trailed a long fingernail from the tiny drawing of the guard station along a neon green line to the edge of the forest.

"I think we're here," she said, perforating the paper with a forceful tap.

"Where's here?" Doug inched past a small water hole.

Three decomposing women waded from the shallows to pursue the rolling lunch box full of fresh meat.

"We're next to this pond, right here." She held the map sideways for her husband to see. "Let's head to the swarming barn next."

As the trio of dead bodies neared, Shelley pushed the unfolded map down to the floorboards and lifted her cell phone.

"Oh, they look like sisters." She pressed a few buttons and zoomed in on the stumbling action. "Adorable."

A thump on the back window made them all jump. A lumbering hulk of a man pummeled the glass with his shredded hands. A fractured bone protruding from his finger clicked on the glass with each strike. Doug pressed the accelerator. The minivan sputtered before picking up speed and leaving the four cadavers in its eight mile an hour dust.

As the vehicle rounded a bend in the road, an enormous wooden barn loomed behind a broken rail fence. Remnants of red paint flaked from the plank walls.

"Some swarm," Tom said. The minivan crept up on the tranquil scene. It clattered over a rumble strip, and the barn door opened on creaking hinges that hadn't seen a drop of oil in years. Corpses poured into the sunlight and careened across a trampled dirt path toward the vacationing family.

"Here they come," Doug said in a Christmas morning voice. He pounded his palms on the steering wheel and squealed like a hungry piglet. "This is so exciting! Just like being a kid again."

His wife grabbed his hand and squeezed as she watched the horde surging toward the vehicle. "Pictures, Shel," the delighted man said as the first putrid face collided with the closed window. "Pictures!"

Shelley lifted her cell phone and framed a shot of a dead woman's empty eye socket. As she continued her photo shoot, the minivan's interior darkened. The automatic flash flickered as the walking dead blocked out the sun.

Dotty thrashed at her bindings and screamed.

"Don't worry, dear. We're safe," Shelley said as she aimed for the opposite window. "They're only zombies."

"Your pictures are gonna suck," Tom said. He ripped the phone from his mother's hand and tapped the digital screen.

A scowl grew on Doug's face. "Tom, that's no way to talk to your mother."

Climbing over the bodies, a lanky dead boy pounced onto the minivan's squat hood. The pop of bent metal reverberated through the interior. As the zombie stared through the windshield, it tilted its head to the side. Skin flaps swayed around the hole where a nose had been. Dotty blubbered from the backseat.

"All you would have gotten was a big white blob of reflection." Tom shoved the camera over his mother's shoulder. "I turned off the flash."

The zombie on the hood placed a maggot-infested palm directly on the glass and held it there. Instead of pounding like the others, it petted the glass as if handling a stray kitten. Dotty gulped quick sobs and slobbered lines of drool down the front of her jumper.

"What's wrong with him, Mom?" Jamie asked, as he leaned between the two front seats.

"I don't know, dear, but he's nothing like the ones I remember when I was little," she said, clicking another shot. "All they did was hammer on things until they got inside or got killed trying."

The creature on the hood placed the nub of a missing finger against its decayed lips. Several grinning teeth flashed through a hole in its cheek. Dotty screeched and trembled. Tears flowed in rivulets down her cheeks. The staring figure swayed as the minivan began to rock.

"Time to go," Doug said.

He gunned the engine and shifted into drive. The surrounding dead didn't move. Doug switched on the wipers and smacked the rotting hand from the glass. The corpse crawled in front of him and smacked the barrier between them. Its remaining facial muscles attempted a scowl. One bald eyebrow lowered. Dotty howled louder.

Lifting his head to see all angles in the rearview mirror, Doug yanked the lever into reverse and stomped on the gas pedal. The minivan lurched and bucked and the abominable hood ornament slid backwards into the mass of walking dead and disappeared under their shuffling feet. Two bodies remained immobile after the dead parade had passed, their heads crushed like pumpkins fallen off a truck.

"I hope we don't have to pay for that," Doug said, cranking the wheel.

Dotty's weeping slowed as the van wound around the clump of decomposing pursuers and continued at a snail's pace. One by one, the zombies fell back and returned to the barn.

"I wonder how they keep them in there," Jamie said. He craned his neck to watch the barn disappear behind a stand of trees.

"They probably keep some live kid in a cage," Tom said in his best villain voice. "Maybe I'll volunteer you."

They traveled in relative silence as they passed a line of burnt-out bungalows. Dotty's breathing slowed and her head lolled to the side, as she began to spout short, wheezing snores.

When the minivan reached a crumbling outbuilding under a sprawling oak tree, Shelley said, "Stop the car, Doug. Stop."

Doug pressed the brake pedal. The countryside was still.

"Kids, go stand next to the front door of that building and I'll take your picture." She rolled down her window and draped an elbow over the sill. "It's the perfect spot, and the light is phenomenal."

"Mom," Jamie said. "We're not supposed to get out of the car."

"Rules are for fools." Shelley surveyed the area. The shambling forms in the distance were not an immediate threat. "It won't take a second."

"But Dotty is sleeping," Jamie whispered.

"Well, I guess I'll get a picture of my two handsome boys then."

"What are you, chicken?" Tom wrenched open the door and ran toward the painted door, the once bright red color now faded and peeling.

"Do I have to?" Jamie asked.

Shelley spun in her seat, a frown drawing wrinkles on her forehead. "Yes. Now, go."

Jamie stretched his head through the minivan's doorway and scanned the overgrown lawn. It seemed clear enough. He tested the ground with the toe of a shoe, as if testing the water for the first summer swim. His arms pumped as he ran after Tom. Tripping over a clump of dirt, he sailed across the tall lawn, leaving a landing strip behind him.

"Way to go loser," Tom said while he slapped his knee and doubled over laughing.

Grass stains streaked the front of Jamie's white t-shirt. A few small pebbles stung where they'd lodged in his palms and his scraped chin dripped a bright splash of blood onto his already ruined clothes.

"Shut up, Tom," he said.

"Make me." Tom put his arm around his brother and sneered at the camera.

They froze for a full minute as their mother captured every nuance of the fading light.

"All done," she said. "I think I got some good shots. We can send them to the relatives."

Tom punched Jamie in the stomach and ran around the weathered building. Holding his midsection, Jamie trotted after him.

"Stop fooling around and get back in the car!" Doug yelled. "I don't want to get locked in here after closing!"

Reemerging from the same side of the building where he'd disappeared, Jamie sprinted for the minivan, his face covered in terror. His screams went up and down in pitch with every stride he took. Tom reappeared, favoring his right leg, as, he too, ran toward the vehicle.

Behind both boys, a herd of frenzied zombies rounded the corner, only a few steps behind Tom and closing fast.

"Come on, Tom, run!" Jamie called through the open door, waving his brother on as if the motion would give Tom an edge over his attackers. "Hurry!"

When Tom reached the minivan, he fell to the carpeted floorboard. Jamie slammed the door and pressed the lock button with his finger. Tom rolled onto his back. A stale French fry was stuck to his cheek. Plucking it from his face, he flicked it under the seat.

"What happened?" Shelley asked as she locked her own door.

Tom's chest heaved as he tried to catch his breath. "I was running," he gasped. "And...my leg...fell through...a hole covered with rotting wood, I think it was an old well." He rested a hand on his stomach. "When I got up, those things…were coming after me. They tried to grab me, bite me, but I got away."

"Are you hurt?" Shelley asked. She placed a hand on his clammy forehead and smoothed the hair out of his eyes.

Tom brushed her away and shrugged. "Naw, Mom, I think it's just a sprain." He wrapped his fingers around his ankle.

"I've got some rocks stuck in my hand," Jamie said. His bruised palm throbbed.

Dotty grunted and fussed in her sleep.

"I think I've seen enough zombies for one day, thank you," Doug said. The engine whined as they pulled away from the gathering crowd. "Ready to go, everyone?"

"Feed zombies," Dotty muttered in a dream.

Jamie nodded and Tom climbed onto his own side of the bench seat. Flopping back on the headrest, he stared at the sagging fabric ceiling. Perspiration erupted across his nose and cheeks. His flushed face burned with fever. He scratched his sprained ankle without glancing down at the torn, droopy sock against his leg. A speck of bright red bloomed like a rosebud across the white cotton weave. The minivan bounced over a speed bump and Dotty stirred. Her mouth gaped in a wide yawn as her arms stretched and quivered. "Thirsty," she slurred.

"We'll get you some juice from the cooler when we get outside the gate," Shelley said. "Hang tight, dear."

"Jamie," Doug said. "What was that dark S word you'd spied?"

The boy tilted his head and squinted at his father's bald spot.

"Shadow," Jamie said with a snap of his fingers.

The hairless patch nodded.

"Good one," Doug replied. "I never would have guessed."

Shelley patted her helmet of motionless hair as she eyed herself in the visor's flip down mirror. "It's still your turn, Jamie." She wiped a smear of lipstick from her teeth before she slapped the sunshade closed. "Pick another word to distract your sister."

Staring through the windshield at the barbed wire that bobbed as the gate opened, Jamie chewed his ragged thumbnail. Tom squeezed his eyes closed and clenched his fists, his fingernails digging into his fleshy palms.

His body flinched once and then relaxed. A line of saliva dribbled down his chin. The chain links jingled as they trapped the minivan between the inner and the outer exit doors. A bell clanged as the solid metal panel slid away and allowed them back into the uninfected world.

"I…spy…with…my…little…eye," Jamie said, glimpsing a tooth mark through the tear in Tom's bloody sock. "Something that begins with Z."

GUARDING THE CEMETERY

ALAN SPENCER

"Why take the job, Gary? It's dangerous. And aren't you scared? The steady work isn't worth risking your ass, is it? Maybe you're not smart enough to know what's best for you. I guess your father's not around to set you straight anymore, so I will. What do you really get out of it, Gary? Fulfillment? I don't think so. I mean, don't you feel wrong for guarding a cemetery forty hours a week?"

Gary Whitehead walked the plush green stretch of Golden Acres Cemetery with only his thoughts to entertain himself while on the clock. His thoughts, and of course, the hum of electricity running through the iron bars of the perimeter.

The crackle.

The pop.

The hum.

The promise of damage.

No corpse would escape the cemetery without frying itself first. He'd seen dead men crawl up from the dirt, and once topside, they would stagger straight for the nearest fence.

He remembered one in particular that had clutched the bars and poised itself to jump the fence. Sparks shot so high once skin met iron. Flesh to flesh. Juice to juice. Burning decay filled the air; the worst kind of death scent—the kind that would send the hungriest flies to some other place. The body had been launched backwards after a healthy dose of shock treatment; every inch of the poor bastard aflame.

After burning a full minute, the coffin garb became diminishing cinders floating high in the air. The flesh soon followed, smoldering to the bone, until it was a blackened and lifeless husk.

Dead for good.

He'd still put a bullet through its head with his .38 Clarke pistol that day, just as a precaution. He'd pressed the cold steel barrel up to its skull and let a slug tear through that crispy skull and out its crunchy face.

Roger Proctor, the funeral director—his boss—did everything to warn him from taking the job during the interview: *"This job's not for the faint hearted. The faint stomached. The faint of anything, Gary. Catching my drift? It's as hot out there as a jailed Tijuana whore's ass crack, and she'd be happy to trade places with you. You've got some trees for shade, sure. Can't give you much else; County says the fences are costing them up their butts in electricity. You're simply a clean-up guy—a glorified security guard. I know you've made a small career out of being a security guard at other joints, but do you really want to do this? No one will thank you at the end of the day. They probably didn't thank you at your other jobs, but you know what I mean...*

"And I know you're not as prolific in the brains as your brother. I knew you since you were fifteen. You wrecked that motorcycle you stole from your poor neighbor, that old man who used to be a daredevil, except he broke his back doing one of those jumps off a gorge and retired early. You don't have the best judgment is what I'm saying. I know you've been laid off from that cannery a while back—and man, talk about a shitty job. And I see how you didn't graduate high school on your application. It's hard to get anything over ten dollars an hour, but shit, Gary; you're not that stupid to take this job. I knew your father, and I know what he'd be thinking of this choice you're making. But hey, I need employees, so if you want the job, I'll give it to you...maybe you are dumb enough to pit yourself alone against those disease carrying bags of shit. By that stupe-

fied look you're giving me, I guess you are. Well, shake my hand, 'cause you're hired!"

Dr. Procter viewed Gary like the rest of the people in the town of Mill Brook, Kansas. He was a man with an I.Q. a spit's shot shy of retarded. The apple that fell the farthest from the tree despite having a father who owned his own law firm, made six figures in the big city, and could have any woman in bed and often did. Gary was the family letdown. The burden. The idiot who couldn't take care of himself.

His brother Joseph, the brilliant tax attorney his father called him 'golden boy,' had a few words of wisdom for him when he found out about the job.

"Why take a job like this? Think about it. Shitty pay. Shittier hours. Barely any benefits. I know you like to work by yourself and everything, but Gary, you're risking getting bit by one of those things. You might as well punch out for good then. I heard about one of those guards like you getting bit. He rotted while he was alive. A slow death. He melted like a candle to the wick. He was only bones when they found him in his trailer out in the country, and that was after he'd shot his own head off. Fucker rotted until he was a peach-colored puddle stuck in the carpet fibers. We've all seen pictures of it on the Internet. Or do you look at too much porn to enjoy the other conveniences of the information superhighway, eh, little brother?"

But Gary was so down and out for money he'd had no choice but to take the cemetery job. He was an ex-con. He'd botched a robbery attempt four years back when he was thirty-five. Robbed a 'Go Mart' with a brown paper bag over his head with holes cut out for eyes and a mean looking double barreled shotgun in his hands. When he'd gotten out, getting decent work was impossible, and he'd done the worst of the worst of jobs to scrape by. And once he was on Golden Acres Cemetery's payroll long enough, he would be fine.

Besides, he loved the job a lot.

But he wouldn't tell anyone why.

They wouldn't understand, and he knew it, too.

Besides, he was on five years parole; he had to keep a job to avoid his parole officer's scrutiny and a possible return visit to prison. This was working out real fine for him.

"Pour concrete like you did way back when," his brother had reasoned with him. "Stand in line at the Labor Ready agency like the other drifters, but the cemetery job, I can't support that. I know you hold it against me that I'm a tax attorney and I'm making good money and Dad loved me more and everything, but come on. Even Dad wouldn't support your decision to do this. I know he's not around to give you money anymore but that's no excuse."

But Gary couldn't take the highway construction job that had recently become available. He'd gotten into a fight with the company's owner a month after he'd been paroled over a pay discrepancy. Clarke Jenkins thought he was too stupid to read over his pay stub and notice too much was being taken out; it was in fact the owner of the boardinghouse he stayed at, a June Merriman, who pointed it out to him.

"You may be stupid, Gary, but you can read, so look at what I'm showing you! You're being docked pay for no reason. Your boss is nothing but a no good shyster."

Gary had landed two good hooks to Clarke's face and the snide bastard went down spitting out blood from both his nostrils and mouth. It took his brother bailing him out of jail and pulling a favor to get his attorney—the one paid by his brother—to pull some strings to keep him out of jail.

* * *

Gary looked up, realizing he'd lost himself in his thoughts again. Finally coming back to reality, he focused on the job of walking the cemetery grounds.

He checked the time; it was eleven thirty in the morning.

Lunch time.

He approached the break station. It was simply a block carved out of the back marble wall of the Parker Mausoleum. It had a lock and he had the key. Unlocking it, he opened a medicine cabinet sized square that was refrigerated. He removed his lunch: a wrapped turkey and Swiss sandwich with extra mayo, a bag of Lay's chips, and a bottle of Coke. He ate it all quickly, being hungry six hours into an eighteen hour stretch. It would be morning before his shift ended and Arnie Zuckerman replaced him.

With his stomach full, he returned to work. He was dressed in a white collared shirt, beige pants, and black boots. He wore a black leather holster holding his .38 pistol. Hanging on his other hip was a long wooden rod with a razor sharp metal tip. If the dead reached out from the earth, he'd give them a good poke.

Sometimes the tactic worked and they'd crawl back into the ground. Other times, he'd have to wait for the body to work itself free completely before he could shoot it in the head. After that, a crew would dig up the coffin, repair the plot, and re-bury the body.

State law prohibited the dead from being dug up and put down for good before they escaped on their own volition. It was a human rights issue, and the government fought tooth and nail to come up with a good solution to the rising dead problem.

All cemeteries were now required to have metal bar perimeters hooked up to electricity, and people like himself at the ready, to dispatch them if necessary. It was the most humane way of going about it, and Gary agreed.

The dead crawled out of their graves for no apparent reason. The first case occurred during a funeral in Idaho. Four people were bitten, and they were sent to the hospital only to be dismissed home after their wounds were treated. Overnight, they were found as puddles in their beds, having melted from a flesh-eating disease. Panic broke out and this is what had come of it.

Here he was getting lost in his head again, thinking.

"Damn it, you have to focus," he derided himself. "You're at work."

Thoughts. They were all he had, being alone during this gig, and he couldn't help but get caught up in them. The time was swallowed up by the consternation of voices from the people who constantly berated him.

How could they understand a man who was okay with walking the cemetery grounds for eighteen hour shifts alone with dead people shifting beneath his feet?

What could such a man get out of it?

Only Gary knew.

Barry Levinson, one of those mean voices in his head, was his parole officer, and he'd given his two cents about Gary's occupation: *"I knew your father, Gary. He was a good man. A hard worker. Money and success didn't slow that man down at all, and by the way things are going, it sounds like you never sped up, son. Some people are born with reason, judgment and the skills to be successful, and you're not one of them, I'm afraid to say. I deal with your kind of people all the time. I call them no-brainers. No-brainers take what job they can and leave it at that. Whatever it pays, it pays. As long as they can drink a bottle of cheap something or other at the end of the day, who cares? It's a no-brainer. But taking this job is a mistake, son. You'll quit it one of these days."*

His brother chimed in again soon after his parole officer was gone, *"How's Wynona? Yeah, the one you met at the titty bar. The one you thought wanted to date you, but she asked for money after you gave her the business in the backseat of your car. You should get a blood test. Condoms break, man. I see why Dad worried about you so much. Don't expect me to coddle you like he did. At least you've kept that job, even if it's at that goddamn cemetery..."*

Gary stopped in his tracks. He was walking along a row of marble headstones. He caught the faintest shift in the grass ahead of him. A square of grass would bulge, as if bubbling up, and then it would stay motionless. They could detect his footsteps, he'd learned, and this corpse was no different. It looked like the escape-attempter was a Mrs. Velma Johanson.

He gave the raised section of turf a good poke with his sharp stick.

"Stay where you belong, Mrs. Johanson."

Gary left the spot after several minutes and made a point of walking right back to the grave, and of course, what he found was no surprise. Two graying, bone weathered fingers had poked out of the turf.

She didn't heed his warning… they never did.

With a snarl forming on his lips, he slapped the sharp stick over those fingers until he'd split the middle one in two halves, the white bone of the knuckle exposed.

The hand shirked from the attack like a worm slipping back into the wet ground.

"Stick your head up, you old bitch. You just try it!"

Mrs. Johanson had been his first grade teacher. She'd caught him stealing the dessert items from the lunch boxes in the coat room. He had a Hostess cupcake half shoved in his mouth when she'd slapped the back of his head.

"You spit that out, young man, you derelict idiot! I'd tell your father, but he'd make excuses for you. I say there's nothing wrong with your brain. It's your morality. Kids either want to be good or they want to be bad, and you, Mr. Whiteford, want to be bad."

He was sent to the principal's office and his father was called in. The man talked to the principal and got him out of trouble. Easy fix. Talk of sending him to a special school was squelched by his father who didn't want Gary to feel alienated. He wasn't mentally retarded, just not as quick to learn as the others, his father insisted.

Gary moved on from the grave; Velma wasn't coming back up—for tonight at least.

He checked his pedometer strapped to his ankle. He'd walked twelve miles today. He was lean. No pot belly. Tight muscled, he was ripped from the push-ups and sit-ups he did at the public park behind Regency Hospital. He had nothing else to do during his off hours. No real friends or lady friends. He'd go to the movies and see every flick on the bill except for the romantic ones.

"Why do you guard that cemetery?" a clerk at the 'Burger Boy' asked him weeks ago, after looking over Gary's uniform. *"Isn't it scary? Did the state make you?"*

"No," he'd told the pimply faced geek. *"I work there on my own free will. Mind your own business."*

The clerk gave him an eyeful. *"But, but why?"*

He didn't bother answering the question. The guy wouldn't understand.

Crossing through the mausoleums, Gary unlocked the slot on the back wall and enjoyed a hearty gulp of water. After eating a candy bar, he continued his rounds. It would be dark soon, and he'd have to use a flashlight to see. His eyes would ache in their sockets. He got the worst headaches during this part of the job. Blaring migraines. Dr. Summers had prescribed medication for the pain.

The doctor told him: *"You're an able-bodied man. You can work anywhere. You shouldn't be in a place that damages your health. Stress can kill you as easily as too much alcohol or smoking. Why put yourself through the pain? Take the easy way out. Quit the cemetery job."*

The sun went down over the horizon, going out in a blaze of glory before the bright purple sky turned into the deepest black. There were no buildings or lights for miles.

His brother cringed when Gary described his work during the night. The darkness. The constant watching of his back. The headaches.

Joseph's reaction was, *"Listen to me, Gary, I can get you a job working construction again. Stop doing that shit work. There's another construction company, and I'm good friends with the owner. Give it a shot. Get out of the cemetery business. No? You won't? And you won't tell me why? Okay, well how about this: why don't you pull your head out of your ass? I've helped you every step of your life. I'm tired of it. Aren't you supposed to take care of me, too? I know brothers who get along famously. I guess we'll never have that, huh? I guess when your brother's half retarded, it's hard to be equals. I give up. You're on your own. But I can't give up on you! I made a promise to Dad on his deathbed. When his lung cancer was real bad, he made me promise him that I'd take care of you. I should've acted like I didn't understand him. Now he's gone and I'm stuck here with your stupid ass. Mom doesn't even bother with you after you waved that gun around in that gas station like a crazy man and got yourself arrested. You wanna keep that stupid fucking job, it's your misfortune, you're an idiot!"*

The shadows would play tricks on his eyes during his patrol. He thought the moving shadows were fingers coming up from the ground. He rubbed at his eyes so much during his shift to rid his vision of the mirages that he had to smear Vaseline onto his eye-lids, they were so raw.

The wind also played tricks on him. It sounded like the grumble of a corpse who'd just escaped the ground as it wafted through the trees. Like air escaping deflated lungs; gases popping in the body that sounded like fetid burps.

On especially boring nights, he'd fire the gun into the air. It was like a set of two-by-fours clapping together, but it would echo for a full minute before dissipating.

Sometimes, he sensed the ground shift after firing a shot; hands retracting from the surface of the ground, bodies halfway to the surface returning back to their graves.

Warning shots had that kind of power over the dead.

With nothing better to do, he decided it was a good time to visit his father's grave. Glenn Whitehead's plot was just up ahead.

Gary stood in front of it, knowing his father cared about him. The man understood his rages; his mental shortcomings.

"Your mind isn't like everyone else's, Gary. It's wired differently, only slightly off. You're not retarded, son. It's not your fault. But they don't understand you, because they don't have a son or daughter who suffers what you're going through. No one's empathetic. That's why you need to find happiness on your own. Your life will be hard, son, but you have to enjoy what you can. Don't stop trying."

While on his deathbed, his father was more outspoken in private company:

"I know you buy hookers, Gary—well, keep doing it! Let them fuck you ten ways to Sunday. Get a team of them to service you. Drink until you piss barley hops. When you're in my position and about to die, you'll see the need to really live life. Life's too short to be bogged down with bullshit. Find what makes you happy, and keep doing it, son."

Then the man turned serious. *"Remember, death is the great equalizer. At some point in time, we're all in the same shit together. One person's not better than the other when we're all dead."*

Gary used to cry when standing in front of his father's grave. Now he was happy to be here.

He returned to the Parker Mausoleum and retrieved another Coke from the wall slot. The fizz burned on the way down. He wanted booze, but to be impaired on the job was asking to be bitten. Ray Felter, an old co-worker, had been bit on the ankle. A head had popped out of the dirt like a groundhog and had taken a chunk from his ankle. The man didn't tell anyone.

He was found the next day in his car in an empty parking lot, nothing but a skeleton sitting in the front seat. The rest of him: skin, guts, and muscle tissue, had all dripped down the seat and filled the floorboard with the ripest, ungodly stink anyone had ever smelled.

That wouldn't be him, Gary vowed, because he was in charge here. He was the smartest of them on the property. The one with his shit together. It didn't matter that he'd been incarcerated. That his motor neurons weren't firing at their optimum potential. None of it mattered here...among the dead.

Feeling a sense of empowerment overtake him, he advanced deeper into the Whitehead plot. Uncles, aunts, cousins, and distant relatives were each buried here along this stretch. He came here every shift numerous times to check on his family.

He scanned his flashlight and stopped on Joseph Whitehead's tombstone. His brother had died only two months ago in a terrible car accident. On the interstate, a semi-truck driver hadn't checked his blind spot and had smashed Joseph into the median. Despite the damage, what had killed him was a brain hemorrhage; the rest of him was fairly unharmed.

The ground before his brother's marker was still. Joseph wasn't trying to escape tonight, but Gary would check it every shift.

Death was the great equalizer, as his father had said. And here he was waiting for each and every asshole that had ever crossed him to pop up out of the ground. He'd blow out their brains with his .38.

Death was the equalizer.

He was the equalizer.

It was the ultimate perk of the job.

He unholstered his .38, checked the chamber for bullets, then spun it in his hand like a gunslinger.

Holstering his gun, and about to continue his rounds, he said, "I know you're down there, brother. Come on up when you feel like it. The same invitation goes for the rest of you assholes. One by one, I'll blow all of your fucking heads off!"

D. N. R.

ADAM P. LEWIS

 The kitchen lights dimmed, followed by a chorus of loud and off key singing, *"Happy birthday to you, happy birthday dear Jamie, happy birthday to you!"*

Flickering candlelight lit up the kitchen. Jamie sat at the head of the kitchen table, smiling ear to ear as her friends cheered and clapped. A large cake trimmed with hard yellow and red alternating sugar flowers, and blue cursive writing reading *Happy Birthday Jamie* was placed before the birthday girl.

Over the merriment, Jamie's friend Anna yelled, "Make a wish, Jamie! I hope it comes true. You deserve it!"

Without hesitation, or thinking up a quirky wish for millions of dollars or a new sports car, Jamie closed her eyes, took a deep breath, and blew out all the birthday candles in one deep breath. When she opened her eyes, the top of each candle plumed a thin gray trail of smoke.

How childish, Jamie thought as she opened her eyes. *Birthday wishes are just that, ideas and thoughts never to come true.* She sighed. *This is one that won't.*

Later, hours after the final guest had left the house, Jamie cleaned up the empty wine bottles, glasses, plastic forks and dirty paper plates. She tied up the draw strings on the garbage bag and took it out to the garage. After turning on the dishwasher, she stretched, yawned and got ready for bed.

When she climbed into bed, she pulled the covers up to her chin and smiled. After three years she'd finally started feeling good about her life for a change. It wasn't often that her birthday was made more important than the following day, Christmas. She was born thirty-one years ago on Christmas Eve.

When she was younger, her parents made a point to separate her birthday from Christmas. But as she grew older, her birthday and Christmas fused together in one celebration. She received combined birthday and Christmas gifts and watched as her family opened gifts while they smiled legitimately or faked them at the sight of their presents. They forgot what and who they were truly celebrating.

On this birthday the presents she received, the cake, and enjoying the company of her friends, was just what she needed. She didn't cry herself to sleep as she'd done every night for the past three years. She fell asleep with a smile on her face. As her eyelids fluttered, she looked at the framed photograph of her husband, Mike, on the nightstand and drifted off to sleep.

She dreamt of Mike returning home from work. She could see his grinning face and his blue eyes—full of love—staring at her through the screen door. She could even feel the way his body felt against hers as he hugged her and said hello through a kiss, warm and secure with a feeling of relaxation and joy.

He never talked about his day nor did he complain about work or traffic. Even in her dream, he asked her how her day was and if there was laundry, dishes, or any other house chore that needed to be done. She could even smell his musky cologne and the fabric softener used on his clothes. But then her dream went from a happy greeting to the hospital where her husband lay dead.

Mike grew up taking Digoxin and other medications that staved off complications from his enlarged heart. They weren't enough. Three weeks before Labor Day, he suffered a massive heart attack. The paramedics did nothing to revive him after his heart stopped; he had filed a 'Do Not Resuscitate' form years earlier. He always said he was going to void the form because Jamie was worth taking medication daily, the risk of open heart surgery and potential transplants. He even joked he'd get a pig's heart to stay alive for her.

But something as simple as voiding a form was put off. He'd say things like, "I'll do it tomorrow," or "I'll be fine for another day." But he wasn't. His last minutes were spent staring at the ceiling of an ambulance before his vision slowly faded to darkness. He was dead on arrival.

A loud thud on the front door woke Jamie from her dream. She lifted her head and cocked it slightly like a confused dog. She didn't know where the noise came from and figured it to be the strong winds from a Nor'easter sweeping through the Adirondack region.

She laid her head back on her pillow and closed her eyes, wanting to return to her dream. Then she opened them upon hearing a thud again. It wasn't snowing nor was there any wind outside this night. The forecast called for low temperatures only.

It's only the dishes in the washer settling, she thought.

Minutes later, she heard yet another loud thud. She couldn't tell if it was the dishwasher or not. She didn't hear a clank or a rattle, she'd heard a bang, and it sounded more like it was coming from the front door.

She reached for the lamp on her nightstand and turned it on, then got out of bed, pulled on her bathrobe, and slowly walked down the hall to the front door.

As she approached the door, she froze at the sound of three more thuds. They were hard bangs roughly three seconds apart. This time she definitely knew it wasn't the wind or the dishwasher. It was someone at the front door. Keeping her bathrobe closed tightly in her shaking hands, she stopped a few feet from the door. Ever since Mike had died, she'd been wary of visitors during late hours.

"Who's there?" she called in a shaky voice.

There was no answer.

"Who is it?" she asked again louder.

There was still no response.

Jamie breathed deep and turned and headed back to her bedroom, now frightened. She considered calling the police but felt she was being overdramatic. It was probably just the screen door, it had popped open from an errant breeze.

It was well after midnight and the streets were empty. Soon it would be Christmas morning and she'd be at her mother's house, in the kitchen helping make pumpkin pie and preparing the turkey dinner. She figured that if she ignored the noise it would eventually go away. It was a tactic she'd used when she heard her car making noises. It had worked then so maybe it would work now.

Two steps down the hallway, three more loud thuds smacked against the door. Jamie turned and faced it, knowing it wasn't the screen door. She crept towards it and pushed up on her tiptoes. Closing one eye, she peered through the peephole with the other. Through the fisheye view she saw a man standing on her porch. His back was turned from the door and the neighbor's Christmas lights were blinking behind him.

"Can I help you?" Jamie called through the door.

The man didn't answer. He slowly turned around and slammed an open palm against the painted wood. The bang scared Jamie, causing her to jump away from the door. Her hands folded over each other atop her breasts. Her heart pounded and her chest heaved while she breathed deep and hard.

From the other side of the door, she heard a low moaning voice grumble slowly, "D…N…R." Though the voice wasn't garbled, she recognized it immediately.

"It can't be," she whispered, her lower lip quivering, her eyes watering.

The man's voice was definitely familiar to her; it was a voice she hadn't heard in over three years. It was Mike's voice. Or at least she thought it was. Mike's voice was slightly mid-toned and clear, though this man's voice was deep with raspy undertones. It was his Yonkers accent that made the impression on her. He was the only person she knew in upstate New York to have that particular accent.

Frozen in fear, she stood staring at the tiny peephole. She squinted to try and see through the hole but her eye needed to be pressed against it to see. She wanted to pull back the curtains and look out through the side window but she was too frightened.

Then she remembered her wish hours earlier when she'd blown out her birthday candles. The thought of her wish coming true and it actually being Mike was something she couldn't ignore. Her curiosity and hope that Mike had come back forced her to look through the peephole again. At the same time though, she was too afraid to look.

Her conflicting emotions subsided within seconds. The excitement of having Mike back built up enough courage to look. She slowly leveled her eye with the peephole. She breathed in deep and opened her eye.

Through the peephole she saw a man walking in erratic circles through the snow until he stumbled towards the front door. He tripped over the first step and fell face first onto the porch. He pushed up on his hands and grunted as he straightened out his back and stood up.

Knowing it was impossible for Mike to be on her doorstep, she rationalized what was happening. One time, shortly after his death, heartless teenagers from the neighborhood had tried to pull a practical joke on her. While the rest hid in the bushes, one of the teens pretended to be her husband by knocking on the front door and calling for her. Even then, when she hadn't accepted his death, she was too frightened and reluctant to believe he'd come back.

"Go away, you little bastards! Stop messing with me!" she yelled.

The man pounded on the front door again, angering Jamie. She flung it open and screamed, "Get off my damn porch!"

She switched on the porch light and nearly fainted at the sight of the man standing before her. It wasn't teenagers playing another joke. It was Mike. The sight of him caused her heart to skip a beat. She grabbed the door handle so she wouldn't collapse at the morbid sight of him.

Three years in the grave had taken its toll. His skin was shriveled and dried, and had turned gray with patches of black and brown. His face looked starved, his cheeks sunken in, and the skin was wrapped tight around the jawbone. Most of his once thick head of hair had fallen out in clumps. The lips had shrunken back, exposing his blackened teeth. His ears had turned cauliflower, his nose having rotted away, and his shrunken eyes had sunk deep into their sockets. The clothes he was buried in hung loosely and were moist from the clinging snow. When he lifted his arm to grab the screen door, she noticed similar decay on his hands. They were boney and gray; his fingernails looked as though they'd grown as the skin had shriveled back.

Mike opened the screen door. His knees crackled as he stepped over the threshold.

"You can't be alive. I held your hand after you died!" Jamie gasped, backing away and whimpering.

She backed up and fell over an ottoman in the living room. Mike stood over his wife and straddled her body. Worms and other insects fell from open cracks hidden under his clothes onto her bathrobe. She quickly brushed off the bugs, cringing in disgust.

"D…N…R." Mike grumbled. "Jamie, D…N…R!"

Jamie crawled away on her hands and knees away from Mike. He lumbered after her, his boney hands outstretched, trying to grab hold of her leg.

"Get away from me!" she screamed, kicking at his hands. She rolled over and quickly crawled a few feet away until she was able to regain her composure and stand. Without looking back, she ran down the hallway to her bedroom. She closed the door but realized it had no lock.

Mike followed. His footfalls pounded the floor as he staggered down the hallway, moaning her name. Jamie looked around her bedroom unsure of where to hide. She was heavy set and wouldn't fit under the bed. Her closet was filled with boxes containing Mike's belongings, items she couldn't part with. Her only option was the bathroom, knowing it had a lock on the door.

She hurried inside, slammed the door, and locked it. She climbed into the tub, closed the shower curtain, and curled up in a ball like a frightened animal. From in the tub, she heard the bedroom door creek open, followed by the rumble of the sliding closet door. Next, she heard the bathroom door handle jiggle. Mike was trying to get in, to find her.

"Leave me alone, get out of here! Get out, you monster!" she cried.

Upon hearing his wife's screams, Mike began banging on the bathroom door with such force it jostled shampoo and conditioner bottles hanging from a shower caddy down upon Jamie's head. He tried forcing himself into the bathroom. He rammed his shoulder into the door, kicked his feet and pounded his hands on the wood. But it was Old Word construction, solid wood, not a cheap flimsy door made of cardboard and pressboard. Unable to get in, he picked up a lamp and smashed the base against the door. The white paint on the facade cracked and chips fell to the floor, but the door held.

Suddenly, the banging stopped and only Jamie's crying could be heard.

All was quiet over the next ten minutes. Jamie built up enough nerve to pull open the shower curtain and creep across the bathroom floor. She pressed her ear up to the door, listening for any signs that Mike was still in the bedroom.

She heard nothing but her own heavy breathing. Dropping to her knees, she peeked under the door. There was nothing visible but the thick shag of the carpet and the bed legs. She unlocked and opened the door a few inches and peered through the crack. On the floor, she saw the soles of Mike's shoes. He was lying face down and motionless next to his side of the bed.

She exited the bathroom and sidestepped around Mike's corpse, then removed a wire coat hanger from the closet. Unraveling it, she poked his shoulder.

Mike didn't flinch.

Jamie was lightly tapping her foot on his shoulder when suddenly he grabbed her ankle. She screamed and shook her leg violently but Mike's grip was too strong. Harder and harder she kicked her leg until it tugged on Mike's arm hard enough to rip it from his body. The hole on his shoulder didn't bleed, but the tearing sound made Jamie vomit. The separation of the arm from the shoulder had sounded like a popping and crackling fire.

She crawled over the bed and fell to the floor on the opposite side, then after she'd emptied her stomach, she ran out of the bedroom and down the hallway into the kitchen. Opening the broom closet, she hid inside while holding a broom tightly to use as a weapon if she was found.

Mike staggered down the hallway and slammed open each door, peering in and checking for his wife. Guttural moans called out Jamie's name as he entered each room, searching. Upon entering each room, he knocked over tables and chairs, trying to find where she was hiding. Lamps shattered on the floor, books were thrown from the shelves, televisions overturned and smashed, and closets ransacked. No piece of furniture was left standing.

Mike found nothing so he kept searching. Jamie kept whimpering and praying Mike wouldn't find her, and she knew it was only a matter of time before he did. She decided she had to make a break for it, so closing her eyes and gritting her teeth, she said a prayer.

She breathed in deep, held her breath, and flung open the door. Upon jumping out, she stopped dead in her tracks as Mike's arm rammed into her.

Knocked back into the broom closet, her shoulder blades slammed against the rear of the closet, spilling cleaning chemicals, toppling over buckets, and knocking dustpans off their shelves on top of her head

Mike reached in for her but she kicked her legs at him as if she was riding a bicycle, tearing through his clothes and puncturing his skin. Ash and dried organs crumbled from the gaping holes she made. Mike staggered backward into the kitchen counter, giving her enough time to get on her feet, grab the broom, and thrust it into his chest like a spear.

Mike ignored the broom in his chest, pushed off the counter, and walked toward her as she held the broom. The handle continued pushing through his decayed body; she was unable to stop him. He ripped the broom from her grasp, pulled it out of his body, and flung it across the kitchen.

Jamie ran across the room and into the small hallway leading to the garage. Once there, she flung open the door to the garage and slammed it behind her. She looked around for something hard and heavy to use to fight off Mike.

From across the garage she saw a coal shovel hanging on the wall. She ran across the garage, grabbed the shovel, and stood next to her car. She stood, crying and shivering and waiting for Mike to find her.

"Do Not Resuscitate!" Mike moaned from the other side of the door.

"I'm in here, you monster, come and get me!" Jamie yelled, then turned the lights on to the garage to signal where she was.

The door to the garage opened and Mike stood in the doorway. His left arm was barely attached at the shoulder, his lower jaw was broken, and other body parts had crumbled away. His torso was twisted, due to the spine turning to the right, and his back was hunched over. The jacket he was wearing had torn off, only a tattered dress shirt covering parts of his crushed and torn-apart chest.

"Do Not Resuscitate."

"No, you're dead!" she cried. "Your mother signed your D.N.R. form as a witness. You're dead, you weren't resuscitated. This isn't real!"

"Do Not Resuscitate," Mike grumbled in anger.

Mike slowly walked down the small staircase to the garage floor and walked toward Jamie. She started swinging the coal shovel as he neared. Each of her swings missed him until he was in reach, then the shovelhead smashed into his left arm, passed through it, and embedded into his chest.

Mike was knocked off balance from the blow and fell onto his right side. Jamie tried to pull the shovel from his torso as he fell but it was caught on his shirt. The shirt tugged with enough force to jostle Jamie from her feet and fall on top of the shovel handle. Her weight was enough to snap the handle in half. She stood up and ripped the broken shovel out of Mike and backed away.

Mike stood and staggered forward, throwing himself at her. She sidestepped him, swung the broken shovel like a baseball bat and made contact with his back. The blow sent him forward into the garage door, this time the one leading to the driveway. Jamie pressed the automatic door opener and swung the shovel again, hitting Mike in the back of his legs and causing them to buckle and knock him onto his butt.

She jumped up and pulled the garage door shut. The door made a loud rumbling sound as it slammed down like a guillotine, cutting into Mike's pelvis and shattering the brittle bones to dust as it severed his body in half.

Mike grabbed Jamie's ankle, trying to pull her to him, but his ravaged body was too weak. She ripped her ankle from his grip, stood over his head, and thrust the broken shovel with all her might between his teeth, chopping though his jaw and severing the upper half of his skull from his body. He went limp.

She knelt on one knee as she rested to catch her breath. Just then, the garage door flung open, and police officers with guns drawn yelled for her to back away from the body and drop the shovel.

"Lay on the ground with your hands and feet spread apart!" an officer yelled.

"Man, look at this! Poor soul, she digs him up and brings him back here and mutilates him," another officer said.

A female officer patted her down then read Jamie her rights. "You have the right to remain silent. Anything you say can and will be used against you in a court of law. You have the right to have an attorney present during questioning. If you cannot afford an attorney, one will be appointed for you. Do you understand the rights I have just read to you? With these rights in mind, do you wish to speak to me?"

"I…I didn't do anything," Jamie said, shocked. "He came after me; he came back from the grave to get me! I just tried to save myself; he was trying to kill me!"

The female officer said, "You were seen removing the body from the casket by a trucker parked on the side of the road. We traced the name on the headstone back to this address."

"Please, let me go, I didn't dig up my husband, he came back to life. I swear to you, he came back to be with me. I wished him alive when I blew out my birthday candles and made a wish," she said, tears welling up in her eyes.

The female officer closed the squad car door and locked Jamie inside. Then the officer walked into the house. Behind the front door, the woman saw signs of struggling and madness.

It was obvious Jamie had lost all sense of judgment and reality. Her imagination and unwillingness to let go of her husband and fully accept his death had clouded her mental well-being.

The house was trashed; every room looked as though a burglar had been searching for hidden jewelry or money, and parts of Mike's body were found everywhere.

The female cop exited the house and joined one of the other officers. She shook her head as she cast a glance at a crying Jamie and said, "Her mind must have snapped. There's a room in Bellevue Asylum waiting for her, that's for sure."

BELL AND WILL:
TRUE LOVE NEVER DIES

AARON GUDMUNSON

The department-mandated retirement became a good thing, once he bought the house on Red Pointe Road. At first he resented it, taking the measure as Captain Benson's personal rejection. It wasn't until he was three weeks in that he realized how good he felt. Retirement, Will Markley came to understand, had saved his life.

He wheeled into the driveway of his new house and tried to think ahead because his therapist deemed dwelling on the past unhealthy.

Happy thoughts—doctor's orders.

Will sighed. Happy thoughts were in short supply these days. Except for the house, of course.

He punched the Suburban into PARK. Yes, the house qualified as a happy thought. It went one step better. It had become happy reality. After so long in the cramped city, this little country tract felt right. It felt free.

Of course, freedom was never Will's primary motivation for purchasing the property. He hadn't bothered to tell anyone where he was moving, and no one had asked, which saved him lies. Because anyone who knew the Shelton murders as intimately as he did would certainly view his acquisition of the house in which they'd occurred as a misstep toward getting healthy.

Gregory Lee Shelton was Will's final case. He had taken it on after the first murder occurred eight years previous, and hadn't stopped until the verdict had been read in court last February. Will's testimony, based on the copious evidence he'd collected, had been easily enough for the DA to bring Shelton down. The jury had deliberated less than three hours before coming to the decision to send the killer to D Block up at Bosco Correctional: Death Row.

The department had thrown Will a party where everyone cheered and drank till dawn. The Commissioner gave him a commendation for outstanding service and every major newspaper printed a write-up about Will's involvement in closing the case. Some of the victims' families showed their gratitude by bringing food or flowers to his door. One sent him a check, as if money might resurrect their beloved daughter, and one bereaved mother even offered her body, which Will gently but firmly declined.

Then, as is the case with every great tragedy, the furor died off and life moved on.

Except, that is, for William Markley, former Area 2 homicide detective, now retired. He wished he could forget it all and sometimes tried drowning it with whiskey. He knew some street folk who could get him high and spent some of his bloated pension each month on cocaine, and once, heroin. Nothing worked. He'd wallowed seven months before realizing the only way to be truly rid of his final case was to buy the Shelton house.

It had been on the market since the case closed. No one showed interest. Not one person. Until Will's inquiry, the realtor had told him, the plan had been to raze the structure and hope someone would purchase the newly-turned land.

"I'll buy the property," Will had said. "I want it whole, though, house and all."

The realtor, reluctant to enter the place even for a brief showing, had balked. "You *do* know what happened there, right?"

"Of course. I was the lead investigator," he had replied and then, sensing the realtor's sustained discomfort, told her he didn't require a look at the property. He'd been there before, often.

They closed the following Tuesday, and after tying up loose ends in the city, Will moved in Saturday.

He hired a restoration crew ahead of the movers and the place appeared spotless upon reentry: curtains laundered, windows washed, hardwood floors swept free of even the minutest crumb and waxed to a high-gloss shine. The lawn was mowed and edged, and a fresh coat of paint adorned the clapboard siding. The roof had even been patched where a scattering of shingles had fallen away sometime over the years.

Will stood for a time in the driveway, one hand gripping the driver's door, while the interior bell of the SUV dinged and dinged, as he stared at the old place. If his goal had been the same as his doctor's, which was to avoid dwelling on the past, he had failed. But his goal was, in fact, the opposite. He wished to embrace these memories, to court them, to take them out for dinner, because for him, the case had never truly closed.

"Isabella Donahue," he whispered. The final victim, abducted only a month before Shelton's capture, was the only body to go unfound. The remains of Maggie Parsons, Elizabeth Tramer, Cassandra McGavin, Maria Gamez, and Barbara Clements had been unearthed in the basement after Shelton confessed their whereabouts. But on the final resting place of Isabella Donahue, he refused to speak.

Will had gone rounds with Shelton in a closed room. Warden Scott had permitted him that much. Shelton had required seventeen stitches and caps to cover the teeth Will had broken off. But still the maniac denied him this final bit of information; the last piece in the insane jigsaw puzzle. Shelton's reason had been simple: he loved Isabella Donahue and wished to remember her as she was, at rest in the place Shelton had kept her.

Will had realized something, too, and was awed by the fact he'd known it for some time: he loved Isabella Donahue as well.

Her face haunted his dreams. He'd seen it in three dozen photos her family provided to aid the investigation. He'd viewed Isabella Donahue from every possible angle and loved every glance, every action, every smile for the camera. She was his motivation in bringing Shelton down. None of the other victims had inspired such action in him, nor had any victim in any of the hundreds of other cases he'd solved during his career. It was something in the confident way she carried herself in each square of celluloid. It was the way her smile dominated each frame—even group shots in which, for some reason unknown to him, she had been relegated to the background.

Will had supervised the retrieval of the bodies from the basement of the Shelton property—now the Markley property. No matter what state of decomposition, he knew he would recognize Isabella on sight.

"We're missing one," the lead forensics investigator had reported.

"Isabella Donahue," Will had replied. Forensics had been skeptical about Will's certainty, but the pathology report confirmed his conclusion.

The consensus was that her body must be offsite, but Will knew this was wrong. Something told him she was still on the premises, even after methane probes of the basement and yard turned up only the body of a long-deceased housecat in a shoebox on the edge of the lawn where the grass gave way to corn.

Will had made it his ongoing mission to discover the whereabouts of Isabella Donahue. For her family's sake, he claimed. For as much as they needed closure on the death of their loved one, he needed it, too.

His days became devoted to the task. After Shelton's repeated denial to speak on the subject, the warden relinquished Will's access to the condemned man. Will argued that by doing so, he was hindering an ongoing investigation. The rebuttal was that his investigation had long since moved to harassment, and Will was forced to concede.

He cashed in some of the favors owed him by various officers and gained access to Shelton's confiscated belongings. He sifted through drawers full of seemingly meaningless items and studied Shelton's journals obsessively.

By the second month of his personal investigation, which had not yet begun to conflict with his work, Will was approached one evening by a man in a trenchcoat and dark glasses who advised the detective to desist in his search. Surprised, Will had demanded the man's identity and reason for his request.

"I'm an associate of Mr. Shelton's," was the man's reply. He displayed a small caliber pistol. "He wishes Ms. Donahue a peaceful sleep, and she can't do so with you nosing around."

Will had eyed the weapon, then stared at the man's face. "Obstructing justice is a serious crime, not to mention threatening a peace officer."

The man didn't waver. "I care little for what's considered a crime. This is your only warning, Detective." He stuck the pistol against Will's right side and squeezed the trigger.

The shot had done no real damage. The bullet had broken two ribs before glancing away, and required only a brief stay at Stroger Hospital. Neither the threat nor the wound much bothered him; it was the fact that his investigation had been temporarily halted that had him angry.

They hadn't found the man who shot Will, but this fact didn't trouble him. He decided to be prepared for the next encounter; stopping the search for Isabella Donahue wasn't an option. If Trenchcoat showed up again, Will would simply shoot him and continue on his way.

The captain had warned Will of Shelton's celebrity status on Death Row. He was approaching godhood, it seemed. Many of the inmates revered the man who the media insisted on keeping on display. The courtroom sessions on TruTV. The series of articles in the major papers. He had many followers; the man in the trench-coat was only one of a Rogue's Gallery of scumbags who wished to prove themselves worthy to Shelton. The son of a bitch had his own cult, it seemed.

None of that concerned Will. He kept focused on moving into his new house. He didn't bother to have the phone turned on—he wanted no distractions. His intention was to comb the house for clues. Top to bottom, rafter to root cellar. Isabella was in the house—he knew it.

First things first. He embarked on a shopping spree for sup-plies. He purchased a pickaxe, a shovel, a spade, a hardhat with a flashlight attachment like miners wore when going into the depths of the earth. There was excavation to be done.

Will's second stop was at the Shop n' Save on Route 47, where he purchased a week's worth of groceries and a bottle of the finest champagne in the store. He predicted heavy celebration ahead, for when he liberated Isabella.

No time was wasted. As soon as the foodstuffs were stashed, he began. Already well acquainted with the basement, he decided to start in the attic. It was the one room in the house in which he'd visited least during the investigation and as he pulled open the trapdoor, he felt a thrill of excitement. Could she be up there? Probably not. But there might be something in the attic he'd overlooked before. Doubtful, but maybe. Now that he knew Shelton's mind a bit better, he thought there just might be something of interest.

He climbed the ladder and felt around in the darkness above his head for the string that would bring light into the godforsaken place. When he yanked it, nothing happened.

Blown bulb. He wasn't surprised. Who knew how long the bulb had been there, collecting dust along its gossamer contours while Shelton's victims screamed themselves hoarse below. This very same bulb had sat dark and indifferent while Isabella Donahue endured nightmares beyond comprehension. Will decided he would change all the bulbs in the house the first chance he got.

In the meantime, he clicked on his helmet light and peered around. It was much as he remembered it: an unsanded plank floor framed by walls of two-by-fours and pink insulation. The ceiling came to a peak high above. The only difference was the cigar box lying in the center of the floor.

Pulse quickening, he rushed to it. The lid featured an image of a steamboat gliding through tropical waters. The stern bore the name brand of the cigar, but Will would have bet his left foot the box didn't contain tobacco. He flipped it open and focused the light.

There were illustrations on sheets of paper drawn in heavy black ink, odd symbols that meant nothing to him. A small lockbox revealed glass vials of colored powders. It looked like Shelton had been dabbling in witchcraft.

He decided now to re-analyze the medical reports on the bodies to see if they would be consistent with known black magic rituals. Of course, gaining access to them would require him to cash in another favor with Records, but he thought he could swing it.

Something occurred to him. How had the box gotten here? The answer came, sharp and immediate. One of Shelton's disciples had placed it here for Will to find.

This thought led back to one he'd had many times before: how was Shelton converting people to servitude? In light of recent discoveries, Will decided maybe it had something to do with black magic. Sure, Shelton was a charmer and a talker—Ted Bundy and Charles Manson rolled into one six foot package of death—but the sudden devotion of so many seemed too left field to be attributed to mere charisma.

"Maybe there's something to this shit," he muttered, thumbing again through the symbols.

He paused at one and stared at it. Had it moved? That was crazy, but for a moment it appeared as though the pentacles and lines and deranged curly-Qs had crawled across the page, stopping like a deer in a clearing that has sensed a hunter watching it.

Will uttered a sharp, barking laugh. "Benson was right, idiot. You needed to retire. You're going crazy in your old age."

Still, he watched the paper to make sure the markings remained still. They did, and after a few minutes, he folded them back into the box, closed the lid, and took it downstairs to the kitchen.

He placed the box on the table and clicked off the flashlight.

Autumn wind whined around the high peaks of the roof and rattled the windows in their panes. He looked at the refrigerator and tried to remember when last he'd eaten.

He couldn't. Not that he was the least bit hungry now. He thought about Isabella Donahue, what her last meal might have been before the abduction. Whether she enjoyed it. Who she enjoyed it with. Her family? A girlfriend? A boyfriend? Alone?

No, not alone. That girl couldn't have spent a lonely moment in her life. She would have always been surrounded by people, such was her radiance. That was the way, at least, Will perceived her. Apparently Shelton had, too.

Except she had been alone, the night of February 28th. While walking home from the library after drama club rehearsal for an upcoming production of *Dracula* in which she was to play Mina Harker, Shelton had approached and walked alongside her a few blocks. He'd introduced himself and the two had begun talking. He invited her to a local club for a drink, which she accepted. According to the bartender, the two had seemed completely at ease: "Ask me, I'd have thought they were man and wife," he was quoted in the investigation narrative.

When they left, Isabella had been intoxicated to the point of requiring assistance. The bartender had asked Shelton if he should call a cab, but Shelton politely declined.

The rest could be read in the record archives. Will knew because he'd studied the reports so often he could recite them like poetry.

Despite his lack of appetite, he needed to eat. With the hard work ahead, he had to keep up his strength. He pulled together sandwich makings: salami, Muenster, Dijon, cucumbers, onions. He slapped it all between slices of rye and chewed absently, staring out the window into the dark yard.

How many times had Shelton walked up that driveway after collecting the mail from the box by the road? How often had he left his victims screaming behind him while he got into his car to drive to the supermarket? How many?

"Too many," Will said around a mouthful. He sat at the table and stared at the cigar box, waiting for it to move. If it did, he thought, he would lose his mind. It would snap, like a dry switch across a knee. Part of him wanted the box to move. Sweet insanity might just be the retirement he required.

The box remained still. Will brushed crumbs off his hands, then went to the basement steps and looked down into darkness. Isabella was down there. He was sure of it.

Why they hadn't found her upon the initial and subsequent inspections, he couldn't fathom. But in his gut, he knew she awaited discovery.

"I'm coming, Bell," he whispered into the darkness. He gathered the tools he'd purchased at the hardware store, stepped into the basement still smelling of turned earth, and set to work.

After two hours of steady excavation, the only thing Will managed to unearth was a clutch of nightcrawlers. He leaned on his shovel, wiped sweat from his brow with his sleeve, and surveyed the scene. Chaos. And not a lick closer to finding her.

With a curse, he flung the shovel at the wall. It sent a small avalanche of crumbling brickwork to the wrecked floor beneath. He swore again, but not because of the damage he'd inflicted upon his wall. It was because of the sound the tool made when it struck.

Instead of a cracking thud, he'd heard a resonant clang. Head cocked, he approached this new development.

He rubbed at the old mortar with his fingers and it sifted away. With sudden passion, he clawed away masonry until he saw rust-pitted steel beneath. Could it be? Yes, it was.

A door. It was a solid steel door.

It could have been to a root cellar or a sealed up coal chute, but he knew better. When he could no longer move bricks by hand, he grabbed up the pickaxe and drove its point again and again into the wall.

Sweat poured off him. At the end of half an hour, he'd opened a man-sized aperture and revealed the prize.

The door was a plate of steel inches thick that hung on an enormous hinge. There was no discernible handle and it had been welded neatly to its iron jamb.

Another hieroglyph had been etched on the surface, meaningless to him. He set his ear against it and heard a hollow thrum, like the sound of the ocean in a conch.

She was there. He knew it.

"I'm coming, Bell," he whispered again. "Don't worry, honey, I'm coming."

He hauled up the pickaxe and began to hammer at the door.

The kitchen door opened, its spring squeaking gently. Had Will been capable of hearing anything other than the resonant echoes of steel on steel, he would have heard heavy footfalls crossing the tile to the basement stairs. The intruder drew a .44 from the waistband of his dungarees and started down. His instructions had been clear: kill Markley before he recovered the master's sleeping bride. Two shots, head and heart, then bury him in the cellar. The master had told him the earthen floor would already be turned due to the detective's futile searching, and the assassin was pleased to discover this was true. A smile broke across the grizzled face and he took the steps slowly, one by one.

Will Markley continued his onslaught. Aside from a few shallow scratches, his progress remained fruitless and he spat curses between ragged breaths. His shirt had soaked through and he stopped to strip it away.

It was instinct alone that saved his life. Only the smallest sliver of shadow from the kitchen fluorescents appeared on the iron door before him, but that was all he needed. His body, a coiled machine, jerked around in a half circle. He used the momentum to fling the pickaxe before he even knew he was doing it—before he even fully perceived the threat.

A man stood at the bottom of the steps, revolver gripped in one gloved fist. Shock braced his face before the blunt edge of the pickaxe struck his forehead, and throwing him backward against the steps. The man opened his mouth to scream, but nothing came out except a brief geyser of gore. He stared at Will in disbelief and then lay still.

Will approached cautiously, sensing no ruse but taking no chances. It wasn't the trenchcoat man, he noted. He snatched up the revolver and unloaded the cylinder into one of the furrows in the floor. He tossed the gun into another, then rolled the body into a third. He would be calling in his final favors and paying Mr. Shelton a visit soon enough.

He took fifteen minutes to cover the grave before allowing himself a break. He checked the yard through the kitchen window, studying the shadows thrown by the floodlight. No movement. Shelton had again sent only one disciple. He would need to send an army to kill Will Markley. He gulped two tumblers of water from the tap, then returned to work.

Will went to bed at dawn no closer to liberating the body of Isabella Donahue. His arms and abs felt as though they were filled with shards of fired glass and his hands were gloved in blisters. He fell asleep immediately and dreamed of something small and dark with bright eyes and stiletto teeth stalking him through a cornfield maze. He ran through rows of ghostly stalks while paper-thin leaves whipped his face. The thing crashed through the vegetation behind him in pursuit, mewling low in its throat as it came.

The next day was a waste. He could not work for the condition of his hands. Will spent all day in the cellar nonetheless, watching the steel door as if it might open itself. At noon he spread a table-cloth across the uneven floor and ate a picnic lunch of ham salad, Pringles, carrot sticks, Oreos, and bottled beer. He watched the door. Occasionally he would whisper to Isabella, as if his voice could penetrate the barrier between them. As if she could hear him.

In the evening, he dragged himself upstairs, cracked a bottle of Wild Turkey, and downed shot after shot while sitting on the porch swing where Gregory Lee Shelton had undoubtedly perched on warm evenings such as this. The world held still. No cars passed and no creature showed itself, not even a crow in the corn.

He studied the cornfields. He saw no further signs of any Shel-ton-sent assailants. If he did, he would be ready, but for now he remained alone. The idea frightened him more than he expected.

For twenty minutes, he busied himself carving words into the wooden arm of the swing with his pocketknife. It said: ***Bell and Will: True Love Never Dies.*** He scratched a heart around it, blew away the dust, and smiled.

When the stars winked on in the night sky, he went inside and turned on the television. He stopped at a program on pets that attacked their owners. Biting the hand that feeds, as the saying went.

He drank whiskey and listened to the house. The damnable house with all the unimaginable misery in its walls. He thought of Isabella Donahue, of her tilted smile, and whispered her name before stumbling to the kitchen. The basement light still burned and he reached to turn it off, then changed his mind. He would leave a nightlight on for her. The idea made him happy. He slurred a soft goodnight before going up to bed.

He didn't hear the soft scraping sound below.

Will came awake with all sense of isolation gone. Someone else was in the house; years of cop instinct could not be denied. He fumbled at the nightstand, head pounding, and gripped his .38 Special. His hand stung at the butt where it pressed the blisters. He found his slippers, toed them on, and listened.

The house remained silent, save the minor creaks and groans all old structures emit in the dead of night. A quiet scratching from somewhere below sent a thrum of adrenaline bursting through him like ungrounded electricity. Someone was here, no doubt.

He crept to the top of the stairs. He swallowed, fully awake and fully aware. Any trace of intoxication was gone. It came again, the scrape of something on wood. The bottom of the staircase was a black pool. Anything could be crouched there, waiting. His dream recurred, the small predator with the cannibal's leer.

He reached for the light, then thought better of it. Surprise was of the element. He started down the steps, settling his weight on the outer edges to minimize creaking. After what felt like half an eternity, he reached the bottom and stared into the kitchen. Dark.

But he'd left the light on in the cellar. He remembered doing it, despite being drunk—or perhaps because of it. Someone had turned it off.

The sound came again, louder, and Will took a step backward into the living room. Someone moved on the basement stairs.

Slowly, as if the person were a child, he heard the small slap of first one foot and then another finding the next riser.

A beleaguered gust of air issued forth and then a forced grunt of effort. The sound carried an undoubtedly feminine quality. The shuffle-thump came again, only now he rushed forward, accepting, understanding the identity of the person who came up the stairs.

Wanting to call her name, but unable to muster the will to do so, he fumbled for the light switch. Nothing happened when he snapped it up and down, and he realized his guest must have somehow accidentally broken the bare hanging bulb in a bid for freedom.

"Isabella?" he rasped. He didn't know how it was possible, some black magic ritual he could never understand, but he didn't care.

The figure on the stairwell moaned, the sound of an October breeze through hollow reeds. Will stepped away long enough to switch on the overhead fluorescents, and when they buzzed to life, illuminating the narrow throat leading to the cellar, all his hopes materialized.

She was there.

Isabella Donahue appeared well-preserved, her skin intact if grayer than her pictures—even those in black and white. Her hair had lost some of its luster, but still maintained a semblance of life. The eyes, though closed, looked not at all sunken and her lips appeared soft and full. One small hand felt along the plaster for some handhold, to pull the body forward, upward, back into the world of the living.

Will took that hand and helped the maiden into the kitchen of his new home. Her limbs trembled as if remembering some horror that had occurred in this particular room.

Will placed a tentative arm around her shoulders and was inwardly delighted when Isabella leaned into him.

The skin felt cool but not cold beneath his fingers, the muscles retaining the suppleness of life. Her smell was earthen, of course, but not entirely unpleasant; a hint of cinnamon and honeysuckle lingered in her hair.

As he led her into the living room, Will didn't care through what means Isabella Donahue remained animated. It was enough for him that she was.

There would be time to worry over details later. For now, he worked to contain his delight. His greatest dream—to find her body and lay it to proper rest—had been surpassed, for here she was now, in his arms. Here she *was*.

"It's all right, honey," Will murmured, the way he'd done with a hundred rape victims. "It's okay. Sit down on the sofa. Are you thirsty?"

The jaw dropped open, expelling a moan on a draft of rank breath. She seemed eager to reply, but her disused vocal cords had forgotten how to create speech.

Will took this in stride. He patted her hand and went to the kitchen for a glass of water. When he returned, Isabella had wandered halfway across the room and into the southwest corner, facing inward.

She made a slight stutter step, turned left, then back to the corner.

"Let me help you, darling," he said, setting the glass on the coffee table and guiding her back to the sofa. He offered the water, holding the cup to her lips. She sipped at it, the liquid tracing silvery rivulets down her chin. Isabella took the glass in both hands, childlike, and gulped. Most spilled down the blouse she wore the day she disappeared, now caked with grime and blood.

"We should get you cleaned up," he told her and led her gently to the bathroom, where he drew a warm bath and helped her in. He washed her hair, working out the tangles with his fingers. He wished he had something better than Head & Shoulders and decided a leave-in conditioner would appear on the next grocery list. He scrubbed her body with a wash cloth and his Irish Spring soap. A tear in her skin appeared on her thigh when he rubbed too hard, but it didn't bleed and Isabella made no sign she had felt it. Will cursed himself and made sure to complete his task more gently.

This poor creature had endured enough.

When they were done, he toweled her off and tucked her into a pair of his pajamas. "Are you tired, Bell?" he asked.

She opened her mouth, but again speech failed her. He searched her eyes, but found no answers in their muddy stare.

He took her to his bed, tucked her in, then lay down on the floor with a pillow and a sheet.

He placed the .38 within easy reach and then tried to sleep, but his pounding heart refused such nonsense. At last, with dawn easing over the slaughtered cornfields, he sat with his back against the dressing bureau and watched his darling sleep.

The desk sergeant snatched the phone up on the first ring. "Bosco Correctional. Hedge speaking."

"Transfer me to the shift commander," barked a gruff voice through the earpiece.

"Who's calling?" Sgt. Hedge demanded. He disliked putting any call through to Commander Phillips if it could be avoided.

"Never mind," the voice growled. "Transfer me."

"You'll have to state your name and purpose for calling if you want to…"

"If you don't want your star revoked by morning, Sergeant Hedge, I suggest you transfer the fucking call."

Hedge considered. There was a strong possibility this person was bluffing. It could be the family member of an inmate. Sometimes they dialed this number—he'd pleaded with I.T. repeatedly to remove it from the Web site—and had to be redirected to the visitor line.

But this guy sounded like he meant business and by the tone was probably a cop.

Hedge sniffed as though he could determine the caller's identity by scent, then pressed TRANSFER and dialed the extension. It was forty minutes to quitting time. Let Phillips deal with this asshole.

Phillips listened to the request with mounting anxiety. By the call's conclusion, the request had become a demand. He knew Detective Markley through rumor and reporters, and had formed an ill opinion of the man.

Now the former detective—Phillips knew of the mandatory retirement—was asking to be allowed unsupervised access to an inmate and Phillips was in a position to grant or deny it.

But not just any inmate. The belle of the ball, Gregory Lee Shelton.

Before Markley finished speaking, Phillips had made up his mind not to help him. It was too risky. He could lose his badge over it. He knew Warden Scott and Markley sometimes played a few hands of poker on Saturday nights.

That was fine. He would report this incident to the warden at 0800 and let him decide if the rules should be broken.

Phillips certainly wasn't going to put his ass on the line.

"I'm sorry," Phillips said. "I can't help you."

A pause through the phone and Phillips thought he heard Markley snicker. "Do you know who I am, Phillips?"

"Of course. You're the guy who sent Shelton here. My question is: what do you want with him now? He's serving his time. He doesn't need some whack-job ex-cop hounding him."

Now Markley did laugh. The sound was low, drawn out, and terrifying. "I'll remember this, Phillips."

The connection dropped and Phillips found himself staring at a dead phone.

Will pulled into the driveway as the last rays of sunlight hit his yard, having come from making his call at the payphone outside the 7-11 in town. He sat a moment, drumming his fingers on the steering wheel, then looked at Isabella. She sat signpost-straight in the passenger seat. Her eyes were closed, giving her the startling appearance of a corpse.

She's a corpse, Will's mind whispered.

"Shut up," he said aloud and Isabella twitched at the sound.

He helped her inside. She took each step slowly, like a drunk with the spins. He had seen a dozen zombie movies over the years and realized what every one of them had gotten wrong: the undead did not become murderous savages upon reawakening. If anything, they became passively handicapped.

The front door closed and Will stood thinking. Isabella waited, her ponytail hanging motionless to the middle of her back like a strangled snake. Just what had he expected to do if he'd gotten to Shelton this morning? Kill him? Yes, probably. For Isabella. He didn't care about consequences anymore, now that his beloved had been liberated.

But why had he brought her with him today? Why, as a witness. To see firsthand that justice had been done.

Getting at Shelton wasn't an option, it had to be done. He would have to call Warden Scott himself and try to drag down one last favor. If need be, he could offer Bosco Correctional a sizeable donation made out to Thomas Scott. But that could wait.

"Isabella?" he whispered. A smile twitched at the corners of her lips in response and she made a half-turn toward him. "Honey, is there anything you want? Anything I can get you?"

Her lips parted—her beautiful, full lips—and she tried to speak, but nothing came out except a dry click. A tip of grayish tongue lapped at the surrounding tissue in an action remembered from a different time, though now she produced no saliva with which to wet them. Will longed to kiss her, his true love, but didn't wish to frighten her.

"It's okay, Bell. Take your time. I'll give you anything you desire. You'll want for nothing ever again."

He tried to get her to sip some water, but most of it dribbled down her chin.

Afterward, he had her stretch out on the sofa but the appearance of a cadaver was too much and he stood her up again. She didn't appear to require rest in the traditional sense anyway.

But Will did. He couldn't recall a time in which he'd felt more exhausted. After locking the doors, he settled back onto the couch and watched Isabella. She simply stood in the same spot, a strand of her hair hanging against one sallow cheek, fine as a cobweb. Before long, his eyes closed and he dreamed of tunnels twisting through the core of the world.

When he woke the next morning, he knew what must be done. He stood, stretched, and went to find Isabella. She was standing in the tub of the lower level bathroom, one hand pressed to the cold tiles. She stiffened slightly when he entered the room, but otherwise gave no sign she was aware of him.

"Bell, want to go for another drive tonight? Want to take care of some unfinished business?" he asked. Now her head came fully up, her drab eyes finding his with a look that made him shiver. She understood.

They spent the day playing house, Will preparing her meals and placing them before her as if she might eat them. She did not. He bathed her again and dressed her in a pair of his shorts and a button-down shirt. He kissed her and she didn't resist. They made love, gently, Isabella giving no reaction outside of a quickening in her breath. In another world, they might have been man and wife. Will had never been happier.

At eight-thirty, with the sun low on the horizon, he helped her to the car, and after buckling her in, drove straight and fast toward Bosco. The prison stood forty miles north. Along the way he explained the plan to Isabella. Her part would be easy, so he wasn't worried about a foul up. But they had to do it quick, before he over-thought it. Before he fully considered this may well be his last day on Earth.

Isabella sat rigid, but moaned occasionally in what Will could only describe as anticipation. He took this as a good sign as he drove into the employee parking lot and parked far away from the floodlights. He turned off the engine, got out, and opened the passenger door. It took a few minutes to get his old Chicago Bears sweatshirt pulled over Isabella's head and get the hood just right to hide her face.

"Now listen, honey. This is just acting, all right? Like in your drama club? Do you remember that? It's not real. You know I'd never put you in danger. It's just a way to get us what we both want. Okay?"

"Yeeeeessss…" she said. The sound was that of an autumn wind through moss and it thrilled him as much as it chilled him.

"Good, baby. It will be over soon and we can live happily ever after," he said, guiding her toward the access door at the back of the administrative block. He had used this entrance dozens of times as an officer, but was fairly certain a civilian would be denied access without proper credentials. That's why he'd brought his own, which he withdrew from the waistband of his jeans.

He pressed the buzzer.

"Yes?" Even through the speaker, Will identified the voice of Hedge.

"Open up, Sarge," Will said. He knew he was on camera and held the gun to Isabella's head. "It's Will Markley. I've got a hostage. I came for Shelton."

A moment of shocked silence. Then, "I'll get Commander Phillips."

"No," Will said. "Open now or I'll put a bullet in her head. Don't call for backup or she dies."

"I don't even know who that is!" Hedge blurted. "It could be an accomplice, for God's sake!"

"Is that a chance you want to take?"

More silence. Then the door buzzed and Will pushed his way in, guiding Isabella in front of him. They made their way down a short corridor that opened into an office area. Will knew what he would find when they pushed through the door. Hedge had drawn his weapon and took aim at Will's head.

"Put it down, asshole, and get Phillips out here," Will snarled.

Hedge ignored him. "Ma'am? Are you all right? Have you been hurt?"

"I said put your fucking gun down and call Phillips!"

Hedge looked from Isabella to Will and back again, squinting to see beneath the hood. Finally, he set his revolver on the desk, picked up the phone, and dialed the Shift Commander's extension.

* * *

Will was proud of himself. He'd expected Phillips to balk at commanding his guards off the block and locking them out, but he made the call and they obeyed. He ordered Phillips and Hedge to handcuff one another to the heavy desk in the center of the room.

Isabella kept tugging at Will's hand. She had priorities.

They stepped up to the single corridor of cells housing inmates sentenced to death. A ring of keys jingled in Will's fist; he was able to manually override the automatic locks.

Fortunately, the other inmates had so far slept through the invasion. He wanted this done fast and needed no further distraction. When it was over, maybe he and Isabella would make for Canada. He knew of a little clutch of cabins in the woods of British Columbia they could spend the rest of their lives in. That would be nice.

But first things first.

He knew from experience which cell was Shelton's and he wasn't surprised to find the man waiting for him at the bars when they stepped up to it. The collar of his orange jumpsuit was popped up, as if Shelton expected to be attending a party, and his hair was neatly combed. He grinned, making his face both handsome and horrible.

"I wondered when you'd visit again, Detective Markley. I've missed you. Another wasted trip, of course. I'll never divulge the whereabouts of…" Shelton stopped talking. His eyes shifted and found Will's companion. His jaw fell open.

"Of who? Your blushing bride? She's mine now, Shelton," Will said. He couldn't remember something that had given him greater satisfaction than the look on the killer's face at this moment, not even when he'd beaten Shelton unconscious all those months ago.

"Izzy? Are you all right, my love? God, has he hurt you?" Shelton asked, quaking.

"She's fine, dickhead," Will said, sliding the key into the cell door. "Which is more than I can say for how you'll be in the next ten seconds. And don't try any of your magic tricks. You won't be alive long enough to wave your little wand again."

Will twisted the key and slid open the door, raising the gun to shoulder height.

But something happened then, too quick to stop.

Isabella ripped back the hood of the sweatshirt, her eyes wide open and glowing with savage hunger. They were *alive*. Her lips peeled back in a terrible rictus, revealing small, perfect teeth.

"Isabella?" both men said. Then she lunged into the cell, hooking her fingers into the flesh of Shelton's cheeks, then pulled his face to hers. Shelton screamed and then Isabella was biting deep, tiny teeth tearing, probing for his tongue, which she promptly chewed free.

Will backed into the corridor, the gun slipping from his fingers. So abrupt was the change in his beloved that he could only bear witness to the slaughter. The victimized had become the victimizer. Justice was served.

The six other inmates on D Block were now awake and howling at the bars. When they realized it was their leader under attack, they screamed for someone—anyone—to intervene. No one did, of course. By the time a detachment of guards figured out what was happening and locked down the block, everything was long over.

When Shelton stopped screaming, Isabella stood up. Her beautiful face was a mask of gore. Most of the hair on the left side of her head was gone, yanked out in the melee. The sweatshirt hung askew at her neck.

As for Shelton, what was left of him could not easily be distinguishable as human.

"Bell?" Will whispered, holding out a hand in comfort or supplication. She looked around at the sound of her name, then marked him standing alone.

Strings of flesh hung from her mouth, the lower half of her face covered in blood.

For a moment, Will entertained the idea that all might still be well, that fairy tales did have happy endings, when the knight would save the damsel, the monster was slain, and true love never died.

Then Isabella launched across the corridor and tore his throat out with her teeth.

THE ZOMBIE'S HAUNT

BENNIE L. NEWSOME

From his customary position at the bottom of the lake, Lawrence stared up at the still water's surface. The light of the full moon glinted off the transparent exterior, almost making it impossible for him to see the figures hovering about the water's edge. If they hadn't been disturbing the water, causing ripples to appear near the bank, he would have never known they were there. However, their carelessness did catch his attention and he was on the move.

The zombie's inability to swim forced him to trudge through the hindering muck that made up the lake bottom. The clinging vegetation inadvertently impeded his movements, but Lawrence's supernatural strength and his overwhelming desire to feed allowed him to plow through the obstacles.

His coming was deadlier than a shark's and he possessed more stealth, for there was no fin to cut through the top of the water, alerting his victims to his arrival. No bubbles broke the surface of the lake, because he had no need to breathe. Although he moved slowly, the zombie made amazing progress; his remaining eye was locked on the shadowy silhouettes.

He continued to wrestle against the force of the water, the tugging of the mire, and the tangles of the aquatic vegetation as he began to climb a rising incline. A few minutes later, and an unreal amount of determination, brought Lawrence right below two sets of leisurely kicking feet.

Distracted by their flirtatious laughter and sexual conversations, the couple didn't see the zombie's grotesque visage staring at them from below the surface. Lawrence had gone undetected and could have continued to do so for a little bit longer, but he saw no need to postpone his attack. The undead creature didn't receive any semblance of a thrill from stalking his victims. In one quick motion, he reached up and grabbed the female by one dainty ankle, snatching her into the water.

The peaceful scene instantly erupted into chaos.

The young woman thrashed about and screamed for help as she was pulled into the murky depths of the lake. Her date jumped to his feet and scampered away from the edge. He wanted to rescue his latest sweetheart, but he valued his life too much to approach the apparent danger. The young man wasn't sure if the girl was being attacked by a giant snake, an oversized fish, or God forbid—the fabled monster of the lake.

Lawrence continued to haul the kicking, clawing girl into the water. Her frantic cries turned into rushing bubbles just before the muddy liquid filled her lungs. As soon as he had his massive, rotten hands on her head, he twisted, breaking the young woman's fragile neck. He was too impatient to let her drown.

The lake went quiet again.

Not wanting to spoil where he slept, Lawrence tossed the dead girl over his right shoulder and slowly strolled out of the water and onto the sandy shore. The zombie's head was the first thing to be seen.

It initially appeared as a large bump on the surface of the lake, then grew until it became a head covered in plant life and mud. Water dripped down his face, which was nothing but skin and bones. His one eye was slanted upwards and his other eye socket was empty except for the leeches that rested inside.

There was no way to tell due to his lipless mouth, but the zombie smiled with pleasure as he watched the young man run away, screaming some nonsense about a lake monster.

With all of the muck and aquatic weed that covered him, Lawrence supposed he did look like the equivalent of a swamp monster, or as some people called him, a mud monster. Nevertheless, he didn't get hung up on titles and could care less about names others gave him. If anything, the confusion only added to the myth that surrounded him, and the less people that believed in him, the greater chance he had of being left to his own devices.

He completed his ascent out of the water with the drenched, limp body still slung over his shoulder. The young woman's colorful attire was in complete contrast to what was left of his dark tattered suit, which was soaking wet and covered with lake refuse.

The zombie staggered over to a section of the wood line that surrounded the lake. His wet apparel created a loud, sloshing sound that filled the nighttime air. It was a noise which continued until he found his favorite sitting spot, beneath an old birch tree, and plopped down on the ground.

The undead creature dropped his victim into his lap and stripped off her clothing. Once again, he smiled.

If he could have formed a coherent sentence with his mouth, he would have said, "This is the life." But Lawrence had lost his tongue in the early stages of his decomposition; therefore, he was only able to groan unintelligibly.

This must be what they mean by simpler times, he thought to himself. *Living off the land. Eating only what you catch and clean with your own hands.*

The hungry zombie situated the now naked girl so her delicate legs were before his face. He took a large bite out of her left thigh and sighed blissfully. He loved females because they kept their bodies moisturized, which made their skin softer. Not like men who were all tough and hairy. The zombie's sensitive gums and few remaining teeth were not fond of man meat.

The phrase 'man meat' made him laugh in a guttural tone. He thought the fact that he was opposed to putting penises in his mouth was hilarious. One would think that the undead were above such trivial qualms, but they were not.

They can keep the men folk, he told himself while taking another bite of the girl's leg. *I'll stick to what I know best, and that's eating women.* The zombie's latest innuendo sent him into another laughing fit. Several minutes passed before he was able to bring himself under control.

Lawrence sighed again and looked up at the night sky as he chewed on a mouthful of blood and raw meat. Because his one eye sat askew, he had to cock his head at an odd angle in order to stare at the twinkling stars dotting the night sky. In the midst of it all sat the full moon, shining its pale light on the land around him.

The majestic scene made Lawrence think about Heaven, a place where he'd spent a brief moment of his afterlife. The zombie hadn't been banished or anything like that. He just opted to return to Earth, assuming that he would reappear in the form of a breathtaking angel, covered in glory and wielding a fiery, double-edged sword.

He looked down at his horrible form and let loose a derisive snort. He was breathtaking all right. Lawrence's spirit had been returned to the body he once knew, only to find that it continued to deteriorate if he failed to consume the flesh of the living. The zombie didn't like the idea of killing innocent people and devouring their bodies, but he refused to waste his return trip to Earth by rotting away in a grave somewhere. He had important business to attend to.

For the first time since his homecoming, he wondered if his purpose was worth sacrificing a comfortable afterlife.

I'll most likely go to Hell after my second death, the zombie lamented as he looked at the dead girl in his lap. He took another bite of his meal and sought comfort in the taste, like a fat person would find solace in a bucket of ice cream.

Lawrence thought about why he'd come back and decided that his sacrifice was well worth the cost. He would have never been able to enjoy his stay in paradise with vengeance on his mind.

One might assume that departed spirits were beyond such trivial qualms as vengeance, but they would be wrong.

About an hour later, Lawrence stared at the mutilated corpse in his lap. Blood was everywhere; the girl's skin had been peeled, flesh was torn, and bones were broken. The zombie knew that there was meat still to be eaten and he hated to waste good food, but he was stuffed.

Separating the meat from a skinny woman's bones was like eating freshly caught fish, or barbecued ribs. He was either going to get a bone stuck in his throat, or come across some meat he couldn't get to.

He let loose a loud burp, while covering his mouth with a bloody fist. Afterwards, he stood up and wiped his hands on the sides of his wet, muddy slacks. Now that he had consumed his after-dark breakfast, he was ready to get down to business.

He bent down and retrieved the bloody mess at his feet. With the torn carcass in tow, he turned around and entered the woods. The zombie whistled a catchy tune as he walked throughout the trunks of the rustling trees, but seeing as he had no lips, the only sound that came out was a droning noise.

A cool breeze blew across the land, and he cherished every minute of it. There was no cold draft in Hell, so he was going to make the most out of his second stay on Earth.

He listened to the crickets as they continued their annoying chirping. The zombie reveled in the sound of the frogs that shared his woods and lake home. The frogs also made a nice snack when human meat wasn't on the menu; that and the abundant fish which also inhabited the waters of Lake Thomas.

Lawrence was quite proud of his new setup, a niche he had carved for himself after rising from the grave. He slept beneath the mud of the lake when the sun took its place above the world, and when nighttime came, he feasted like a king. He had an all you can eat buffet of amphibians and fish, and when a foolish human came to his lake, he had dessert.

Yep, he thought, *the afterlife is good.*

Dry leaves and sticks crunched beneath his feet as he lumbered through the woods. A crackling sound followed him as he dragged his recent meal across the forest floor, leaving a bloody trail.

Lawrence continued to muse over how good he had it. He no longer had to rush to work every morning like he did when he was alive.

There were no taxes to be paid, no law to worry about, and he wasn't registered to vote. He didn't have to worry about working endless hours for a paycheck that barely made ends meet. He was no longer bound by a desire to climb the social ladder, while failing miserably.

He was free from the binds of life.

He came to a halt and looked up. He spotted a sturdy tree branch far above his head and decided to cast his kill into the crook of the limb. With only a fraction of his strength, Lawrence hurled the battered body up into the tree.

The young woman's carcass bashed into several limbs on the way up, failed to catch on anything, and began its descent back to where the zombie stood.

Realizing he was going to be hit with the returning corpse, he tried to get out of the way but the going was slow and the body hit him in the back of his neck and slid down his back.

What a spectacle I must be, he thought, laughing to himself.

Lawrence walked back over to the mutilated corpse and picked it up. He returned to his original spot and slung the body back up into the trees. The second time was the charm.

He stared at his handiwork, proud.

A few minutes later, Lawrence exited the woods and came upon a broken hill that served as the community of Springville's graveyard.

Horizontal and vertical headstones cluttered the area, while scattered leaves and burial flowers—both dead and plastic—added to the shoddiness of the place. That was the very site his body was to have rested in peace.

The zombie scowled at the thought of being buried in that un-kempt wasteland.

Because of his stiff legs, the muck-covered dead man half-slid, half-walked down the steep slope. Eventually, he came to stand before his own headstone. He stared at the words above his final resting place which read, **Lawrence W. Taylor. Born: December 3, 1969 - Died: February 12, 2011.**

Two days before Valentine's Day, he thought angrily while slowly shaking his head.

Below the timeline were the words his widow had asked to be inscribed on the tombstone. **Beloved husband.** Those two simple words made the zombie angrier than his departure date.

He clenched his rotting fingers, then unclenched them as he fought to subdue his rage. Shortly after arriving in Heaven, he had learned of the part his wife had played in his premature demise.

The woman had taken a lover outside of their marriage, and afraid that she would be left with nothing if Lawrence somehow found out and divorced her, she schemed to have him killed for the insurance money. Two days before Valentine's Day.

He tilted his head back and let loose a deafening roar that sent animals scurrying into the nearest, darkest hole and made children tremble beneath their blankets.

After releasing some frustration, he turned to face the small town at the bottom of the hill.

What his wife had done to him wasn't hard to discover after he became a spirit and was privileged to all the secrets of life. And like most restless spirits with a score to settle, Lawrence decided to return to Earth and exact his revenge.

The zombie knew that he would be redirected to Hell once his second life was over, but he was satisfied with the knowledge that he would not be the only one burning in the unquenchable flames.

Nestled within the small community at the bottom of the hill, was a particular house that he'd been keeping his remaining eye on—his old home.

For three months, he'd watched the house and during that long amount of time there had been no activity whatsoever. The zombie figured his wife and her lover had moved away with their blood money, which wasn't even that much in the first place.

Lawrence looked at his grave and thought, *I'm sure she saved a lot of money with the cheap ass funeral she gave me. If she'd spent a little more money on the casket, I probably would still be stuck in that box and she would have been spared the horror I plan on visiting upon her. I suppose I should be grateful for that.*

He turned his gaze back to the house that had served as his sanctuary from the world when he was alive. The same place that he'd been betrayed in.

After three long months of waiting, there was a light on in the upstairs bedroom. After three long months of waiting, he was finally going to exact his revenge.

His bumpy descent through the graveyard and an even longer trek across the country dirt roads took up more of his time than Lawrence liked, but he finally arrived at the rear entrance of his former house.

He angled his head so his one eye could peer through the window pane of the backdoor. He glanced around the moonlit kitchen to find no one in sight.

Eager to proceed with the murder and mayhem, he cocked his decaying arm back and sent it forward with amazing force.

Smash!

The single impact caused the glass to shatter and the wood to splinter. Immunity to pain was an upside to being deceased, and he made use of the beneficial attribute by reaching around the jagged shards of glass, which dug into his flesh. In less than ten seconds, Lawrence undid the three locks that barred entry.

Once his arm was retracted from the window, the zombie turned the doorknob and pushed the door open. Glass crunched beneath his heavy feet as he crossed the threshold, entering the dimly-lit room. Muddy footprints were left behind in his wake.

He found himself sidetracked as he glanced around the kitchen. It had been months since he last stepped foot into his house. He stared at the large kitchen table and thought about all the meals he and his wife had eaten in that room.

He reminisced on the great neighborhood parties they had thrown and how he and his wife went about making love on every surface in the home.

"WHO THE HELL IS IN MY HOUSE?" came a shout from the living room, ultimately yanking Lawrence from his nostalgic moment. The fact that the voice was male only increased his rage tenfold.

"WHO THE HELL IS IN *MY* HOUSE?" the furious zombie re-iterated. His shout sounded more like a bestial yell.

He heard the man in the living room mutter, "What the hell was that?"

I'll show you what the hell I am, he promised while staggering across the kitchen floor as quickly as he could. It wasn't long before he hurried through the doorway that led to the well-lit living room, and caught sight of the man his wife had willingly killed him for.

The man was dark-skinned and his hair was twisted up into well kept dreads. He stood at the bottom of the stairwell with his tattooed arms and bare chest visible, while his gym shorts hung off his rear end, showing the top of his boxers.

Lawrence always suspected that his wife had a thing for thug-gish men. Something he had never been.

"Oh shit!" the half-naked man screamed when he saw the gro-tesque form that was Lawrence. He lifted a pistol held in his right hand and fired.

The mud-covered zombie flinched as the bullet tore through his shoulder, but he felt no real pain. Lawrence straightened back up and fixed the gunman with an evil glare.

The frightened man shot three more times and Lawrence took the bullets without fear.

Realizing his weapon would be of no use against a zombie, the man turned and began to run away. Lawrence became worried. He didn't want to lose sight of his wife's boyfriend, out of fear that the man might escape.

The zombie lumbered over to a small table on the side of the living room couch. He snatched up the table and hurled it at the fleeing man before he had gone three feet.

The table crashed into the man's back and sent him colliding with the wall. Fueled by fear, the injured man managed to stand up, but Lawrence was ready for him.

The zombie reached for the fallen lamp that had been sitting on the table. He yanked the lamp's cord from the wall and threw it at the man's head with enough force to stun an elephant.

The porcelain lamp connected with the back of the man's skull and he fell face first onto the floor.

Lawrence hobbled over to the wounded man. Without hesitation, the zombie grabbed and pulled the man's shorts and underwear down in one swift motion. Lawrence reached between the unconscious man's legs and tore off his penis and testicles. The pain caused the man to wake up suddenly and scream in agony.

"I don't eat man meat!" the zombie growled as he slung the wad of flesh across the room. The meat hit the new flat screen television with a sickening thud before falling to the carpet. Lawrence reached down again and broke the man's neck, silencing his cries.

Once the evil deed was done, the zombie looked up to the top of the stairs.

"And then there was one," he grunted

A low creak filled the room as Lawrence pushed open the bedroom door. He lurched into the room, creating a wet, smacking sound with every step.

His head spun toward a loud gasp and he automatically spotted a dark-skinned woman sitting on the bed, huddled in her covers.

Damn it! Lawrence exclaimed mentally while looking over at the wide-eyed woman. *It's not Theresa. That's not my wife.*

The confused zombie glanced around the room and noticed unpacked boxes sitting against the wall. *Were there move-in boxes downstairs? I don't remember. I was too focused on killing…the wrong man.*

Lawrence's black heart fell to the bottom of his stomach as his entire world began to crash in on him. He'd given up an eternity of bliss in Heaven to exact revenge against his cheating wife and her lover, only to discover they had moved on and he could never possibly find them.

He had returned to the land of the living for nothing.

The frightened woman shivered from fear while sitting in a puddle of urine. Her watery eyes never left the monster that stood within her doorway.

Lawrence, on the other hand, stared down at his muddy shoes, obviously in deep contemplation. All of a sudden, a figurative light bulb clicked on in his head.

Unless… he mused. *Unless her relationship with whoever she's with doesn't work out and she returns to the only place she knows. Theresa will come back here and then I can have my revenge! But I'll have to keep the house empty so she can return.*

His head suddenly lifted and he fixed the whimpering woman with a murderous stare. He no longer felt guilty for killing the innocent man downstairs, nor did he have any remnants of sympathy for the woman before him.

The zombie had made up in his mind that they were standing between him and his only purpose on Earth—revenge.

He hobbled over to the woman and she proceeded to let out a blood-curdling shriek that was heard a great distance throughout the town of Springville. Then the scream ended just as abruptly as it began.

* * *

Six months later, the zombie known as Lawrence W. Taylor staggered through the dense woods humming happily to himself. He was quite content after having just finished eating a hearty breakfast of frogs and fish.

Eventually, he exited the woods and came to stand on the top of a steep hill. Below him was a cemetery, and below that was the small community known as Springville.

The zombie's lone eye immediately focused on one house in particular and a gruesome smile found its way onto his face. His shriveled heart would have been beating rapidly from excitement if it still worked.

He was elated because there were a couple of lights on in the house that used to belong to him and his treacherous wife. After six months of waiting, someone was finally occupying the house.

Lawrence had no idea if Theresa would be there when he arrived. Maybe it would be a single stranger, another couple, or a large family.

There was no way for the zombie to know from that distance, but one thing he did know was that whoever was in the house would die this night.

The only thing Lawrence had left was his thirst for revenge, and one way or another, he would have it.

THE WOODS' FAMILY FAREWELL

P. A. DOUGLAS

Nathan Woods was ten years on the police force and counting. With his dark hair, militaristic crew cut and thick mustache, he looked the part. He even acted it, too. Standing a solid six feet three inches and weighing in at nearly two hundred and thirty-five pounds, Nathan was a force to be reckoned with. Even at the age of forty-seven.

Originally from Atlanta, Nathan and his wife of twelve years had moved to Georgia for three years to be re-stationed, this being his second transfer with a promotion attached. It was a big advancement.

Being a father of two children, Carla age sixteen and Billy age seven, he took a great deal of pride in the idea that he was making his home a safer place for his children. Sure, it was hard on the kids having to move twice already, but he'd promised them that this would be the last time for quite a while. He'd kept his word.

As lead sheriff of the Bay County police force in Panama City and Panama City Beach, Florida, Nathan and his family had made the small tourist town their home. It had only taken four years to get settled and for Billy to make a solid set of real friends.

He'd always had trouble with that, though his sister Carla did not. And with her out on the streets driving this year, there was no telling how many more friends would be added to the list.

This Tuesday was no different for the Woods family than any other. It was seven-thirty in the morning already and Billy was now off to school on the bus, Helen was up and about doing things to upkeep the house and Carla…well, she was sixteen. She was hard to keep up with.

"Come in, Nathan…this is Betty. We have a problem, over!" the radio CB crackled.

Nathan retrieved the handset from the radio attached to his unit next to his locked shotgun.

Sitting in his police car, a fresh set of creamy hot donuts and a steaming cup of coffee in his lap, it was unusual for Betty to call him so early. His routine over the last four years had been relatively the same; see the kids off to school, give the wife a kiss and hit the donut stand before getting to work by eight.

Something had to be wrong.

Nathan clicked the handset with the car door still open. "What do you have for me, Betty? I'm only a few minutes from the station, over."

"We've had a flood of calls coming in all morning and the day is just getting' started, over."

"What do you mean 'a flood of calls'? Over." He leaned back, touching the hot cup of fresh coffee to his lips using his free hand. He surveyed the parking lot around him at the donut stand. Come to think of it, business did seem a little slow, the parking lot empty.

"Over half of our units have already been dispatched to handle various calls this morning. You need to get here fast. This place is a mad house, over."

"I'm on my way." He slammed the clip back onto the radio, putting the car into reverse. Almost forgetting to close the car door, he tossed the box of donuts in the passenger seat and drove while still balancing his hot coffee in one hand.

More than half of the units? That has to be something like fifteen cars or more, he thought, already pulling up to the precinct. He was right and almost all of the police cars were gone, and before the morning meeting. *What the hell is going on?*

He jumped out of the car and dashed inside.

The station was just as Betty had suggested. A mad house of clerks, detectives and police officers frantically moved about in the large building. Phones were ringing off the hook and more than a dozen crazed civilians sat and stood, each handcuffed to various locations. The place was chaotic.

"What the hell is going on, Betty?" Nathan asked as he reached her desk, glancing down at his watch. It was nearly eight. "Get someone to put these people into proper holding cells, for Christ's sake!"

"I wish I could, Nathan. The cells are full." Betty hadn't even looked up from her files as she shuffled through paperwork with the phone glued to her ear and resting on the shoulder. Cupping the mouth piece on the phone, she leaned across the desk, eyeing Nathan intently. "There's a man in your office to see you. He says he is from the CIA or the FBI or something."

Nathan glanced to his office from across the room, down at Betty, then back to his office again. "You're kidding, right?"

She just looked at him.

Responding to one of the many domestic dispute calls, the two man patrol car slowly pulled up to the home where the call was made. The car idled and the two officers hesitantly stepped out of the vehicle.

Without warning, the front door to the home came crashing open. A panicked woman drenched in blood ran out, fleeing to the two men. "On my God, please help me!" she shouted, out of breath. The agitated woman crashed into one of the officers, his arms embracing her.

"Calm down, miss. Calm down!" He clicked the handset on his shoulder. "We need medical response to a domestic dispute, over."

"Location," the voice from the other end asked without hesitation.

"1945 Alabama Ave., Lynn Haven, over."

There was no reply.

"Help is on the way, ma'am. You just need to calm down…"

"Hostile!"

The officer comforting the injured woman looked up, his partner's gun already drawn. At the opened door to the home, a large man stepped out onto the porch. Covered in blood, the man's mouth and arms were drenched in red.

He slowly staggered toward the two cops, arms raised and mouth wide. His milky white gaze fixed on the woman and he moaned low in his throat.

"Hands on top of your head, now!" the police officer yelled with his gun drawn. "Do not move!"

Not realizing that the woman had become limp and heavy in his arms, the officer assisted the woman to the grass while retrieving his side arm, the hostile still approaching. "An ambulance is on the way, ma'am." When he looked down at her, he saw that she was unconscious. The blood from her open wounds soaked the grass under her dying body.

With guns aimed at the hostile, both officers barked and spit a relentless plea of orders at the oncoming man.

"I said, hands on top of your fucking head, now! Before I shoot you right where you stand! Do you hear me?" one officer said.

A single shot rang out.

It went wild, clearly a warning shot. The echo of the handgun's discharge bounced off the surrounding homes, causing the sound of gunfire to linger in the air. The hostile kept coming. He snarled in a vicious fit, closing the distance between him and the cops.

Both officers glanced at one another with weary eyes, then back at the man approaching them.

"Fuck him…" one cop said and fired at the man. Two shots jolted the hostile as each round splintered into his upper thigh. A gush of blood splashed from the open wounds upon impact, the pant leg beginning to saturate with dark red.

The man acted as if the bullets were nothing and still he kept coming, his mouth dripping saliva tinged with crimson.

That should have taken him down. What the hell is…

Suddenly, a sharp piercing pain broke through the policeman's thought, his ankle instantly on fire. Startled and falling forward to his knees, the officer caught himself but not before seeing who his attacker was.

The woman at his feet had lunged forward, taking him to the ground. She gnashed and ripped at his leg violently. His ankle already bleeding from the bite, she bit down again.

Countless jolts of pain shot through him as flesh and muscle was torn from bone.

His gurgling screams were drowned out by the sound of gunfire.

"What the hell do you mean 'dead'?" Nathan stood in his office, the suspicious man dressed in black refusing to show any form of identification.

"It's exactly as I've said, Sheriff. The dead have come back to life and we need you and your men patrolling the surrounding areas. The National Guard has already been notified and should be arriving shortly. We need to make sure that this thing remains contain…"

"You have got to be out of your mind! You don't actually expect me to believe that. Do you honestly presume I tell my men to simply start shooting everyone that doesn't cooperate?"

"No, not just shoot them, Sheriff Woods." The man in black calmly paced around the room, looking at the sheriff's many photos and awards on the wall. He glanced at Nathan with a scowl of seriousness. "Head shots, Sheriff. That's the only finite solution to this devastating situation."

"You have got to be out of your fucking mind!" Before Nathan was able to continue, the phone on his office desk rang, the tension in the room thickening with each if its chimes. "What is it," he said, the phone already to his ear, his eyes still locked with the unidentified man in black.

Betty said, "Nathan, we've already lost contact with more than ten of our units. It's getting worse out there."

His vision slightly blurred and a sense of light headedness slowly took hold. He found himself balanced with one hand against the desk. "Do me a favor Betty, Call every last unit in. We need them back here at the station yesterday. I want everyone still accounted for to rally up and meet in the assignment hall. No less than forty-five minutes. Got that?" He nodded before hanging up the phone and look at the man before him. "You're actually serious about all this, aren't you."

"Deadly serious, Sheriff!" the man replied.

By noon, every unit had been briefed by a man that still refused to identify himself. Had it all not been happening so fast, Nathan might have gone about things a little differently.

He'd already had way too many men unaccounted for and as a result reluctantly gave the mysterious man the floor when briefing the officers at the station. FBI, CIA or whatever form of the government the man was associated with at this point didn't matter.

What did matter was that the information told in the meeting was true. The dead had returned to life and were feasting on the living. Those that died by their hand then in turn became one of them.

After patrolling the surrounding area for only a few hours, Nathan did the unthinkable. He resigned. He may not have made it official, but one thing was sure, before taking care of the citizens of Panama City, Florida, his family came first, and getting to them was what he planned to do.

Turning off his two-way radio, he went to his son's middle school and pulled the boy out of school, then drove home. Nathan hoped that Carla had been let out early and was already headed home. If not, he would get her too.

The drive was gut-wrenching. Countless undead mobs were in the streets, feasting on one another, terrorizing neighborhoods.

It was the same all across town.

When he arrived home, he parked out front and he and Billy got out and ran to the front door. After unlocking it, Nathan burst inside with Billy right behind him.

"Helen! Helen! Are you home, honey?" he called out.

There was no reply.

"Stay here, son. I'm gonna check the rest of the house. Just sit on the couch and don't move, okay?" Before Billy could say anything, Nathan was clear across the room as he began his search.

Carla hadn't made it home yet, and Nathan was beginning to think she wouldn't at all. Helen's car was in the driveway when he'd pulled up, so she had to be home.

But where was she?

He'd already searched the house twice and found nothing. Where could she be?

Suddenly a loud bang jarred the front door on its hinges. Billy jumped to his feet, standing atop the sofa cushions. "Daddy! Someone's at the door!" he yelled out.

Darting across the kitchen and back into the living room, Nathan went to the peephole at the front door.

It was Helen.

"Thank God," he said, reaching for the door handle.

The very second the door swung inward, a very dead and mutilated Helen staggered inside. Catching her husband by surprise, she fell on top of him, forcing him onto his back on the carpet.

With his gun still in his hand, Nathan wrestled with the woman who was most definitely not his wife…not anymore. She spit and snarled with rage, trying her best to sink her teeth into his jugular.

"Helen, no…please, it's me, Nathan," he said as he struggled to keep her at bay.

"Daddy, look out!"

Two zombies stumbled into the house from the open doorway, each bearing similar marks and abrasions, their clothes covered in blood. Their moans filled the house.

"Billy, get in the kitchen!" Nathan snapped at his son, who was frozen in horror as he stood on the couch. "Run, son, run!"

The moment he took to tell Billy to run was a costly one. Helen's teeth sank into Nathan, sending sharp pains into his arm. She tore away skin and tendons, blood gushing out around her snarling lips. He yelped in pain.

Shoving her off, he staggered to his feet. With all three of the zombies trailing him and more steadily making their way across the driveway, the patrol car was no longer an option for escape, so he made his way into the kitchen.

"What's wrong with Mommy, Daddy? Why'd she hurt you?" Billy asked as his father entered the kitchen.

"Everything's fine, son, Mommy's gonna be fine. I promise." As he said this, the three zombies rounded the corner in the hallway and entered the kitchen.

"Daddy, look out!"

Nathan turned with his gun drawn.

Head shots… That's the only finite solution to this devastating situation, he recalled the man in black telling him. His bloodied arm throbbed but he ignored it. His mind raced with the memories of his life with his family.

Images of his marriage to Helen, their first child Carla being born, then Billy. It all flooded his mind in a wave of emotions.

Helen shuffled forward with her arms reaching for him. Her milky eyes were glazed over in death, the others right behind her.

"Why did this happen? Why?" A tear found the corner of Nathan's eye and before it had time to fall, a single shot sounded.

The bullet struck Helen right between the eyes. In slow motion, he watched in horror as the love of his life left him forever. Her head jerked back, blood and brain matter spraying out of the back of her skull.

The small hole above her nose seemed to appear from thin air as it leaked blood down the front of her face.

She was dead.

The living room was crowded with more zombies, their moans snapping the grief-filled sheriff out of his stupor. He sucked back another tear and turned to sweep a crying and terrified Billy into his arms. The sudden throbbing pain in Nathan's arm came to the forefront of his mind as the young boy's weight weighed on him. The wound was deep and bleeding heavily.

"You shot Mommy! You killed Mommy!" Billy cried under wheezing breaths. Nathan was out the back door and halfway across the backyard before the forest zombie was at the back door. Nathan hopped the fence and landed in the alley leading to the street.

Nathan ignored Billy's sobs about Helen. He didn't understand. How could he, he was only seven. With Billy still under his wounded arm, Nathan jogged down a side road leading out and into Mackenzie Park.

It was crawling with zombies, but at least they were thinned out unlike everywhere else, allowing him to avoid them easily.

It was then that Nathan spotted the public bathroom building across the grass by the pavilion. He'd responded to more than a dozen calls in his time as lead sheriff to the park for vandalized property issues.

On most nights when it got called in, kids would break into the restrooms, making a major mess of things which meant it was locked at night.

Dashing across the park and right up to the building, he saw that a handful of stragglers were headed in his direction. He ignored them for now, wanting to get Billy safe. It was all he could do, all he could hope for.

As father and son stood before the building, Nathan flashed back to something that was said by the unidentified agent in his office.

Those that are bitten will turn, you can count on it. He couldn't go with his son, it would be too dangerous. His throbbing arm jarred his train of thought. His wife, she'd been one of them. She'd bit him so he was infected too and sooner or later he would turn as well.

The door was locked as it should be. He couldn't shoot the lock off or there would be no way to secure the door, so he went around to the side of the building where there was a small, wire mesh fold out window six feet off the ground.

He was in luck, it was open and unless zombies could climb, they couldn't get to it, and even if they did, the window was too small to allow an adult to pass through it.

"Okay, now listen to me, son. You need to go through that window. I'll lift you up," he told Billy as he picked him up so that Billy could reach the edge with his hands. Billy did as he was told and began to climb up. When he was halfway through the window, he paused and looked back at Nathan.

"I love you, son," he said as he looked up at Billy. "Now you stay in there till I come back for you. Don't come out for any of the bad people."

"I love you, too, Daddy! Don't leave me." Billy reached out a small hand.

Nathan Woods got underneath his son's feet, and with his hands on Billy's sneakers, he shoved up and pushed his son through the window and into the bathroom.

He heard Billy fall and then his son call out that he was all right. Nathan turned to face the oncoming undead crowd. He had to lead them away from the bathroom, to at least give his son a chance.

A light cough filled his throat and he tasted blood.

He shot the first few zombies to get their attention, then began to move off deeper into the park, shooting one every now and then to keep the walking dead focused on him.

Head shots, he thought. *Head shots!*

Inside the bathroom, the frightened little boy could hear the gunshots as they slowly grew fainter, his father moving away from him.

Billy Woods never saw his father again.

BROTHERS FOREVER

SUZANNE ROBB

"Hey, beautiful, can I get you a drink?" The chick standing next to Jerry was too hot to ignore.

"I already have a drink, but thanks."

Jerry leaned in towards her. "But what happens when you're done with the one you have? You'll need another one."

"Very true, you're Jerry, right?"

"I see you've heard of me" Jerry puffed up his chest with pride.

"Oh yes, I know all about you. Why don't we go do some tequila shooters?"

"A girl after my own heart. What's your name?

"Jen, but it won't really matter later on, will it? Plus, it's not your heart I'm after." She smiled seductively and Jerry followed her like a dog after a bone.

I think, therefore I have to be alive. Jerry kept repeating this to himself. He had no idea what happened, but someone would pay.

He remembered doing tequila shooters with a hot chick, then he'd woken up in an frigging embalming room. Then someone had stabbed him with an unreasonably large needle, apparently to drain his blood.

He tried to scream, but no sound other than weird guttural moans came out. The man sticking him was so shocked he passed out cold, hitting his head on the metal table as he fell.

Jerry took the opportunity to sit up and look around. The process was much harder than it should have been. Not seeing anything exciting or interesting among the medical equipment, he turned his attention to the man on the floor.

He absently licked the spot of blood left by the man's head on the table before realizing he was doing it. He decided being naked wasn't cool and stole the clothes of the unconscious man. His hands were a bit stiff, but after fumbling for several minutes, he got the buttons and zippers to cooperate.

He noticed the Y-incision on his chest as he buttoned the shirt. *What the hell? Did someone actually do an autopsy on me?* he wondered in shocked amazement.

This was getting ridiculous, he'd heard of hazing before, but this went too far for his tastes.

He looked for a mirror, and found one above the corner sink. He tried to look at his reflection, but his eyes, normally a chocolate brown, were now milky white. What he did make out in the reflection didn't make him feel any better.

His hair went out in all directions. His body, which he had worked so hard on in the gym, now looked loose and pale. The only bonus, he now had a cool scar, and chicks dug scars.

All of a sudden, Jerry remembered his girlfriend Holly, he needed to call her. They were supposed to meet up last night, but he'd gotten distracted by something. He looked around the room and saw a rotary phone on a small metal desk. He headed towards it, and after several minutes, succeeded in punching in the number.

When Holly answered, he tried to talk, but only breathy moans came out.

"You disgusting bastard! My boyfriend just died and you're prank calling me? Sicko!"

He heard the click of the phone being disconnected.

He stood still for a moment, holding the phone. Obviously something wasn't right with this situation. He had a Y-incision, he couldn't talk, his eyes were freaky, and he moved slower and clumsier than usual. Now Holly said her boyfriend, Jerry, was 'dead.' Definitely not good.

Jerry stood there for a moment trying to think. Focusing on one thing was harder than he remembered it being. He felt like his head was filled with sand. Only one solution came to mind, zombies. Sometime last night he'd been bit, and now he was one of the undead. But that was impossible because he could reason, and he wasn't even thinking about brains. In fact, he wanted a cheeseburger with fries, or even a steak. Of course he wanted them cooked really rare, but still, they weren't brains. He hung up the phone, and decided what to do next.

Absently he walked over to the man passed out cold on the floor and began gnawing on his arm. Soon, he had blood dripping from his chin and onto his chest, and occasionally his tongue would dart out to catch some of the leakage. Jerry was totally unaware of his actions. He needed to talk to someone from the party he'd attended last night. Who did he talk to last?

Thinking again, it was hard. He'd been talking to a girl, a brunette, a hot chick by the bar. She was way into him, and it wasn't like he and Holly were married. What the hell was her name? He remembered she lived in the Sawyer dorm, so he decided to go there and 'stalk' her, no wait, he wanted to go there and 'talk' to her.

What smelled so horrible? Jerry kept looking around to find the source of the odor he'd been dealing with for the last few hours. He'd chosen to hide in the bushes outside of Jen's dorm. He felt the need to hide and stalk her for some reason.

Did a dog take a crap? He looked at the bottom of his feet, and on the ground around him, but saw nothing. He just had to deal with the smell for now. He had to keep his eyes on the dorm.

Hours passed and he grew bored, and hungry. He didn't have a watch on so he had no idea what time it was, only it that it was dark. He saw a bug on the tree next to him, and ate it.

He felt bad about Holly. He didn't want her to be upset, especially since he'd slept with Jen, or at least he thought he did.

Hopefully Holly didn't know, then again, somewhere in his head he planned on stopping by to see Holly and eat her. Wait, he didn't want to do that, it would be bad. He wanted to 'talk' to her.

Finally, Jen came out of the dorm with a stack of books in one hand, and a cell phone to her ear with the other. Jerry watched which direction she went in, the casually followed her. The fact that it was dark out gave him an advantage, but he knew he stuck out just a bit.

His shirt was half buttoned, the Y-incision visible, and his eyes were milky white. Then again, college campuses were full of all types, so not many people paid attention to him.

When no one else was around except Jen, he hurried his pace. At least he tried to, his left leg dragging behind him. This made him try to speak again, the guttural moaning noises, and hoped when Jen turned around she would recognize him before running off screaming.

He thought Jen might be going to the library, what with all the books she was carrying. She hung up her cell, then took something out of her purse. She slowed her pace, and Jerry tried to talk again as he caught up to her.

She turned around, and he saw the shock in her eyes just before she sprayed him with mace.

Jerry tried to reach out to her; he needed to talk to her. The mace was more of a nuisance than anything else, as he didn't feel any pain, but out of instinct he tried to rub his eyes. As soon as he did, she dropped her books and ran off screaming.

Jerry stood there, trying to clear out his eyes, and looked down at the mess Jen had left behind. Her bag was there so he searched it and grabbed her keys. He would just wait in her room to eat her, he decided. No, he wasn't going to eat her, he would explain what had happened.

Turning around, he dragged himself back to the dorms. This whole zombie thing sucked. Why couldn't he be a vampire, a werewolf, or even a damn leprechaun?

It took a few extra minutes to use the keys on the front door of the ground floor. He had lost a lot of his dexterity and ability to manipulate small things. Finally, he got the door open. He took the elevator up to her room, and had to go through the key process again. He got some odd looks from people, but for the most part no one seemed to say anything as he entered Jen's room. This made Jerry wonder about her a little more.

When he entered the room, what he found shocked him. The interior looked like some sort of demon witch store. There was a cauldron in the corner, some small little voodoo-looking dolls, and lots of bottles with odd things inside. Books littered a small coffee table with pentagrams and other symbols he didn't recognize on their covers.

He moved further inside the room and saw magazines to **Witches Brew Monthly,** and **Men Suck and Should all die!**

He began to think perhaps she had something to do with what had happened to him.

He walked further into the room and saw several pictures of his frat brothers hanging on a wall. There were seventeen total in the picture and five of their faces had a bright red X through them.

He knew them all because there was such a big deal made when they'd disappeared. During the last few weeks, there had been a rash of mysterious disappearances.

Rumors were rampant about some of the guys freaking out and leaving school, or getting a chick pregnant, or a fraternity row serial killer. Looking at the wall, then down at himself, he went with psycho killer witch.

He stopped short when he saw his picture had an X on it. This was bad, very bad. He needed to eat Jen's brains. No, he needed to pick Jen's brains out of his teeth. No, he needed pick Jen's brain about what happened.

Jerry was so hungry. He went to the mini-fridge and opened it and a jar of something disgusting caught his attention. He opened it and ate it. It wasn't bad, but it was no blood-filled liver. Liver? Where did that come from?

Jen was a witch, and not the cool hippy 'let's love the Earth' kind. She obviously did bad things to frat guys for some reason, and he had to kill her. Wait, he had to ask her to reverse it, then kill her. With his plan set, he shambled over to the bed and took a seat. He was trying to keep his wits about him, but it was so hard. Maybe if he took a little nap he could clear up some of the cobwebs. Before he realized it, he was asleep.

When he woke up, he knew trouble was brewing. He opened his milky eyes and saw Jen had returned while he'd slept. She didn't look happy, but oddly she didn't look scared either.

"What the hell are you doing in my room?" She stood in front of him with a hammer in her hand.

"Mmmnhh…mmmmnnnnn..." he said.

"Oh right, you can't talk. You ate my goat embryo from my fridge. Do you know how hard those are to get?"

Jerry tried his best to be coherent. Usually not a fan of talking, he really wished he could right about now. Unfortunately, he continued to make horrible, breathy, moaning noises.

He tried to stand up so he could attack her, and eat her brains. No wait, he just wanted to calm her down. He couldn't stand though, because she had tied him up. He looked at her, pleading with his eyes to explain to him what the hell happened.

"All you guys are the same. You see a chick, think she's hot, bang her, then forget about her. Or you have a girlfriend who actually loves you, and you cheat on her at a party because you got wasted on tequila shooters."

Jerry's eyes widened, he'd been doing tequila shooters with Jen when things went dark. He started to motion frantically to the photo of frat guys.

"Those are my targets. Every single one of them has pissed off a girl on this campus. I'm sort of the 'go to' girl for revenge. I don't mean to brag or anything, but I'm quite good at my job."

Jerry looked down at himself, then back up to her and nodded. He hoped she'd made a mistake with him, and would clear everything up. Then he remembered he'd cheated on Holly with one of her sorority pledges last week, and one time with her best friend. Okay, he'd been a target.

"Jerry, you weren't supposed to get up and walk around. My goal is the most suffering possible. The other guys I took care of myself. I like the look of horror on your faces when you realize nothing will ever be the same. There's just something so satisfying in a job well done." She smiled. "You, on the other hand, got so wasted you fell off the balcony. People saw, paramedics came, you were pronounced dead, blah, blah, blah."

Jerry really wanted her to fill in more of the blah part of the story. The part where he became a zombie.

"But you woke up, and felt no pain from the autopsy: blood draining, embalming, any of it. You're not supposed to wake up, Jerry. You just totally screwed my average. If you let word of this get out so help me I'll…"

He had no idea how she planned on finishing the sentence since he was already dead. He tried to raise an eyebrow, but couldn't. In fact, he had a hard time moving anything. He tried looking at her with sad eyes again, willing to try anything to get this sadistic psycho to undo what she did.

"See, once I make enough of you into zombies, I'm turning you loose on campus. Can you imagine the pure chaos? There will be blood and carnage everywhere. It's enough to get me all hot and bothered." He watched as she began to get aroused.

He might have been a zombie, but things still affected him. Listening to the way she talked about the carnage and blood that would be rampant aroused him, too. He had no idea zombies could be aroused, but the grumbling in his stomach and the drool coming out of his mouth let him know he could still get happy. He looked towards the photo on the wall, then back to Jen.

"Oh yes, the others are zombies, too. Different than you though. I must have given you too much or too little, or it might have to do with your fall of the balcony. Everyone else is totally brain dead with no thought other than eating brains. You though, you're special. I don't know what to do about that."

Jerry knew that was bad. Most people thought thinking was a good thing, but right now he knew his brain function was bad. He knew any plans she had to fix him were not going to be beneficial to him. He decided to act as if he'd finally turned into a full-fledged brain obsessed zombie. He made the guttural noises and tried to raise his tied hands up in the motion zombies often did in the movies.

"Nice try, Jerry, but you won't have to worry much longer. I can't have a thinking zombie. I'll be putting you out of your misery soon. By the way, no offense, but you smell terrible. You could've at least let the embalmer drain and embalm you."

So, 'he' was the smell. Great he was a smelly zombie with no plan, and in all likelihood this psycho would find something worse to do to him. He had a hard time imagining worse, until she walked over to him with a sharp metal device.

"Don't worry, you won't feel a thing. Buck up, Jerry, it's one of the bonuses of being a zombie, you don't feel any pain, although, it's probably the only bonus."

Jerry closed his eyes as he felt his body being pulled one way, then another. It didn't hurt, it actually tickled in a weird way. He cracked an eye open and saw Jen had cut the sutures on his Y-incision. His insides were now outside, and he really hoped she would do him a solid and put them away when she was finished.

She poked around his insides and Jerry thought with the smell they would be halfway decomposed, but they actually looked quite healthy.

"Well, Jerry, you lucked out. Whatever happened to you is unique. I need to study it, seems like you get to live a little longer. A brainless decomposing zombie is one thing, but a zombie that can think with a slower decomposition rate is a whole new game."

Jerry watched happily as she shoved his insides back where they belonged. They might not be in the right location exactly, but they were inside and that's what mattered.

He flinched when she pulled out a medical staple gun, and closed his incision. He looked down at her work. Not too bad, but he didn't think there should be things sticking out of the staples.

"You interest me, Jerry. I'm not going to put you in the pit with the others. I'm going to have some fun instead."

He knew that meant more tests, and after watching her play with his insides like it was Play-doh, he really didn't like that option. He would have to escape. Problems with that plan were many. He was tied up, lacking physical strength, and his thoughts kept roaming to eating her.

"Hmm, I bet you're hungry."

Jerry looked up at her from the bed, nodding in agreement.

Jen walked over to the kitchen counter, and returned with a knife. He started to get nervous. A psycho with a knife; not a good thing in his book. She knelt between his legs. If he wasn't so scared he might have been turned on.

"There, the ankle bindings are undone, now let's do the wrist ones. And, Jerry, before I do this, you need to know I'm faster, stronger, and can kill you very easily. You're going to do exactly as I say. Understand?"

He nodded his head in agreement, it was his only chance for escape and he couldn't waste it. She cut the binds on his wrists and he lunged for her immediately. At least he thought he did. Jen reached a hand out to steady him when he stood up. He seemed to lean in one direction.

"Looks like you aren't too steady on your feet right now. Let's get you some food."

Jerry shrugged his shoulders, and followed her out of the apartment. She slowed her pace so he could keep up. Obviously, he wouldn't be outrunning her. He kept looking at the back of her head and thinking about the tasty brains inside.

"Okay, I have a specific target in mind. Look over there."

Jerry glanced in the direction she pointed and saw Sean, one of his frat brothers.

"I want you to go attack and eat him, but don't eat his brains. I want to see if you can infect someone so they turn out the same way you did."

Jerry had no idea what she was talking about. He did know Sean was a prick, and he would happily eat his brains. He started to make his way over to where Sean was having a cigarette with some chick. Fifteen feet away the two turned towards Jerry.

Sean turned around and the chick screamed and ran. Sean stood still for a moment before he started to laugh.

"Wow, Jerry, that is the coolest costume ever."

Jerry just continued to shamble.

"Jerry, you okay, man? That was a nasty fall last night, and hey, aren't you supposed to be dead?"

Jerry reached Sean just as he realized what was going on. Jerry tore into his throat, and started to gorge himself. He enjoyed his meal, about to go in for the brainy goodness when he felt a tap on the shoulder.

"Uh-uh, no brains, remember?"

Jerry didn't remember that. Dammit he wanted the brains, to taste their creamy goodness. The way they would feel in his mouth. He'd never actually eaten brains before, but he assumed they were yummy, because there was no other reason for him to crave them like an eight month pregnant woman craved sardines and ice cream.

Another tap on his shoulder indicated he would be wise to avoid said brains.

"Good boy, now let's go. I promise you can have the brains of the next person."

He perked up at this, and his shamble seemed to have a bit of a lift in it. He followed her all over the campus. He bit dogs, couples making out, teachers in their offices, and janitors. Jen seemed to be an equal opportunity infector.

Personally, Jerry didn't care, but then he started to feel full in a weird spot other than his abdomen. Biology had never been his best subject, in fact he failed it twice. He did know however, that his stomach should not even remotely be close to his armpit. The bulge and full feeling he developed there convinced him Jen had put his stomach back in the wrong spot.

He would have to ask her to fix it. As they were walking back to the dorm, he made some groans and moans until Jen looked at him.

"What is it? I'm tired. I need to tie you up and get ready for a chemistry final."

"Mnnnnnmm…ghee."

"Jerry I don't have time for this, you can play with more brains tomorrow."

Jerry pointed to his armpit.

"What the hell is that? What did you do? You better hope the swelling goes down."

He gave up and followed behind her. His head felt heavy again. He had a total food high. This was like nothing he'd ever experienced before. Perhaps being a zombie wasn't as bad as he thought. The food was awesome, and he got off on the fear he seemed to evoke in people.

When they arrived back at Jen's room, she tied him up just like she said she would and then cracked open her chemistry book. Jerry watched for a few moments. Watching someone study was less interesting than watching paint dry. Letting his eyes wander, he noticed a metal nail file on the table next to the chair he was tied to.

The thing about being a normal zombie, you got bored very easily, and your thought process revolved around brains. Since Jerry was different, he could think about other things, for a short while at least. The thinking part came in handy because he had planned to escape tonight. Whatever Jen had planned, he wanted no part of it.

"I'm going to bed. Make any noise and I'll put you downstairs with your frat brothers, or kill you," she said.

He nodded his head like a good zombie, and tried to smile.

"Don't you dare make a threatening face at me." She started to advance on him with a knife.

Jerry tried to hold his hands up in supplication, keeping his face neutral. Jen slowed her approach, then stopped altogether.

"Good boy." She turned and walked away.

He would have gulped, or let out a breath of relief if he did those things still. Instead he waited for what felt like an eternity, but had really only been ten minutes. He reached over to grab the nail file, glad he could reach it.

He started with his wrists. The sawing was much harder than the movies made it out to be. The fact he wasn't very adept at it didn't help.

After an hour, and several cuts to his wrists, which would have ended his life were he alive, his hands were free of his bindings. Getting through the rope on his feet was significantly easier. Within moments he freed himself. He stood slowly, not on purpose, he was just slow.

He ambled over to the door, keeping the nail file in his hand. He turned the knob and made it into the hallway. He left the door open behind him and made a dash/rapid shamble for the stairs.

He felt like things were finally going his way. When he'd reached the main floor of the dorm, there as still no sign of Jen behind him. He looked around, and then remembered something she'd said about his frat brothers in the basement. He decided he would stop whatever plans she had; it would really annoy her and he liked doing that.

After going down another set of stairs, he found himself on some sort of maintenance floor. There were some boilers, heating and water pipes, random things he couldn't remember the name of, and a door with a huge sign, *Keep Out!*

He figured that was the door he needed to go through. As he headed towards it, he heard familiar sounds. As he got closer the sounds began to make sense.

Jerry ambled faster and flung the door open. He saw his missing frat brothers, at least he thought so. They were badly decomposed, and covered in rotten flesh from whatever they were eating.

"Jerry is that you?"

"Yeah, is that you, Mike?" he said.

"No, I'm Kyle, Mike is over there. The other two are Carl and John."

"Man, it's good to see you guys. I thought I was going crazy." Jerry leaned on the doorframe in relief as he spoke.

"Same here. Jen's a whack job. She seems to be collecting us." Kyle indicated the ropes keeping them all in place.

"I'm just glad I have someone to talk to. I felt like no one understood me, ya know? Like no one knew what I was saying, or even cared."

"Yeah, I get that, Jerry. Say, think you could do us a favor and untie us?" Kyle looked hungry.

"No problem, I got it," he said and started to untie Kyle first. Jen had only tied the hands of the four down here. He remembered her saying something about these guys being all about the brains. If she had only taken the time to try and understand them, she might have a totally different perspective.

Several minutes later, all the zombie frat brothers were free. Kyle, Carl, John, and Mike were in bad shape. They were falling apart, literally. Jerry figured the best thing for them would be a good meal. He knew after he'd eaten ate he'd felt a lot better, and the world didn't seem so bleak.

"Hey, I bet you guys are hungry. Wanna go eat Jen?"

All four nodded and followed behind him.

Jerry had to slow his shamble so they could keep up. It took almost ten minutes to climb one floor. Jerry motioned them to the elevator to do the next three floors. They looked at him with nothing short of awe.

"Wow, never would have thought of that. Since when were you the smart one, Jerry?"

"I don't know. Jen apparently messed up when she did whatever it is she does, to me anyway."

"That's kind of cool. So what are we doing? We're hungry."

"We're going to eat Jen to get our revenge," he said with a smile.

"Awesome, why didn't you say so."

He just smiled at them, and made his way off the elevator towards Jen's room. Her door was still open, and he assumed she was still asleep. He and the others made their way into her room and headed towards her bed. She woke up at the last minute, there was no time to scream.

Jerry watched the others eat.

The four zombies tore and ripped at Jen's flesh. He watched closely, making sure they didn't eat her brains. He still felt full, and as tempting as brains were, he had a better idea. He felt the bulge by his armpit, annoyed it had not gone down in size. What if Jen had put those necessary parts of his anatomy where his lungs should be? He wondered if he should be worried about what would happen when he went to the bathroom. Did he go to the bathroom?

"Jerry, you really gotta have some of this."

"No thanks, I'm full," he said.

As soon as Jerry thought enough of Jen had been eaten, he told them to stop. Difficult to stop them at first, he only got them to ease off when he mentioned a hot chick in the room next door. The guys disappeared.

Jerry checked Jen's head, her brain thankfully intact. Screams came from the room next door as his buddies began their attack. He knew he had inadvertently started Jen's plan early, but with his guidance and leadership, they might have a shot at creating some major carnage, or die trying. Either way, he was happy to get his revenge on Jen.

It took several hours, but when she finally opened her eyes, Jerry smiled at her. She looked down at her body and screamed.

"You bastard, what did you do to me? I'm going to kill you?"

"I'm already dead, you made sure of that."

"I can understand you?"

"Of course you can, you're a zombie now. We're the same."

"Dammit." She tried to stand up, but one of the other zombies had chewed off her left foot.

Jerry just smiled, or at least he tried to. Jen struggled to get up, which had to be difficult. Her foot was not the only thing missing, most of her insides were outside, or gone. One of her arms was gnawed off at the elbow, and her other leg had been eaten down to the femur.

"Well, are you just going to sit there? Help me."

"I'll help you if you tell me how we undo this. I want to be alive again. Brains are great, but I don't want this."

"Jerry, there's no undoing this, once a zombie always a zombie."

"So you created a fraternity from Hell then. Well, that's all I needed to know."

She tried to maneuver away as Jerry moved in towards her. He opened his mouth wide, and moments later finally got the tasty brains he'd been waiting for. The screams were still coming from the lower floors as his frat buddies did their thing, and from Jen. She struggled for a bit under him, then stopped.

As soon as she stopped struggling, he stopped eating. Dead brains really didn't taste good.

Standing up, he looked down at her and shook his head. He started towards the door, and saw the mayhem in the hallway. People were covered in blood, some had bite marks, others were just confused.

He saw that his frat brothers had enjoyed themselves.

He smiled.

They were going to be brothers forever now.

He planned on seeing how long things could be this way. His first stop was his own frat house, say hello to some of his old brothers, and make them zombies of course.

He also wanted to see what had happened with all the people Jen had told him to bite. The entire campus had to be in chaos by now.

Last stop was Holly. He had a special present for the girl who had made him a target. The girl who had him turned into a zombie. They were going to spend forever eating brains together.

Being a zombie wasn't so bad after all.

KILOMBA LIVES

DANE T. HATCHELL

Nakima slept soundly on a bed made of thatch in his grandfather's hut. Deep drumbeats pounded out an enchanting rhythm, while the tribe's Shaman danced and grunted incantations to bring back the departed spirit of their fallen god.

Nonstop for the past three days, the Shaman performed his ancient ritual, believing that he alone had the power to restore the faith of his village, a faith untested over the eons of time.

Kilomba had always been there to care for them. He brought the rains for the crops and provided the abundance of fish caught in the sea. The loving god's only requirement, an annual human sacrifice. Of which the village was eager to comply in order to continue the blessing of plentiful food and fertile women.

The future was in question now that Kilomba lay dead and rotting where the bolt of lightning had struck him down.

The Shaman stumbled as he stepped to his right to complete the ceremonial dance. Two ebony warriors rushed to his side. One gave him a drink from an animal skin.

"It is no use, Barlak. Kilomba is forever asleep. It is time for you to rest," one of the warriors said.

"A god can never die. This is trickery of the Devil, to test our faith. Kilomba's spirit is waiting from above. I can feel it in my heart," Barlak said.

Thunder rolled in the distance, the eastern horizon lit briefly in a warm glow. Fresh winds pushed the ceremonial flames sideways; a damp coolness washed over the villagers in their wake.

"The time is approaching. We must not lose faith now. Prepare the *terrikitu*, quickly, for the final time," Barlak said, weakly waving his hand.

"Kilomba's body has started to rot. This is a waste of time. Better to declare the death of a god than allow the people to cling to false hope," the warrior said.

With his last remaining strength, Barlak slapped the warrior on his cheek with his open palm. "Devil, get behind me." Then he called out with closed eyes, "Start the *terrikitu*!"

Sanctified disciples of the Shaman mashed a large bladder filled with extracts of fermented leaves and roots, pumping the potion directly into a vein leading to Kilomba's heart, through a small piece of sharpened bamboo.

Two others stood on the chest of the massive beast directly above its heart. In unison, they flexed their legs and bounced up and down, using the heart as a pump, circulating the potion throughout the body. They continued a ritual they had performed four times a day for the last three days.

The mighty beast was magnificent to behold in death as it was in life. It lay on its back with its arms stretched out from its side, reaching out nearly twenty-five feet, slightly longer than it was tall.

The head was larger than that of ten humans. The face was a black leathery mask surrounded by short black hair. The nostrils were so large that two fists side by side could fit inside each one. The teeth were long yellowing spikes able to slice through the toughest of animal hides, and jaws that were strong enough to crush the sweet milk from coconuts.

The bladder went empty as the last of the potion entered Kilomba. The two disciples stepped off the mighty chest, kneeled, and gave a short prayer before departing.

Barlak sat upright with the two warriors supporting him on either side. Lightning crackled across the sky, the earth rumbling from the reverberating thunder. The winds intensified, extinguishing a few of the torches that outlined the body of Kilomba.

Near the head of the fallen god towered a memorial made of bamboo. It was a beacon erected by the villagers to announce to the heavens that Kilomba was dead. The tower rose some fifty feet in the air.

The clouds blocked the light of the moon and gobbled the stars as it rolled in. Darkness prevailed, split only by the branching arms of lightning that flashed above.

Barlak raised both of his hands to calm the mourners, then clapped twice for the drummers to stop. He then nodded for them to invoke the power of the gods.

The drumbeat rolled over and over, leaving a space of silence between each outburst, then stopped abruptly. The cadence pleaded, it begged, it demanded the gods above to give an ear and answer the prayers of the faithful.

The drums played, the drums stopped, the lightning crashed in the space of the silence. The drums played, the drums stopped, the lighting crashed again.

The drums resumed, and before the second beat, the lightning struck the shrine of Kilomba.

Ethereal spirits poured down the tower and pooled around the mighty god. Jagged sprites and fairies of electrical energy joined hands and danced upon the body of the giant ape.

The clouds continued to roll overhead but no rain fell. The hairs of the mourners stood on end, tingling the skin at the root.

Barlak's eyes widened, his heart pounding in his chest in awe of the fantastic event. Standing with the aid of the warriors, he lifted his hands and spoke the final chant.

Waves of energy flowed through Kilomba's body, glowing like burning embers. Barlak couldn't tell if the body was actually starting to twitch, or if the flow of the energy only made it look so.

Then, there was no mistaking this was so, the body was moving. Kilomba's entire body began to quiver in rhythm with the otherworldly force, shaking like a string puppet with a frenzied master.

A high-pitched whine filled the air and grew in intensity. A bolt of electricity jumped out of Kilomba, flowed up into the towering shrine, and left the body of the fallen god.

The top of the tower erupted in a celestial shower of sparks that the heavens absorbed, leaving an eerie silence behind. The clouds evaporated, unveiling the light of the moon and the twinkling stars.

Kilomba's eyes opened.

Cries of surprise and thanks went out from the faithful. The gods in heaven had heard them. Many fell to their knees in reverence, but a few backed away in fear.

Barlak hobbled toward the mighty giant. "Praise be to Bumba and Shango. Kilomba has returned from his visit in the heavens. He has come back to protect his children. He has come back to preserve our way of life. It is assured that the hunt will be plentiful. The fields will bloom and produce a wealth of fruit to feed our children."

Kilomba sat upright, releasing putrid gas trapped in his bowels. Two of his worshipers wretched and vomited. He looked at the people of the tribe with lifeless eyes, and opened and closed his mouth as if learning how to do so for the first time.

Barlak felt a cold fear crawl up his spine and rest in the back of his head.

Kilomba brought his fist to his side and put his knuckles on the ground. Slowly, he pushed himself up, placing his legs underneath him, then stood erect. The giant ape wobbled, shifting his body to stay upright.

More of the villagers backed away. Barlak remained with hands uplifted, praying for a merciful outcome.

Kilomba leaned his head back, spread his arms, and let out a horrific cry. The sound echoed in the still night air. He put his knuckles to the ground, took an unsure step forward, hesitated, then continued.

Barlak backed away as the giant figure began to move. He was unsure what to do next. He had expected Kilomba to go back into the jungle and rest in his mountain abode.

Something was still wrong with him. He walked as if he were asleep. His movements were stiff, and the rotting parts of his body began to tear.

The walking dead god reached out to grab Barlak. He easily stepped out of the way as the giant hand missed him by several feet. Kilomba tried again with the other hand, and missed.

Kilomba let out another loud cry, turning everyone on their heels to flee back to the village.

Jarobi, Nakima's grandfather, leaned against the outside of his hut with his left hand, while directing his urine stream with his right. Aging had him waking frequently in the night to relieve himself.

An enlarged prostate reduced his once powerful stream into a trickle. Still feeling half-asleep, he raised his one open eye to the direction of his brother's screams as they fled back into the village.

"Wake up! Kilomba lives and is angry. Wake up!" the first man to cross the village perimeter yelled.

Jarobi shook his leaking member dry and went back into the hut. "Wake up, little Nakima, there is something wrong. We must leave."

Nakima was a deep sleeper, and didn't respond. More commotion filled the village as those awoke in surprise and the others fleeing Kilomba returned.

"You must wake up now. Danger is coming." Jarobi leaned on his cane as he shook little Nakima.

Kilomba howled, engulfing the village in pandemonium. Brush and small trees crunched as his knuckles and feet hit the earth.

"You must wake now, Nakima!" Jarobi pleaded.

Nakima's eyes opened and stared into the distance, mouth open, and struggled back into consciousness.

Kilomba roared again, this time sounding just outside the hut.

Jarobi helped his grandson to his feet, and pushed him out of the door. Not twenty-feet away stood the lofty figure of the Ape God, silhouetted against the moonlit night.

"Run, Nakima! Run!" Jarobi yelled.

Nakima looked about the empty village, confused, then did as his grandfather instructed as Kilomba moved forward.

Jarobi pushed off his cane as fast as he could. As the distance between he and Nakima grew further, the distance between he and Kilomba drew nearer.

Jarobi fell to the ground as the sweeping hand of Kilomba caught him across his right ankle. He lay on his back, looking up at an unfamiliar husk of what his loving god had once been.

It was a cruel joke of the Devil that had drained the life of their vibrant deity, replacing it with an imposter, one that had broken the covenant protecting the village by entering it for the first time.

The hand of Kilomba wrapped around half of Jarobi's body as it lifted him into the air. Nakima stopped and turned upon realization that his grandfather was no longer behind him.

Kilomba shoved Jarobi's head in his mouth, tore it from the body, and chewed greedily, all the while staring into nothing with a vacant gaze.

Nakima watched in shock as the god he'd worshipped all of his life ate his grandfather. He was aware of the annual sacrifice, but never really understood the real implications of the ritual. Kilomba ate to the sound of crunching bones until every morsel was gone.

When finished, he felt the call of his mountain cave to rest, leaving nothing to the memory of Jarobi but his cane and the blood-stained ground.

"I can't believe that I let you talk me into coming on this stupid trip," Mary said, after swatting a biting fly on the back of her neck. "You need to get me on the shore. This up and down on this old bucket makes me want to puke."

Professor David Brigtsen, famed National Geographic explorer and her husband, ignored her, as he compared the shoreline to the photographs in his hand.

"How are you going to make this up to me when you find out it's a bust? David, I'm talking to you."

Prof. Brigtsen held a photo towards the shore. "Yes, you are talking to me. I'm standing next to you. I couldn't escape the sound of your voice if I wanted to."

Mary frowned, crossing her arms across her short, fat, frame. "Why couldn't you be content with teaching?" she asked. "We're too old for this crap. But no, you have to be off halfway across the world chasing the African Bigfoot. You're only going to be remembered as an old fool that was tricked by a prankster. Ever hear of Photoshop? That big monkey in those satellite photos was created by a ten-year-old on a computer."

Prof. Brigtsen pushed his gray hair under his safari hat. "It was standing right over there, by that tree to the left of that large rock. My God, it must be twenty-five to thirty feet tall."

"David! Get your head out of your ass and answer me," Mary said, her arms by her side, her hands balled into fists.

A thin Chinese girl with long legs glistening with a combination of insect repellent and sun block stepped up behind Prof. Brigtsen. She wore khaki shorts that were cuffed at mid-thigh, an olive-colored shirt with the sleeves cut off at the shoulders, and the shirt-tails tied in a knot at her waist. "Prof. Brigtsen, Capt. Roscoe radioed in that the team has made contact and will be back to pick us up shortly. He sounded really excited."

Prof. Brigtsen spun around at the sound of her voice. "Why thank you so much, Changchang." He smiled and gave her a wink, and could feel Mary's eyes burning a hole in his back. "Tell the others to ready the equipment. We shall move as soon as the boat returns. We don't want to delay."

Changchang smiled back and nodded, her almond-shaped eyes nearly closing, and turned to carry out the professor's instructions. Prof. Brigtsen looked back at Mary. Her mouth was drawn in so tight that all he could think of was a sphincter muscle.

"You just had to bring your little Geisha with you," Mary said.

"Geishas are Japanese. Changchang is Chinese," the professor said.

"Whatever. Changchang Chow, what a stupid name."

"Her name is actually Chow Changchang. In China, the surname is written first."

"Whatever. Her face is still mashed like a Chow or a Pekingese dog."

"Mary! How dare you act in such a way about my best student! I do believe this voyage has taken a toll to your basic reasoning. Get a hold of yourself, woman. Don't embarrass yourself any further. And for God's sake, don't embarrass me. This expedition may very well be my last. It may also prove to be my greatest claim of discovery. My professionalism needs never to be in question." He gazed off onto the shore. "National Geographic has given me the opportunity because of my reputation from the past. The Chinese government is funding half of this expedition because Changchang is my student, and because her father is well connected in the government. Please don't do or say anything that might jeopardize the success of my mission."

Mary stewed a while longer, looking at her husband through narrow eyes. Her upper lip quivered, showing glimpses of her front teeth.

"Make use of yourself and go and pack. We'll be leaving shortly, and I want you to be at my side for this historic moment."

The scowl on Mary's face softened. "Why is it so important to have me with you?"

He took her hand. "My dear, we've been together for over thirty years. This will prove to be my finest moment in history. This will be my last adventure. I cannot think of a better way to honor our marriage than by sharing this moment with you. That the world may remember David and Mary Brigtsen together, as they present the Eighth Wonder of the World."

"You're a fool," she said softly. "But you are a charmer." She leaned over and hugged him tightly.

He returned the hug and kissed her on top of her head. He looked towards the shore as the dinghies sped back to the ship. His future was now in his hands, he couldn't afford to make the slightest of mistakes.

Not only for him, but for Changchang also.

* * *

Barlak greeted the male strangers with the custom of shaking hands while smiling and making eye contact, the same with the two women, adding a kiss on the cheek.

Prof. Brigtsen listened to Barlak's fantastic tale of the Ape God that shared the island. He was familiar with the tribe's dialect and followed the story up until lightning struck and killed Kilomba, then had Barlak retell and explain the part where Kilomba returned from the dead.

"So you're saying that your God died, and then you brought him back to life. But that he's not alive as he once was, that he is now a *nzambi*, and seeks a daily human sacrifice instead of his annual one? Do I understand you correctly?" the professor asked.

"Yes. Once each day we leave him an offering by the sacred ground near his cave. If we do not, he returns to the village and creates havoc until capturing one for his meal. Many people die, much destruction is done. It is better to offer sacrifice, then only one die," Barlak said.

Prof. Brigtsen noticed the disproportionate ratio of women to men, having counted less than fifty males on arrival.

"Is that what happened to all of your men?" he asked.

"In the beginning, we tried to return Kilomba to the grave. Many brave warriors died in the attempt. Our men sacrificed themselves for the women and children."

"You will have no men left in a matter of months. What will your women and children do then?"

Barlak looked to the ground and shook his head. "I do not know. We have no boats to leave the island. There is no place we can hide forever. We can only fight and win, or we will die. Will you help us fight, Brigtsen?"

The professor's entourage of twenty had come well equipped for the mission. More than half carried rifles, some fully automatic. The expedition also carried explosives meant to tame the rugged terrain of the jungle, along with tranquillizer darts and specialty grenades designed to confuse an adversary without lethal consequences.

"We will assist you any way we can. I ask only that I be allowed to take photographs of the encounter and for the remains of Kilomba once he's defeated," the professor said.

Barlak hesitated, finding it difficult to believe that he was negotiating the destruction of his god. His spirit was worn down to the point that he didn't care if he lived or died. He knew he had to hang on until his village was safe, or in the end die trying.

"I agree to your terms. The thing that lives in the cave is not our god anymore, it is not Kilomba. It is an imitation created by the Devil. Better to be rid of it, and out of our memories," Barlak said, sealing the commitment with a handshake.

Changchang raised the tripod slightly, and tilted the camera forward. The LCD screen on the back framed the mouth of the cave and she pressed the control to zoom in on the view.

"I have it ready, Professor," Changchang said.

"I've just finished with the video, the camera is rolling," the professor said. "The perspective from this ridge is perfect." He stood with his arms up in the air as he looked down below.

A series of hills bordered the eastern side of the cave of Kilomba. Prof. Brigtsen, Mary, and Changchang were in position to capture images of the beast as it emerged from its lair.

The cave itself faced a large, mostly clear area, with the dense jungle surrounding some fifty-yards away. It was a perfect place for Roscoe and his men to lay and wait.

"Excuse me, you two, am I getting in your way?" Mary asked with her hands on her hips, her binoculars hanging from her neck.

"Not at all, Mary, carry on," Prof. Brigtsen said, testing the pan of the camera.

"I was being sarcastic," Mary added. "I'm being ignored. Why did you want me to come again? To be a pack mule? You could have used one of the natives to help haul the equipment."

"The natives consider this sacred ground, and will not venture this far, my dear," he said.

"Whatever. You bring me up here to do what? Watch you and *Chingaling* scurry around like ants while I stand back here looking at your rear end."

"Mary! Her name is Changchang, and please stop with your incessant whining. Changchang, please excuse my wife." He turned his head and stared at Mary. "Her hormones are obviously imbalanced, and she should seek medical attention as soon as we get stateside."

Changchang wiped the sweat from her forehead. "It's okay."

"Come in, Professor," Capt. Roscoe's voice sounded tinny as it blasted over the radio speaker.

Prof. Brigtsen unclipped the radio from his belt and lowered the volume before speaking. "Brigtsen here; is it a go?"

"Set your watch for ten minutes. We'll send in some bait, let you get a few pictures, then we'll try to bring him down in one piece."

"Use plan B only as a last resort."

"I know, Professor. Don't worry, my men have been informed. Roscoe out."

Prof. Brigtsen looked at Changchang and smiled, then reached for her hand and squeezed it for reassurance. Changchang smiled back, and pulled him into her for a hug.

Mary suddenly felt alone, as if she were intruding on their special moment.

Something below caught Mary's eye. "David…oh my…David, when you find the time to pull yourself off her, look."

Prof. Brigtsen and Changchang looked at Mary, and then below where she pointed. A saber-toothed tiger trotted through low foliage toward the cave of Kilomba.

"I don't believe it! Changchang, get some video while I snap some pictures," he said as he headed for the equipment. "That cat became extinct over ten thousand years ago. Look at it!" He lowered the camera and focused in on the saber-tooth, taking shots as fast as he could before it escaped from view. "It looks as if it's over ten feet long. I imagine it tips the scale at over four hundred pounds."

Mary watched through her binoculars as the cat slinked its way across the valley. This truly was a historical moment. For the first time she was happy she'd made the trip.

As the saber-tooth neared the entrance of the cave, it dropped to a crouching position, fur standing on the end of its spine.

Kilomba exited from the cave knuckles first, turning its lifeless eyes toward the savage beast.

"Oh my God," the professor said, looking away from the camera, mesmerized by the sight of Kilomba.

Changchang quickly turned her video camera towards the ape. Mary let out a cry of surprise and dropped her binoculars.

Kilomba looked like a hairy, withered, bag of bones. His lips were peeled away from his teeth, his foot long canines on ghastly display. Some of his fur had split away from the skin, exposing rotting flesh. The maggots infesting the wounds were too small for the observers to see.

The saber-tooth twitched its tail, then sprang on the huge ape.

In four quick leaps, the saber-tooth had the left arm of Kilomba in its jaws. It jerked its head about, trying to throw him to the ground. Kilomba hissed, grabbed the tiger with his free hand, and tossed it to the side.

The saber-tooth tumbled through the air with a large flap of hair-matted skin held tightly in its teeth. It hit the ground on all fours, and ran off into the dense cover of the jungle.

Kilomba stood and banged his chest as he let out a roar. Birds scattered from all directions, looking like a black cloud emerging from the treetops.

The radio squawked to life. "I was going to use one of my men for bait, but he's out of the cave now. We're going in. Copy?"

"Copy, Captain Roscoe. Good luck," the professor said, replacing the radio on his belt. Then he turned to the women. "You might want to cover your ears."

Five concussion grenades flew out of the jungle and landed on either side of Kilomba. The professor and his party were far away enough that all they heard were five short *pops.*

Kilomba's body shuddered as the sudden blast of kinetic energy hit him. Prof. Brigtsen thought he could see the shock waves roll through the giant ape's skin.

Three of Roscoe's men emerged from the jungle with rifles raised. The tranquilizer darts flew through the air, finding their targets on the confused zombie ape. As fast as they were able, the three men reloaded and fired again.

"The men did a fine job," the professor said. "I can see all six bright red darts sticking in the torso."

"How long will it take for him to go under?" Changchang asked.

"Hopefully in just minutes. Each tranquilizer carries enough punch to stop a bull elephant."

"I can't believe this is happening," Mary said.

Kilomba turned his gazed towards the men who had shot him, having recovered from the blast. The tranquilizers were having no effect.

The men fell back into the jungle. One narrowly escaped the sweeping arm of Kilomba.

"Fall back! Fall back!" Capt. Roscoe screamed to the three men. "All right mates, green light for plan B. Fire when ready."

Prof. Brigtsen watched as small orange flashes lit the jungle perimeter from Roscoe's men, filling the valley with the sound of a chain of automatic gunfire.

"That bloody bastard isn't slowing down at all. *Nzambi*, what we call zombie. I now understand. I'm finally starting to believe that perhaps that beast is somehow dead and yet has been reanimated back to life."

"He's going into the jungle after the men. Oh David, what if he can't be stopped. What will we do? He'll kill us all." Mary ran to her husband and held his arm.

"Now, now, Mary, don't worry. Capt. Roscoe has a plan, one where the terrain will come into play and will defeat the monster." Prof. Brigtsen signaled to Changchang with a nod.

"Do you really think so? I've never been so scared in my whole life. This is like a living nightmare," Mary said.

Prof. Brigtsen grasped her by her shoulders and gently pushed her away as he looked into her eyes. "You have absolutely nothing to be concerned about, my dear. I'm here by your side. To have and to hold, till death do us part."

Changchang smashed the side of Mary's head from behind with a large chunk of limestone, sending her straight to the ground.

"Thank goodness. I don't believe I could have stood to hear that annoying voice for another second," the professor said, wiping his palms on his shirt.

"I have dreamed of this moment for a long time. We won't have to sneak around anymore, pretending only to be teacher and student," Changchang said.

"No too fast, my dear. I must play the role of the grieving widower long enough to avoid suspicion. You better learn how to fake a tear or two if you know what's good for you."

Changchang nodded. "I know...I just want us to be happy. Do you think the others are far enough away to go ahead with our plan and roll her down the hill?"

"Alas, I have thought of it. Now that it's a reality, I can't bring myself to watch her simply tumble down like a rag doll." He narrowed his eyes. "I want that bitch to suffer."

Changchang bit her lower lip. "What do you mean?"

"I want to tie her up and leave her in Kilomba's cave. Capt. Roscoe will either be unsuccessful and Kilomba will return to the cave and find her as a tasty snack, or he will kill the beast, and she will wake in darkness. All alone, her only companions will be the creepy crawlers of the earth to pick at her soft flesh bit by bit." He removed his hat and slicked back his hair. "Either way, it still won't equal the years of misery I've endured thanks to her. And the best part, we won't have to worry about her being found, the villagers wouldn't dare trod on sacred ground."

He wrapped Mary's hands and legs with thick packing cord while Changchang circled duct tape around her mouth and head.

They now shared a secret that would bind them tighter than the sacred oath of marriage.

"That was a truly dreadful thing to happen, Prof. Brigtsen. I can't imagine how you must feel," Capt. Roscoe said, his hand on the professor's shoulder as they sat in the hut in the village.

"It happened so fast...it didn't seem real. Mary was lagging behind on our way back to the village when the saber-tooth sprang out of nowhere and dragged her off. I was in total shock." His voice broke. "Perhaps if I'd reacted faster, I could have given her a chance." He stopped and rubbed his eyes until they were red.

"Now, Professor, you didn't have a prayer against that prehistoric beast," Capt. Roscoe said.

"By...by the time Changchang and I tracked it down...she'd been torn to pieces. I wanted to kill the beast with my bare hands, but knew it would be foolhardy to even attempt such a thing." He hesitated. "Then it looked at me and roared, showing me its blood-stained teeth. I knew I could do nothing to help Mary. Not wanting to make matters worse, I realized my responsibility was to lead Changchang to safety. And here we are now, God forgive me..."

"You did the right thing, Professor. You had no other choice." Capt. Roscoe slapped him on the back. "At least the ape is no more. We filled him with so much lead that he probably weighed twice what he should have. Fortunately the plan worked. We coaxed him to the edge of the cliff and sent him plunging five-hundred feet over the edge to the rocks below. The ship should be in position right about now to haul the carcass on board. I hope his remains are still worth something to you."

"Come in, Captain Roscoe," came over the two-way radio.

"You see, right on time." Roscoe keyed the microphone. "Roscoe here, go 'head."

"Captain, we're at the coordinates you provided. There's nothing here, sir. Are you sure the coordinates are correct?"

"Of course they're correct. Did the tide pull the body out to sea?"

"No, sir," the voice on the radio replied. "The tide won't roll out for another five hours."

"Hold your position and wait for further instruction," Roscoe said while he stroked the stubble on his chin.

A young warrior ran into the village, speaking franticly and making elaborate gestures with his arms.

"What now?" Roscoe asked.

The professor went to investigate and Captain Roscoe followed.

Changchang was waiting outside the hut. She wanted to run to his side, but thought better of it. The earth shook slightly, the jungle rumbling with the sounds of brush and small trees being crushed under a massive weight.

"I don't believe it," Prof. Brigtsen said.

The jungle parted and the Ape God emerged to claim his sacrifice. His body was flayed from bullet fire and his left leg dragged as he lumbered forward.

"Kilomba lives," the professor said to himself. "Or worse, Kilomba cannot die."

Then the professor saw a sight that startled him more than the combined surprise of seeing the saber-tooth and the zombie ape. Mary was hanging on tightly around Kilomba's neck.

"There!" she yelled into the god's ear.

Prof. Brigtsen was frozen in shock, numb in horror, as he stood with his mouth open wide. Capt. Roscoe and Changchang backed away as Kilomba snatched Prof. Brigtsen up and bit off his left arm at the shoulder.

His pain-filled screams filled the air. He was only a few feet from Mary as she clung to Kilomba's neck. She gave him an evil grin.

"Like you said, David, 'until death do us part.' " She laughed, her eyes filled with madness.

Prof. Brigtsen's screams ended abruptly as the next bite took off his head, blood shooting into the air to rain down on the ground below. Mary wished his suffering had lasted longer.

Satisfied with the daily sacrifice, Kilomba turned away from the village and headed back to the solace of his cave. Mary slid from his neck and down his back to land on the ground.

Changchang backed away as Mary approached her, and halted when she bumped into Capt. Roscoe.

Mary stopped when she was within arm's distance, and slugged Changchang with her right fist. Changchang fell to her backside on the ground, rubbing her chin.

"You two should have planned this better," Mary said with a crooked grin. "You should have paid more attention to the details. You see, Kilomba only eats men."

HUNT OR BE HUNTED

MICHAEL C. DICK

These freaking zombies, living impaired, walking dead or even mutants. I really don't care what you call them. I call them a pain in the ass and they've destroyed everything that gave my life meaning, self worth and happiness.

How did it happen? Well, pretty damn fast, that's how!

Two nights ago I'm coming home from work and on my way I'm seeing and witnessing all sorts of bizarre stuff. What looked like people attacking other people, but instead of using their fists in your typical manner, they were biting, ripping and tearing into one another!

There were also numerous car accidents and no rescue workers on the scene to help. Also, I saw people being burned alive inside their burning cars, the flames then spreading to nearby buildings, the entire time everyone on the street—that is the ones not being attacked—seeming completely oblivious to all that was transpiring around them.

I left the area as quickly as possible and eventually pulled into my development, but when I turned onto my street and started approaching my house, I noticed a lot of my neighbors were packing up their belongings and loading them into their cars.

As I reached my driveway, I looked up at my neighbor's house, who seemed to be the only one not packing. I waved to their son who was in one of the upstairs windows. He either didn't see me or he just didn't care because he didn't respond to my wave.

They're a really nice family but have had a bit of bad luck lately, ever since their daughter was attacked and becoming sicker by the day.

After parking the car, I hurried into my house to be greeted by my wife and beautiful, loving six-year-old daughter, as well as the blaring of the television set announcing some very unbelievable breaking news.

I'm quite sure you have all heard it by now, but for me it was the first and most shocking time. The police and military were being overrun by untold amounts of rioters, leaving fires burning unchecked throughout most of the city and those that had recently died, unbelievably, were returning to life, which you can imagine added to the chaos.

I fell backwards into my comfy chair and thought to myself that this explained a lot of what I'd seen and witnessed on my way home from work today, as well as some of the strange absentees from work over the last couple of days.

I sat lost in thought and I was brought out of my reverie by the sound of my wife clearing her throat and drying her eyes. It was evident she was waiting for me to make some kind of decision.

"Well," she said, "what do you propose we do?"

Yeah! Like I had the fucking answers because Zombie Apocalypses come around just about everyday.

I sat there for a few more minutes until a plan began to form in my mind.

The first thing we needed to do was get as many boxes and bags together that we could find as well as plastic containers. These things, I explained to my wife and daughter, were to hold our food and water. We needed to get it stashed away down in the storm cellar

On top of these items I told my wife to collect plenty of blankets and bedding as well as any type of medical supplies she could find. It was a simple plan but we could elaborate as we went along. The thing that was important was we were getting started and being proactive in trying to stay alive.

As I said the plan was simple, we would load all of our supplies and equipment into the storm cellar and hope to wait it out, whatever this was.

The storm cellar had two entrances to it, one on the inside of the house and one on the outside, located in the backyard. As my daughter and wife gathered up the supplies, I pushed and heaved as many heavy objects I could find and placed them in front of all the lower windows and doors. Then I went back into the storm cellar, boarded up all the windows with the extra nails and boards, and went back upstairs to seal the interior door that lead to the storm cellar.

After this was accomplished I pushed a large hutch in front of the door, placed a rug down in front of it, and effectively made it invisible. The way I was looking at this thing was that zombies weren't the only bad thing to be worried about. There were bound to be looters and other people trying to take advantage of this situation, and this way if a looter broke into the house, they would never find the opening to the cellar.

Next we needed to get all the food, water, clothes, linens and medical supplies downstairs, and if we were lucky and had enough time, I was going to try and wrestle a couple of mattresses downstairs as well. I also wanted to get enough toys, board games and art supplies to help Zoe pass some of the time away down there, so she wouldn't get bored and want to go outside and play.

We had plenty of stuff but the most important things I thought we had were our old camping radio and television, which was going to be our only link to the outside world for who knew how long. I had guns and ammunition, and we had each other. The last thing we needed to do was seal the door behind us as we crawled into the storm cellar, which to me felt too much like a tomb.

As it turned out we weren't down there for very long, only a couple of hours of our self imposed exile, when we heard a series of loud crashes drifting down from the front of the house.

Against my wife's better judgment, I peeled back one of the boards blocking one of the windows and was horrified by what I saw. There were literally a small army of those creatures roaming the street, breaking into houses where they perceived a human might be. Once inside the house, they tore into the residents and literally ripped the people apart. Then they began eating their blood-soaked corpses. But what made the situation even worse were that the corpses of the recently eaten would rise up and join in the ever swelling ranks of undead.

I stared at the carnage in morbid fascination, unable to take my eyes away from the horror that was unfolding in front of me, as the army of the dead slowly made their way across the street, heading to my neighbor's house.

Without thinking about what I was doing, I loaded up with two pistols and a shotgun and hung a bat across my back. I filled my pockets with as much ammunition as I could carry and when I finished, I looked up and into my wife's watery eyes.

Taking a deep breath, I started to tell her why I needed to do this but she stopped me and said she understood. We hugged, neither of us talking. Then the silence was broken by a blood-curdling scream. I quickly ran to the window and looked out and saw my neighbor's wife lying on the ground, being torn to pieces by at least three zombies.

Without any further hesitation, I rushed up the stairs, burst through the storm door and started blasting zombies away as I made my way to the front of the house with the intent on helping my friends and neighbors.

As I rounded the front of the house, I heard a roar of pure hatred and rage and looked up in time to see my neighbor's husband burst out of the broken screen door, swinging a baseball bat as if he was swinging for a homerun. He was doing a good job, too, but there were just too many zombies and he was soon overwhelmed by their sheer mass.

But where were his son and daughter? I was debating if I should leave, to return to my family, but my conscience got the better of me and I was soon shooting zombies again as I made my way to the screen door and into the house to search for them.

Within moments I was covered in blood and gore but I managed to gain entrance to the house without any injury. I took a quick look around the kitchen and first floor to make sure there were no zombies prowling around, and once I was convinced there were none, I made my way slowly upstairs to the second floor.

As I reached the top of the stairs and entered the hallway, I was overcome by the worst odor I had ever had the misfortune of smelling. It was a mix of bodily sweat, puke, piss and something very acidic.

As I went down the hall, the first door I encountered was open and I took a quick look inside. It was the bathroom and lucky for me, it was unoccupied. I pressed on and the next door I came to was closed, so I placed my ear up against it to see if I could hear anything from inside. I thought I heard something but I wasn't a hundred percent sure, so I decided to check the rest of the floor first then return to this door.

I searched three more rooms and they were all empty. The only room I spent any time in appeared to be a small boy's room. As I entered it, I made my way over to the window that overlooked out on the front yard and street.

The situation outside was getting worse by the moment and the lady of the house, even though she had been ripped into two pieces, was now clawing away from her house to God only knows where. Her husband, even though he was missing an arm and his neck had been eaten almost completely through, leaving his head resting on his shoulder, was also getting up from the ground and starting to move away.

I quickly took stock of the ammunition I was carrying and calculated that I had more than enough to get back home as long as I didn't have to deal with too many zombies, but first things first; I needed to find those kids.

I cautiously made my way out of the room and back down the hallway to the closed door. Standing outside it, I wondered why that particular door was the only one closed. Maybe it was paranoia, but before I opened the door, I made sure that both pistols were in my hand and ready to go.

As soon as I cracked the door, I was instantly assaulted by the same hideous odor I'd smelled when first setting foot upstairs, except now it was much stronger. From the small opening I peered inside, but I could only see shadows, the room swallowed in darkness except for a small patch of light on the opposite side of the room. I saw what looked to be a bed in the far corner.

As for the noise I'd heard earlier coming from the room, I discovered it to be a child's record player, the vinyl record skipping over and over again after it had reached the last song on that side of the album.

I pushed the door open the rest of the way and entered with both guns out in front of me. Without taking my eyes off the bed, I reached for the wall and tried to find the light switch for the room. I eventually located it but my luck was holding true and the light fixture didn't work. I wondered if the power was out.

Slowly I scanned the room and made my way over to the bed with the intent of checking the closet door that was located on the other side, but what I saw as I rounded the foot of the bed made me almost lose the contents of my stomach. I dry heaved but managed to regain my composure.

As I rounded the bed, I saw on the floor, crouching in a pool of blood, gnawing and ripping into various dismembered parts of her brother, was the daughter of the house.

As bad as it looked, it was made even more disgusting because even though his head had been bitten clear through and lay off to the side—it was still freaking alive—its mouth was moving up and down, snapping open and closed while its eyes were focused on me.

From that day on my motto was 'don't think, just react,' and it all started on that day when I lifted both guns and fired several shots into the head of the boy and then the little girl.

After I'd done this I reloaded and realized that this was probably not the smartest thing to do. In a neighborhood filled with zombies as ours was now, I may as well have hung a neon sign out the window that said 'Fresh Meat Inside.'

No sooner did those gunshots stop echoing around the room and my ears stopped ringing, then I heard from downstairs the sounds of doors being battered down, furniture being pushed out of the way or knocked over and windows being smashed. I quickly turned, lost my balance in the blood on the floor, and ran out into the hallway and to the top of the stairs.

There at the bottom, packed like sardines in a can and all trying to get up the stairs at once, were a dozen zombies, with more moving around in the rooms behind them.

So much for leaving that way, I thought. I needed to slow them down while I tried to figure another way out of the house. Quickly, I looked around and grabbed a hallway table and launched it down the stairs, where it crashed into several of the zombies, knocking them backwards and into the others.

Unfortunately, that was going to have to do. I turned and fled down the hallway and entered one of the rooms, looking for heavy objects to help barricade the door. I settled on a long dresser and a large bureau. That being done I now needed to find a way out.

There were two windows in the room. I ran over to the first one but it looked out over the side of my house where the drive-way was, and if I was to leave this way, I would be exposed to the street. So much for that option. But then realization kicked in. If the first window faced the side and front of my house next door, then the back window should logically look down into my back-yard.

And that was where the entrance to my storm cellar was, and the locked gate and my yard completely free of zombies. Without any further hesitation, I opened the drapes so I would have an unrestrictive view of the yard.

As I stared down into my yard, something didn't seem right. I just knew something was off, I just couldn't place it and I didn't have time to figure it out because at that moment, from out in the hallway, I began to hear things crashing to the ground and a moaning that was growing louder and closer by the minute.

Without any further hesitation, I opened the window and looked down into my neighbor's yard. It was only a two-story drop. Not high enough to break a leg if I landed right, but I could sprain my foot or hurt my knee easily.

There was no time like the present, especially now that the zombies were practically outside my doorway. Tucking the guns securely into my waist band, I closed my eyes and took a leap of faith.

Luck was on my side today, and the fact that my neighbors were lousy gardeners helped as well, because on my landing all I managed to do was sink several inches into the soil before I rolled to absorb the impact. As I shook off the numbing tingling, sensation, I stumbled out and hopped over the fence and ran directly for my storm cellar door before any of the creatures inside the house knew I was there.

It wasn't until I had entered the stairwell and secured the doors behind me that I realized what had seemed wrong to me back at my neighbor's house.

Before I'd left the storm cellar, I remember telling my wife numerous times that as soon as I left, she was to close and lock the storm door. I even went so far as to even have my daughter repeat it as well, but as the padlock made an unearthly click as it was locked into place, I knew instantly she didn't do as I'd instructed.

Reluctantly, I pulled both guns out of my pants, and then slowly turned around to face the darkness of the basement.

At the bottom of the third and final step, I saw that the basement was shrouded in darkness. As I ducked under a low support beam, I could see the single light bulb swinging ominously back and forth on the other side of the cellar.

Fear gripped my heart and my throat went dry, making it impossible to call out for my wife and daughter. With feet made of stone, I slowly moved deeper into the cellar.

As I crossed the floor and traversed the numerous canning tables, I made quick, darting glances under them to make sure nothing was hiding there. When I rounded the final table, I saw a pair of men's legs protruding out and lying motionless. I allowed myself a glimmer of hope that my family had come out of this unscathed, but that hope was short-lived.

Cautiously, I stepped over the legs, making sure not to slip in any of the blood that had pooled around its torso and head. As I neared the front of the table, I heard the slurping, smacking sounds of someone with very poor table manners.

In a daze and with both guns pointed in front of me, I turned the corner of the table and nearly lost consciousness at what I'd found.

On the cold cement floor, bent over the corpse of my wife, was my little girl, her face buried deeply into the gaping, red hole that was my wife's abdomen and until recently was the home of my unborn child of six months. The unborn child that my daughter had ripped from my wife's womb, and after devouring it, had started in on her mother.

The thought of all the carnage, especially to those that I loved and cared for so much, became too much and my mind went to a nice safe spot as I unloaded both guns into the thing that had once been my daughter. Her body and mine both slumped to the floor, one lifeless and the other limp.

The horror I'd just seen and done was too much for me to handle, and as I sat with tears welling up in my eyes, I heard a loud clanging noise as the creatures outside my house tried to gain entrance to my shelter. My gunshots had attracted unwanted attention it seemed.

Casually I reloaded the guns with the intent on taking my own life. All I had ever lived for was now gone, dead in a way I could never have imagined possible. As I raised the gun to my mouth and lovingly laid the warm steel on my tongue, resting the muzzle against the roof of my mouth, I heard a now all too familiar scratching noise.

Slowly I pulled the gun out of my mouth. I wiped the tears from my eyes with the back of my hand, and as my vision cleared, I looked over and saw my disemboweled wife trying desperately to crawl forward and reach one of my legs.

As one of her bloodied hands wrapped itself around my foot, I shed my last tear as I placed a single bullet into her skull. That was my last conscious thought as mercy took hold and I passed out from the trauma my mind had endured.

Unfortunately, reality always comes back to us and when I at last woke up, I was staring into the sightless, still eyes of my wife, daughter and the remains of my unborn child.

Looking at their motionless corpses helped me snap out of my psychotic break, and on weak, trembling legs, I stood up and made myself ready to take my revenge on this new zombie nation.

After loading up with anything that could be used as a weapon such as screwdrivers, for those up close personal moments, I made myself ready to leave. I also loaded a backpack with some nonperishable items and extra ammunition. Then I zipped up my winter coat and climbed the stairs to set forth and seek my revenge on this dark and cold night.

The zombies that had been trying to gain access to my house were the first to go. There were more than twenty but killing them was easy.

When had emerged from the cellar, they hardly took notice of me, and even after I had dispensed several of them using an aluminum baseball bat, the others barely reacted at all. I'm not entirely sure why, but my theory is that they were more than likely partially frozen into immobility because they had no body temperature and tonight was extremely cold.

I put this theory to the test, and as soon as I'd killed those in the backyard, I opened the gate leading to my front yard and walked out onto my front lawn.

The moon was full and the sky was clear of any clouds, so I was able to see up and down the street easily. Scattered throughout the street, in both directions, were at least thirty more zombies, all of them standing still.

Taking my time, I approached the first one closest to me, and as its eyes settled upon me, I brought the bat down hard on his head, splitting it open and sending brain matter flying in all directions. The zombie fell to the ground, dead, but for good this time.

So it went from zombie to zombie, me whistling softly the Rainbow song, as I would bring the bat down upon their heads again and again.

But then something happened that I wasn't expecting nor was I prepared for. As I approached the last one, the front door of the house it was standing in front of burst open and I saw silhouetted in the doorframe at least two zombies that were moving.

Upon seeing me they pushed and shoved their way through the doorway in their rush to get to me. Their shoulders jammed together as they tried to get through the door and for a few seconds they were stuck. If this hadn't been such a serious situation I think I might have broken out in laughter at the slap stick routine they were performing but as it was real and not some movie. I was forced to drop the bat and draw my pistols.

Carefully I walked forward to allow myself the opportunity to make all my shots count, and within moments I'd dispensed two more zombies, but this time there were consequences.

I hadn't been thinking clearly when I'd shot them and the gunfire had alerted more of the creatures. As I was admiring my handiwork, I noticed that the stillness of the night was now filled with the constant wail of the undead.

I looked around, and standing in the doorway of at least seven houses, were more and more zombies. I couldn't tell from where I was how many were actually there, but I figured retreat would be prudent at this time. I could seek out my revenge another time. Picking up the baseball bat, I made sure my guns were fully loaded, then started running down the street.

As I ran, I would take pot shots at any of the zombies I'd encounter or any that tried to grab me. Eventually I exited my neighborhood and ran up one of the on ramps that would take me onto the expressway, hoping to find someone else alive or at the very least a workable vehicle.

My hopes were soon dashed as I reached the top of the ramp and looked in both directions to see nothing but abandoned and crashed vehicles littering the expressway, stretching out for as far as I could see in both directions.

At this point I really didn't have many options available to me, so I decided to go in the direction of the Peace Bridge. As I weaved in and out and between the cars, I was especially careful just in case there were any zombies trapped inside any of them. As it happened, there were quite a few of them, and each one I came across found a bullet placed nicely in its head.

On several occasions I had let my guard down, and in those times a hand or two would reach through an opened car window and grab at me, desperately trying to draw me closer to its mouth. I was lucky each time, dispatching them in the normal way.

I lost track of time on how long I had traveled, and looked back and was surprised to see I'd only gone a mile or two. It was getting darker and colder by the minute as the night progressed, so I decided to exit the expressway near Lafayette Park and try to locate some secure shelter.

The problem was going to be finding a building free of zombies. This by far was my most major concern since leaving and setting out on my journey. Just the thought of being trapped in a ruined or empty house and having to go room by room and do a search with only a flashlight, checking to make sure there were no undead lurking around, chilled me to the bone.

Later, I was lucky that the building I'd found and took a chance on only had two floors. The ground floor was clear of any zombies but there was no way I could cover all the windows and doors to make it safe. I started climbing the narrow stairwell up to the second floor and began my search again. As I neared the last room, my stomach did some serious flip flops as I heard several noises coming from inside the room.

I turned off my flashlight, placed it in my back pocket, and drew my second gun, ready to take out as many zombies as I could.

Taking short, shallow breaths to calm myself, I counted to three and kicked the door in. As I charged into the room, ready to shoot, I was forced to stop at the last second when I discovered the people before me were all still living, breathing humans.

Their eyes went wide in fear as I burst in with guns aimed at them.

Slowly I lowered the guns. From where I stood, I could see three teenage girls and an older woman and man, who were stretched out on a filthy mattress on the floor nearest me.

"Sorry," I simply said as way of an apology, then introduced myself. The man on the mattress sat up and started making introductions, and it turned out that the group was a family. Just to break the ice, I asked them how they managed to be here or if this was their house.

Tom, the man on the mattress, just shook his head and said they came in here, like me, trying to find shelter from both the cold night air and the horde of zombies on the street. He then went on to tell his story.

Tom's Tale

"The section of the city my family and I lived in was one of the first to fall victim to the zombies. At the time, no one knew it was zombies. Everyone thought it was just another gang dispute, but things escalated too quickly and before we knew what was happening, the police that were sent in to stop the riot became overrun, but even worse than that they were now helping the original attackers. At the time it wasn't understood that once killed by a zombie, the person would then rise from the dead.

"I gathered my family together and we quickly left to try and find someplace safer. Eventually we found ourselves at another police check point. They had ambulances and medical help set up there along with more police reinforcement and those vultures from the news stations.

"As we were led into one of the tents to make sure we weren't harmed in any way, a commotion started outside. I jumped to my feet after sitting down and saw the horror of the zombie horde approaching the police blockade.

"Among the volley of bullets and yells of the police, my family and I scrambled out the back of the tent and watched from a distance as the police blockade fell under their unrelenting onslaught. It was at that moment my family and one other we met up with made a run for it. It was slow going because the other family had some older folks with them but eventually we were able to put some distance between us.

"As we continued on our journey, we could still hear all around us gunfire and people screaming for help but were powerless to do anything for them.

"Eventually, even these sounds stopped and relief flooded through the group, but I knew better. I knew that if the screaming had stopped then that just meant the zombies had run out of victims and we could be next.

"At this point I don't know who was stupider, me for wanting to go on or listening to the others that were begging to stop and find someplace safe to stay and hide for a while. Against my better judgment, I decided we should find someplace that could accommodate us all and would be easily defended and fortified. Then in the morning when everyone had rested, we would set out again and make our way across the bridge with the hopes of making it to Canada.

"So that's what we did. We located a house in a relatively quiet neighborhood, checked out the upper and lower floors and blocked the windows and doors as best as possible.

"We thought we were safe in the house, so we weren't being as quiet as we should have been while we were making sure everything was sealed up. But during the time we were blocking the doors and the windows, we'd alerted some zombies to our presence that we were down in the cellar. Looking back, I think they must have been the home's original owners, the poor souls.

"In our rush to make the house safe we'd somehow managed to overlook checking the basement. I was upstairs at the time, looking out the windows and checking the neighborhood to make sure no zombies were approaching our location, when suddenly from downstairs I thought I heard a muffled scream and then I definitely heard a single gunshot.

"As I left the room at a run, I grabbed a bedside lamp to use as a weapon, then took the stairs two at a time. As I was heading down, two members of our group ran by the bottom of the stairs, heading for the front of the house.

"I stopped immediately and heard my daughters in the front room crying and struggling to get the furniture away from the front door. From the back of the house I could hear screams of terror but no sounds of retaliation. Then at the bottom of the stairs, three figures shambled by, going into the front room where my family currently was. I hesitated only a moment and then jumped the rest of the way down the stairs, coming up behind the first zombie and bringing the lamp down on its skull. With a satisfying crack, it immediately crumpled to the floor. As the second one started turning around, I swung again, this time hitting it in the face. Other than dislodging its lower jaw bone, it did nothing to stop it, so I took another step back, then lunged forward again, bringing the lamp down on the top of its head.

"As the creature tumbled to the floor, it ripped the lamp from my hands, the base having lodged itself in its skull. I watched in slow motion as the last zombie grabbed my wife, and before I could make a move, it bit deep into her arm. With a primal scream I lunged forward, plowing into the creature and sending it falling away from my wife.

"I quickly looked around for something to hit it with and my hands settled on a large glass ashtray. With all the anger I felt, I leapt upon the downed zombie and started bashing again and again at its head until blood and gore flew from the ashtray as I continued to bring it down. I didn't stop until I felt my wife's hand on my shoulders and I knew it was time for us to leave.

"I struggled to my feet, and with adrenalin still coursing through me, I pushed and shoved the remaining furniture out of the way of the front door. Once it was clear, my family and I fled the house, never once stopping or going back to see if anyone else had survived. Finally, after much running and hiding, we ended up here, exhausted.

"As we settled in, I took a good look at my wife's wound and saw that it was going to need medical attention, so I wrapped it as well as I could and then checked on my daughters. They all seemed fine except my oldest who had suffered numerous scratches and gouges from when she tried to help her mother and younger sisters escape. That's her over in the farthest part of the room."

* * *

I waited a few moments to see if he had anything else to say. When the silence had stretched into more than a minute, I cleared my throat and stood up. Standing in the darkness, I asked him if he could give me a hand downstairs. Reluctant to leave his family, he eventually conceded to my looks and slowly stood up from the mattress and followed me downstairs.

When I thought we were out of ear shot of his family, I turned to face him, but before I could say anything, he looked at me with sadness in his eyes and said, "You don't have to say anything. I already know that my wife and daughter are infected with whatever's causing all of this." He sighed heavily.

"I'm not stupid, but I just can't abandon them. When you leave here, I planned on putting my other daughters in another part of the house and when my wife and daughter change, then and only then will I take care of them. Then the three of us still remaining will leave here together. But I won't leave this house, or my wife and daughter. You on the other hand, my friend, should probably seek shelter elsewhere for the night or at the very least, if you wish to stay, then stay down here where you'll be somewhat safer."

We stared at each other for a few heartbeats. Just before he turned to go, I stopped him and handed him one of my guns. "Here, this beats the hell out of an ashtray." Silently he took the gun from me, stuck it in his waist band, nodded his head in my direction in silent thanks, and turned and went back upstairs.

As for me, I made sure that the front door was locked and all the windows had their shades drawn before sitting down heavily in a chair in the front room. It was much too cold out to continue my journey tonight and besides, I was both mentally and physically exhausted. As I sat drifting in and out of sleep, I could hear Tom's two other daughters crying as they were led from the room and brought to another part of the house.

I'm not sure how long he was inside with them, but before I drifted off to sleep, I did hear him say to his daughters that he would be back later. Then I heard his footfalls and a door open and close, then silence.

Sometime later, I was woken by the sound of a single gunshot and then something large falling heavily onto the floor. I came immediately awake and listened.

The next sounds I heard sounded vaguely like someone dragging their feet on the carpet, followed by a low moaning noise. Then my heart stopped, as I heard someone cry out softly, "Daddy?" Immediately the moaning grew louder, needier, and the shuffling increased in speed. Above this I heard a girl's voice call out, breaking the silence, "Is that you, Daddy?"

Silently I stood and prayed the girl would realize what was happening, but in the next moment I heard a terrified scream. Sadly, I shook my head and turned to make my way to the front door. As I reached out my hand to open it, I heard two distinct different screams ring out across the stillness of the house, then as suddenly as they began, they stopped.

Two more souls for an ever increasing army of the dead, I thought as I pulled open the front door and stepped out into the cold morning air. I wandered around the suburbs, staying hidden as much as possible, trying to find something to eat before continuing on to the Peace Bridge and my hopes of escaping this insanity.

An hour later, I was safe inside a local convenience store. After I'd made sure the place was empty of any possible threats, I pulled the security gate down, locked it in place, then closed the front door and locked it.

The store was untouched; there was plenty of food. As I settled in, casually eating a Twinkie, I noticed a television set mounted on the wall next to the coffee stand.

It took me a few minutes, but I finally located the remote control behind the counter and turned on the TV, only to be met with the sound of white noise. Cursing, I flipped through the channels until I at last came across a station that was still broadcasting, CNN, go figure. It appeared that I'd tuned in at the end of a live feed and the anchorwoman, Sue, was saying they would be back after a short break.

I munched absentmindedly on the sandwich and chips as I waited for the news program to come back on, then sat through some silly ass story about a bunch of kids doing some kind of concert.

By the time I'd finished eating, so had they, and the annoying, smiling anchorwoman came back on with a list of do's and don'ts for when you find yourself in the unfortunate position of meeting a zombie, the most ridiculous of which was the advice they gave about scaring them off.

I shook my head in wonder at the plain silliness and stupidity of the entire thing, wondering how many fools were going to die because they listened to this advice. They honestly expected us to just 'shoo' them away instead of killing them, like that would ever work. I sat patiently through the rest of the broadcast. Instead of rushing back outside and into the cold morning, I decided to rest for a while and get some much needed sleep.

Just before I turned the TV off, the anchorwoman was saying everyone needed to stay tuned for a rare and shocking interview a team of investigative reporters from CNN had done. No thank you.

Off went the television, leaving me alone in silence and I settled down on the floor behind the checkout counter for some much needed rest.

It was hard to get to sleep, as my wife and daughter's faces floated across my mind's eye. Before I knew it, I was sobbing softly and eventually I drifted off to sleep.

I was shaken awake as the ground and building shook around me, the store windows imploding from what could only be from a concussion blast.

I quickly stood up and rushed over to the locked security gate, looking outside to see if I could locate what had happened. Seeing nothing, I relaxed slightly, but then noticed how high the sun was. I must have been more exhausted than I'd originally thought, because the sun's location told me it was close to mid afternoon; half a day wasted and only a few more hours until sunset. I needed to get moving.

I walked over to the radio and set it to scan, hoping it would tune into a broadcast while I rummaged through the store, packing food, water and medical supplies.

By the time I'd loaded up with all I could carry, the radio still hadn't locked onto a station. So shouldering my pack, I checked my weapons and then opened the security gate. It squealed and groaned in protest as it rolled up. The noise set my teeth on edge, as it broke the silence of the day. Before the noise could alert anything within earshot of my presence, I slipped underneath it and hurried away.

The path I decided to take took me into a residential section, but steered clear of the more populated ones. The closer I got to my destination, I was forced to enter more densely populated ones.

I'm not sure if it was the cold, the death of my family or the lack of zombies, but eventually I let my guard down and my mind wandered as I passed by an alleyway which I neglected to check as I proceeded to the next corner.

As I approached the alley, I flattened myself up against the corner of the building and took a quick look down the side street. Halfway down, wandering aimlessly, were at least a dozen zombies. As I checked my gun to make sure it had a full clip, I heard a low guttural groan that drew my attention back the way I'd just come.

Ten zombies had managed to sneak up on me and were nearly within reach of attacking me. Panic set in and without thinking I turned and ran across the street. As I dodged around the rear end of a crashed car, my foot shot out from under me, sending me crashing into the trunk of the vehicle to fall heavily to the ground, jarring my gun loose and sending it skidding away.

Lying prone on the ground, I noticed the zombies from the side street were merging with the others, and all were heading straight for me.

I tried desperately to get to my feet. After several painful attempts, I managed it and took a second to examine my ankle, which was bruised and swelling up.

I carefully set my swollen foot down and applied pressure to it, testing to see if it was broken, and lucky for me it wasn't but it still hurt like hell and was going to slow me down.

I grabbed the baseball bat from off my back to assist me in walking. Glancing backwards, I was shocked at how quickly the zombies had closed the gap between myself and them. At this point it didn't matter how messed up my foot was, for I needed to get moving or become their dinner.

I felt like the pied piper as I limped and staggered out in front of an ever increasing mob of zombies. And so it began as I limped and hobbled, just staying out of their reach as I made my way to the bridge. There were times when they were only a few feet behind me, and then I would get a burst of speed and pull away, only to lose ground yet again. If I stopped walking, I was a dead man. More than an hour after my accident, I saw a large plume of black smoke rising lazily into the air, right where I was heading.

Eventually I made the final turn and started to approach the Peace Bridge. I was stunned by what I saw. There were large sections of the road that had become nothing more than smoking craters, and lying scattered around in a hastily built blockade, were various military and police vehicles that had sustained tremendous damage.

Scattered amongst the field of debris were various bodies and body parts, some of which were still moving. As I walked by the twitching bodies, I brought the bat down with all the force I could muster, destroying their remaining life. I only had one chance to put them down, for if I slowed for a fraction of a second, the zombies behind me would catch up.

My progress up the ramp was slow and the zombies following me started to close the gap once more. The further I traveled, the more bodies I saw littering the bridge: policemen, firemen, National Guardsmen, all now showing signs of re-animation. I did as before and brought the bat down again and again, smashing their skulls in as I took out my hate and anger for what they had stolen from me; my loving wife and little girl.

The amount of damage on the bridge told me a battle had taken place between the living and the dead, and the further I walked up the bridge the more evident that became. As I struggled up the road, limping and swaying from side to side to elevate some of the pressure on my foot, I reached the apex of the bridge and stared down in horror.

Nearly falling several times, I trudged onward, knowing help was close at hand. Finally, I came to a huge gap where the bridge was supposed to be. I knew now what the explosion that had woken me and shaken the store had occurred here. The Canadians had blown the bridge to close the border. There was no where to go! I turned around to see that the zombies were still behind me.

It was all over, I could either jump to my death into the freezing water of the Niagara River below, or remain to be eaten alive and eventually return as one of the walking dead. If only I still had my gun, then I could have at least shot myself in the head and ended my suffering quickly. Either way it seemed like death was a sure thing.

The choice was simple. I turned around and prepared to jump off the edge of the bridge. But I turned too fast and I accidentally put too much pressure on my foot and staggered and nearly fell.

I took a moment to compose myself then began to crawl on my knees to the jagged opening in the bridge. Rebar jutted up at odd angles, the concrete fractured and cracked, and far below the rushing water beckoned.

I'd be lying if I said I wasn't scared about jumping from such a height, and as I tried to get my courage up, I felt a white hot fire erupt in my chest. As I fell to my knees in disbelief, I heard the echoes of gunfire, then cheering as the Canadians guarding the border fired at the zombies behind me. Some overanxious soldier had believed I was one of the living dead and no doubt from a distance I must have looked as such. My hand went to my chest and came back wet and sticky. Tumbling over the jagged edge, the wind whistling in my ears as I fell, I heard the roar of more cheers from the Canadian side, then the icy cold fingers of the Niagara River as I was engulfed and carried away on the currents.

Limply I bounced along, my body hitting the sharp rocks that adorned the river bed. As I drifted lazily away, I felt a strange yet powerful transformation taking place.

THE HIDDEN DEATH

DARREN WJ MILLS

Guarding the Army barracks at night was the worst. Any time spent guarding any part of the outskirts of the base was frightening, day or night, and even though many of the troops often said they had no fear of anything, the fear and readiness for action could clearly be seen in their focused eyes at all times.

This night however, October 3, 2011, had all the troops stationed at the base full of a fear that was easy to see. Two nights before, a priority message had come through, informing the base that a radioactive satellite had lost its orbit, and come crashing down about fifty miles south of the Army base.

Immediately, three squads of troops, nearly forty men and women, were sent out with special equipment to retrieve the satellite. But this wasn't what was concerning everyone on base.

The thoughts filling their minds was that the three squads had come back from their mission empty handed, not finding the satellite. They did find the crash site and serious traces of radioactive material, but no satellite.

Trevor Monroe was stationed on the front gate of the base. A position he, like many others, absolutely hated. In the past two months, three suicide bombers had tried their luck at speeding through the gates in old cars.

Two had failed to get even close, but one had managed to explode the vehicle a matter of meters away from the entrance, badly injuring two of the soldiers on guard that night. One of the men was Trevor's good mate, Paul, and although he felt bad for his mate getting hurt, he felt worse for himself, being one of the replacements for that position.

"Hey, Gaz," Trevor called over to the other soldier on guard with him.

"What's up, Trev?" Gaz replied.

"Can you see that?" Trevor pointed out into the dark night across the desert, directly in a straight line from the gate. "There, in the distance, is that…It looks like people walking this way, bloody loads of people. Can you see them?" He urged Gaz to look harder.

"Nah, what're you talkin' about? You're just shittin' yourself because of what happened the other day," Gaz said, laughing as he spoke.

"Of course I'm not, you cock! There are loads of people out there, look!" Trevor frowned at Gaz, who shook his head as he stared out into the darkness.

Gaz knew Trevor well and could see that he wasn't happy at being put on guard duty at the main gate. He'd been stationed with Trevor for a long time now at the Army base in the Southern Province of Helmand, and although he had no doubt that Trevor would give everything in battle, he knew the guy hated being put in a situation where he could so easily get caught off guard, with no real way of fighting back to overcome the danger.

Trevor was a brilliant soldier if the danger was face on, but if the danger was to come in the form of a friendly figure, pretending to want help, only to have a bomb strapped to their chest, then it just pissed him off. He had a deep belief that honor should be maintained in battle.

It was something that had been drummed into him by his long-serving military mother, and when faced with under-hand tactics such as suicide bombers, he just felt sick to his stomach at the very thought of being taken down like that.

"Shit, yeah, you're right, Trev. There are loads of them! I can see them in the distance now. What the fuck is that all about?" Gaz's voice was filled with curiosity more than anything else.

"I don't know, Gaz, but we need to radio this in and…" Trevor stopped mid-sentence.

"What? Trevor, why'd you stop?" Gaz was on the other side of the main gate, staring right at Trevor, looking for an answer.

"Shit!" Trevor shouted forcefully and began scrambling to get his rifle up.

While the two men had been looking out into the distance at the strange sight of so many people just walking through the desert towards them so slowly and so late at night, they hadn't noticed a speeding vehicle with no lights to reveal it in the darkness, heading straight for them, until it was too late.

Trevor found himself automatically backing up behind the barrier, quickly followed by Gaz. Two other soldiers that were stationed on either side of the gate, manning a stationary heavy machine gun each, were now seeing what had caused the two men to back up so quickly. The speeding vehicle was only a couple of hundred meters away from the main gate now.

One of the soldiers directed a large searchlight out into the darkness, in the direction of what they could all see was a medium-sized truck. But more so than that, they could clearly see the rear of the truck was carrying a very large object, an object that as the truck got closer, looked partially like the satellite that had crash landed to Earth and was stolen three days earlier.

"Stop the vehicle or we'll open fire!" the soldier with the searchlight called out through a megaphone system attached to the searchlight. The truck just kept coming though, with no signs of stopping.

Trevor and Gaz were struggling to hold their positions behind the gate, knowing that unless the truck stopped in the next few seconds, the two soldiers would open fire with the machine guns and then they would all have to deal with a potential fireball crashing through the entrance to the base.

Then the men opened up and all that could be heard for miles in all directions was a continuous burst of gunfire. Both soldiers mounting the heavy machine fired simultaneously, but it was too late. The truck was traveling too fast and was too well-built to be stopped by the barrage of bullets.

Trevor immediately ran for cover, not realizing he was leaving a shocked Gaz standing directly in the path of the oncoming vehicle. As he hit the ground, well positioned behind a concrete building to the side of the gate, he immediately heard a thunderous explosion come from where he'd been standing only seconds earlier.

The explosion was so strong that it lifted him from where he was and slammed him into the guard tower, then back down to the ground again, knocking him unconscious.

After a few minutes, he came to and felt a sigh of relief at the thought that the heavy gunfire had managed to stop the vehicle before it had penetrated the base. Also that he was still alive.

Unfortunately his relief was short-lived as he tried to look up from the ground. The air was filled with dust and he could barely breathe through it, let alone see anything.

As he stood up on weak legs, he began to partially see through the dust cloud that had encompassed the entire area. He could just see that there was no longer a gate to the base, or even an entrance. All that was left was a massive hole where the two soldiers manning the heavy machine guns had been moments before. After a few more steps, he couldn't help falling to his knees, coughing from the dust in the air, but also spitting up a large amount of blood.

He quickly checked himself to see if he he'd been hit by any debris, but he had no wounds. He coughed up more blood again, but this time, instead of thinking he was hit, he put the sight of blood down to possible internal injuries from hitting the ground so hard. He slowly moved through the dust cloud, desperate to see if Gaz had survived the explosion, even though he knew the possibility was unlikely.

As he ventured further into the base, he could hear faint shouts from within the cloud of dust, voices he recognized from other soldiers stationed at the base. He could clearly hear shouts for help from wounded men and women, but he could also hear what sounded like screams of fear too. Not the sort of screams he would expect, but real screams of terror about something within the dust cloud. As he moved deeper into the base, it seemed the entire base was covered in the cloud.

"Hello," Trevor yelled. "Hello, anyone, please, I need help." More blood spluttered through his lips as he called out. "Please, someone…" He almost cried his words out.

He suddenly slipped and fell to the ground in a thud, coughing up more blood. He didn't stay down for long, not after realizing what he'd slipped in. It was his friend Gaz, or what was left of him. All that remained was a pile of mangled limbs, ripped to shreds, with shards of metal embedded throughout the body, the entire body lying in a pool of blood. Trevor knew it was his friend. Though the body was mutilated, the head was still partially intact, making identifying Gaz horribly easy. Trevor retched at the sight, bringing up lumps of vomit mixed with blood.

"Jesus Christ, Gaz…shit…I'm so sorry." Trevor cried. Though the sight was beyond terrible, he couldn't help but look at the mess, realizing that his brief assumption about the truck carrying the lost satellite was correct.

He could see scorched wording on the larger shards of metal embedded in his friend.

Millcase Technologies.

He recognized the name from the description he'd heard of the satellite while he was part of the three squads sent to retrieve it.

He began to move away from the bloody mess on the ground, the mess that was once a man, his friend. Then, when a hand viciously grabbed his shoulder, he practically jumped out of his skin and almost landed back in the mess.

"Fuck!" he shouted as he looked up, hoping to see a fellow soldier ready and willing to help him. He recoiled in shock as a woman dressed in bloodied and torn clothing reached for him. Her mouth was wide open, her teeth ready to bite down into his flesh. He quickly raised his arm to protect his face but the woman bit down hard into his arm, causing him to let out a loud scream of pain.

"Get the hell off me, you bitch!" he yelled. Before the woman could gorge down on his arm anymore than she already had, he grabbed her hair and yanked her over to one side as hard as he could manage, causing her to release the hold on his arm with her teeth.

Before she had the chance to get up and go for another bite, Trevor pulled his side arm out and fired the entire clip into the woman's stomach, pleased with every explosion of blood that sprayed up from the woman's stomach as each bullet made contact.

Not wanting to stay anywhere near her, he quickly began to back away, careful where he stepped, as visibility was low thanks to the dust cloud.

"How do you like that then, hey? Fucking bite me will you. Well, how did that..." He stopped talking and moving. The woman wasn't dead. She was getting back to her feet. He'd pumped her full of bullets but yet she was still alive and still coming after him. His jaw dropped as the woman began approaching him. He was shocked by the fact that she was still alive, but the dust cloud was also beginning to settle and he could see other people approaching him, bloodied, mutilated people.

People he'd never in his life seen before. But also soldiers, his friends, the men and women he'd spent every waking moment with for months on end.

They were with the strangers and acting exactly the same, badly injured and moving slowly, almost dragging their bodies along, moaning and groaning with every step.

Before Trevor could be set upon by the disfigured attackers, he felt himself being pulled backwards, almost lifted off the ground. As he looked up, still in shock, he saw his friend Paul and one of the medics from the infirmary, a woman named Tina.

"Quick, we need to get him back to the infirmary, you need to pull harder, Tina," Paul shouted. "I can't grab him properly, and my leg is still fucked up from the other day. Move quicker, they're getting closer!"

"All right, all right, I'm trying!" Tina replied, crying.

Paul had been in the infirmary when the truck had ripped the base apart. He'd been there since receiving a broken leg after coming under attack from a suicide bomber at the front gate a few weeks ago. Tina was with him and had unsuccessfully tried to stop him from leaving his bed to see what had happened.

"Get the door, Tina! Get the fucking door!" Paul shouted.

Tina ran to the door the three of them had just passed through, slammed it closed, locked it a second later, then collapsed to the floor. Paul struggled to get Trevor on the bed where he himself had been laying in for weeks.

Once Trevor was secure, Paul slumped onto the floor next to the bed, but let out a cry of pain as he felt the bone in his broken leg rub against the piece it had snapped away from a few weeks earlier.

Trevor sat up in bed and spit up some more blood with a coughing fit. He grabbed his arm where the crazy woman had bit him. Squeezing the wound, he tried to feel the pain that should be there, instead of the numbness he was beginning to feel spreading through the entire limb.

"What's going on?" Trevor calmly said. He looked around the room, first towards Tina then to Paul, desperate for an answer but unable to show any real emotion in his face due to shock.

"What's happening? What's happening?" Paul said, as he stood up. "I'll tell you what's happening. The dead are fucking walking around out there!" He paused for a second before carrying on at a slower pace. "There are dead people dragging their bodies around and attacking any living thing that moves. They are either creating more walking dead bastards or just bloody eating the person before they can change! That's what is bloody happening!"

Tina looked at Paul, wanting to tell him to shut up, to tell him he was wrong, that such a thing as the walking dead wasn't possible. But she couldn't, she'd seen it with her own eyes and knew there was no other explanation.

Trevor looked at Paul and smirked. He knew what his friend was saying was true, but he couldn't help himself. It was too much for him to handle. The entire idea was crazy. He coughed again but this time even more blood came out.

"Jesus, Trevor, you're in a bad way," Paul said. "Tina, quickly get over here. Trevor, you need to lie down." Paul ushered Tina over as he gently pushed Trevor onto his back on the bed.

Before Paul or Tina could concentrate on his wounds, they found themselves shuddering in time with every bang that was now coming from the infirmary door—from the walking dead. The pounding was clearly being done by more than one set of hands, and the door was shaking badly with every hit.

"I'm done for Paul," Trevor said.

"What?" Paul replied. "Don't be stupid."

"No, listen to me. Whatever those things are out there, one of them bit me. It hurt like hell at first but now I can't feel it. I can't feel my whole arm now. I think whatever made them the way they are is doing the same thing to me," Trevor said softly. "I can feel it inside me, changing me."

"Don't be stupid, Trev, it can't be that bad, and it's only a small bite," Paul stated as positively as he could manage, but he knew what his friend was saying was true.

"I think I was fucked before the bite, anyway, mate," Trevor said, dropping his head slightly.

"Eh, what do you mean?" Paul asked.

"I think that truck was carrying an explosive weapon made from the satellite we couldn't find the other day." Trevor coughed blood up again.

"What, shit, how do you know?"

"I saw the satellite on the truck, and its debris after the explosion. I think I've got radiation poisoning." Paul and Tina froze at his revelation. "I was right near the explosion when it went off and I can't stop coughing up blood now." He looked away from Paul, the reality of his situation settling in.

As Paul sat on the edge of the bed, upset about his friend's situation, he also felt sick to his stomach that although he and Tina weren't bitten, they must also be contaminated with radiation and would end up dying even if they managed to fight off the walking dead.

Tina immediately ran over to the far side of the infirmary and started tearing through the cupboards, desperate to find a Geiger counter to check herself for radiation. Paul looked over at the frantic woman, ready to tell her it was no use, but he didn't have time to get his words out before he heard her take a really deep breath and blow out a sigh of relief.

She turned around after her breath of happiness, and made her way over to the two men, holding a Geiger counter out in front of each of them, checking both for signs of radiation. Paul quickly stood up when he saw Tina smile.

"Nothing, no radiation, nothing, we're all clean," she said with an enormous grin on her face.

"What? But that can't be. I know what I saw and I know how I feel. There must be radiation," Trevor said, pulling himself upright.

"No, nothing, it couldn't have been the satellite, and if it was, the top brass must have been misleading us when they said it was radioactive," Paul said before Tina could.

Paul and Trevor looked at each other simultaneously, both having the exact same thought. The Taliban must have retrieved the satellite and attached explosives to it, hoping to make it into a weapon of mass destruction. Then when they rammed into the main gate of the base, exploding on contact, it would cause the radiation to spread over the entire base and wipe out thousands of troops.

But the two men also now knew that the Taliban were wrong. Whatever was in the satellite, it was definitely not radioactive material, but something else, something even more terrible. Whatever Millcase Technologies was working on, it had the ability to bring the dead back to life, and had done so where the Taliban had taken the satellite to, before they had the chance to transport it through the desert as a makeshift bomb. Trevor remembered all the people he saw walking slowly towards the base before the truck had appeared.

Trevor pushed himself off the infirmary bed, and started to drag his body towards the door from where the constant banging of bloodied hands and fists was coming from.

"Hey, what the hell are you doing?" Paul began to shuffle after his friend.

"I can't go out like this, Paul. This is no way to die. Let me go out there and take those bastards with me! If I'm going to die, I want to face my enemy." Trevor smiled at Paul and held up a grenade he'd just pulled off his belt.

"Shit, Trevor, please no!" Paul begged. But he had no real intention of stopping his friend. If Trevor wanted to go out this way, he wouldn't stop him. Every man should have the right to choose how he left this world.

Tina dropped the Geiger counter and turned away from Trevor, knowing what he was about to do. Trevor was beginning to lose his grip on life. Whatever had entered his bloodstream from the bite earlier, and from the explosion at the gate, had progressed through his body and was slowly killing him. He gritted his teeth as hard as he could and tensed all his muscles. He then slipped the lock off the door and slammed his body into all the clawing hands outside the infirmary.

Paul quickly pulled the door closed after Trevor had successfully knocked all the disfigured bodies out of the way. "Good luck, mate!" he yelled as the door slammed closed, taking off a few fingers from a hand not fast enough to pull it back. The severed digits fell to the floor and twitched for a few seconds before going still.

He tried his hardest to fight through the mutilated and disfigured horde that was now tearing at his flesh like it was paper. He wanted to get as far away from the infirmary as possible before pulling the pin on the grenade, but his flesh was being torn away at an incredible rate. He screamed in pain and tried to stay focused but it was hard. Blood got in his eyes and blurred his vision.

His thoughts went back to the suicide bombers, and how disgusted he'd felt about them, how there was no honor in their way of fighting an enemy. He realized that he himself was about to be what he hated so much, and though he knew his death would eliminate many of his attackers, he hated the fact that he felt a kinship to what he despised so much.

With his last breath, he managed to pull the pin on the grenade and then fall to the ground in a heap, followed by blood-soaked hands and mouths. As the first teeth sank into him, tearing off chunks of meat, an explosion ripped through dozens of the flesh-hungry creatures that were gorging themselves on Trevor.

A spray of blood, flesh and bone splattered the door of the infirmary and completely coated the ground directly outside the building in a red mess of gore. The image Paul had of Trevor being devoured and then consumed in the explosion, almost knocked him off his feet.

"We have to get out of here." Paul muttered his words, waiting a full minute after the explosion before speaking.

"What? What?" Tina replied, confused.

"We should leave, now, while the door is clear of them. We could make a run for another building and try and find others that are still alive."

"We can't, they'll get us!"

"Goddamn it, Tina, shake that fear off! You're a fucking soldier, start acting like one! Trevor sacrificed himself so we could have a chance; don't let his death be for nothing!" Paul shouted; his thoughts were of his friend's bravery. Tina looked at Paul, realizing what he said was right. She couldn't shake off the fear, but she knew they couldn't stay safe in the infirmary, not with such a flimsy door.

"Okay, you're right, I'm ready," she nodded.

Tina placed Paul's left arm over her shoulder and put her arm around his waist. She pulled out her side arm and began moving towards the locked door, struggling with Paul and his broken leg. Paul wished he had his own gun, but he'd been in the infirmary for weeks and was currently wearing a pair of pajamas. There wasn't another firearm in sight. He thought about suggesting to Tina to give him her gun while she helped him along, but he knew instantly she wouldn't give up her only form of protection.

"Are you ready for this?" he asked, looking into her eyes. She was a pretty woman, something he'd really not noticed till right at this moment.

Tina nodded. She was putting all her concentration into building up as much aggression as possible, to try and overcome her fear.

The two soldiers burst through the infirmary door and immediately almost slipped in all the blood and guts spread across the ground. The immediate area was clear of the walking dead, but more were approaching from all directions. Tina started looking around for an escape route as Paul began to lose his focus. He couldn't help looking at all the gore they were standing in and feel fearful of the danger approaching.

"Come on, Paul, we've got to move, they're getting closer." She began tugging at him to move, but he wasn't responding; he was frozen where he stood.

"Jesus, Paul, please, fucking move, they're right there!" She pointed her gun out and began shooting at the oncoming creatures.

After emptying the clip, and not successfully stopping a single attacker, she managed to get Paul moving again, but they had spent too long in one place; the only route they could take was towards where the gate used to be and out into the desert.

Hundreds of walking dead were now surrounding them and they had no way of getting to another building to check for other survivors or seek safety.

As Paul and Tina reached the destroyed main gate, Paul suddenly fell to the ground and cried out in pain. Tina fell also, knocked over by his weight. As she looked at him, she pulled away in a state of shock.

The reason he'd cried out in pain was because their friend, the man who had sacrificed himself so they could escape, was holding onto Paul's good leg and biting into the flesh at the top of his thigh.

Trevor no longer had any legs. The grenade had succeeded in destroying all the walking dead that were clawing at him, but instead of killing Trevor, too, it had just blown off his legs, leaving him ready to join their ranks as a flesh-hungry creature.

Trevor's intestines were trailing behind him, though the undead man didn't notice or care.

Paul screamed out in pain as Trevor began ripping chunks of flesh away from his leg.

His screams had attracted more walking dead to where he was being feasted upon and he was only moments away from becoming a human buffet.

Tina kept backing away as Paul desperately looked up at her to help him, but there was nothing she could do for him. His screams died away, replaced with shock from his body being ripped apart.

But then Tina had a sudden adrenaline rush as anger built within her at the sight before her, and she felt a need to help the man she'd been looking after for the last few weeks.

Without hesitation, she ran towards Paul, grabbed his arm, and began tugging at his heavy frame to release him from Trevor and four other flesh-hungry creature's grip. All of a sudden she began to feel Trevor's hands claw at her legs as he dragged his legless body towards her, drawing blood on her calves right through her pants.

She desperately tried to kick at him, to knock him away, but after a few more hard pulls on Paul, she suddenly fell back, getting away from Trevor, but still holding Paul's hand.

The adrenaline rush she'd experienced moments before disappeared as she looked into Paul's face. She had managed to pull him away from his attackers, but one of his legs was still in the middle of the four creatures.

As he stared at her, she didn't notice that Trevor had managed to catch up to her. Before she had a chance to get away, Trevor pierced the skin on her ankle with his teeth.

She jumped up in horror at the pain, seeing that he'd drawn blood, but was relieved he hadn't taken a bite of flesh away.

As she moved backwards, she took one last look at Paul's now, pale-white face, before turning and running away as fast as she could, heading out into the desert with no destination or thought other than escaping.

Hours later, all that could be heard around the area where the walking dead onslaught took place, was the rumbling engines of helicopters circling the destroyed Army base.

Tina looked up from where she was, a few hundred meters away from where one of the helicopters was just about to land.

All of the walking dead had moved on from the base during the night, looking for fresh meat after devouring every last living soldier, but she had stayed hidden, knowing that at some point the military would dispatch troops to the base after losing communication.

As she got closer to the helicopter, one of the soldiers jumped out of the aircraft and began jogging towards her, after seeing she was Army personnel.

Once the soldier reached Tina, he had no time to react to her attack as she instantly sank her teeth into his neck.

She'd clung on to life for most of the night, but the small tear in the skin on her ankle from Trevor had been enough to slowly and painfully kill her, to then bring her back as one of the walking dead.

THE DEAD OF WAR

JEREMIAH COE

Six United States Marines walked down the Japanese-made road in a single column. Their lazy march across the Pacific Island called Tarawa looked much less professional than what those on the home front would have expected from them, but after all they had been through, the men really didn't care.

They'd hit the beach two days earlier and the Japanese had put up heavy resistance. All around them, the water and the sandy beach looked like geysers as the U.S. Navy bombarded Japanese positions and the Japanese lobbed artillery fire onto the approaching infantrymen.

Each of them had seen friends killed. Many of their friends hadn't made it to the beach, but instead remained in the water, floating face-down, as the rest of the advancing soldiers passed them. Others had made it to the beach, but no further, having been ripped to bloody shreds by the Japanese machine gun fire that poured on them heavier than a severe thunderstorm.

After furious fighting, the Marines had pushed off the beach and moved inland. That was when things became worse than they ever could have imagined and their training had never prepared them for. While they'd had a rough time coming to terms with it, and still were, their comrades, as well as their enemies who had been killed in the fighting, began returning to life.

But Saint Peter hadn't sent the men back to continue the good fight, instead they had viciously attacked the living.

Many good Marines who had survived without wounds had fallen victim to the cannibalistic bites of their new deceased foes.

It didn't matter if the living dead had been American or Japanese in life, they now attacked anyone alive without discrimination.

The six Marines had all started their adventure on Tarawa with different units, but in the confusion of the dead returning to life, the men had all panicked and scattered. As time went by they had found each other one at a time and teamed up for mutual protection.

Walking with his Reising Model 50 sub-machine gun slung over his shoulder, Private Charles Tiin fished a pack of cigarettes from his breast pocket, pulled one out, lit it, and took a long, much needed drag.

Sergeant Alvin Suust, who was behind Tiin and saw him light the cigarette, quickened his pace, snatched it from between the private's lips, and extinguished it by squeezing it in his hand as tightly as he could. Suust showed no sign of pain from the burning in his palm.

"What was that for, Sarge?" Tiin asked with more confusion in his voice than anything else.

"The Nips could be all around us and the smoke you were letting off would have been enough to bring 'em right down on our heads," the three-stripe sergeant answered in a low, gruff voice.

Tiin laughed. "Come on, Sarge. The dead ain't dead no more and you're worried about the Japs?"

"Trust me, those slanty-eyed bastards are still a threat."

"Nah, they're in this just as deep as we are," Tiin argued.

"When it all happened, four men from my original squad stuck together. We came upon a gaggle of Nip survivors—seven of them. We tried to communicate with them, turned one of my men's undershirts into a white flag and everything. They didn't even give us the chance to say hi. They just opened fire on us. We did the Corps proud. The other three from my squad may have been killed, but all seven Nips are now dead things. Trust me, whatever has happened hasn't made them our friends or our allies."

Realizing that arguing further would be futile at best, Tiin sighed. "Yeah, I guess you're right. When can I smoke though? I'm startin' to hurt here."

"When I tell you it's okay." Suust reached into his pants pocket and pulled out a small, round silver can of smokeless tobacco. "Here, use a pinch of this for now. It comes from my home state of Kentucky. Good stuff," the sergeant said without any compassion showing in his voice for Tiin's nicotine withdrawal symptoms. He tossed the can to Tiin. "Make sure you spit the juice. I don't want you gettin' sick on me."

Tiin caught the can and appreciatively took a small pinch, placing it between his gum and lower lip. "Thanks, Sarge," he said as he tossed the can back to Suust.

On point, Lt. William Huckmen ordered everyone to stop with the motion of one of his hands.

All six Marines instantly halted and knelt with their weapons pointed into the dense foliage surrounding them. Once a few tense seconds had passed without either the lieutenant motioning them forward or hostilities breaking out, Sgt. Suust, while keeping his body low, sprinted up to Huckmen.

As soon as he was next to his superior officer, Suust asked in a whisper, "Why did we stop, sir?"

Huckmen put one finger to his lips in a silent order for Suust to be quiet. He pointed down the road. Once all was quite again, the sergeant heard it too: the sound of shuffling feet coming from around a curve in the road ahead of them.

Suust pointed into the jungle, silently asking the lieutenant if he'd heard anything coming from their flanks. Huckmen shook his head and Suust turned to face the other four Marines. Using only his hands, he silently motioned for them to spread out along the road. Without question, they all did, as quietly as they could, some kneeling, some lying flat on their stomachs, but all ready to fire as soon as the order was given.

It wasn't long until they saw their enemies come around the bend in the road. There were ten of them wearing both the U.S. Marines' OD green uniforms, with the globe and anchor stenciled on the breast pocket, and the drab brown uniform of the Japanese infantry.

Together, despite the fact that the differences in their uniforms had made them enemies not that long ago, they walked like people that were severely drunk. The new arrivals were all in rough shape and were obviously not alive. One Marine had a Japanese bayonet stuck in his chest. Another, a Japanese soldier, had his face torn off when he was attacked by one of the dead things before dying and reanimating himself, giving the living Marines a very good view of his skull. Another one of the undead Marines had had his stomach ripped open and his intestines began to slip out. They were dragging on the ground behind him.

Apparently all at once, the reanimated corpses seemed to realize that more of the living food they all craved had become available. Together, their heads lifted and looked straight at the six Marines, their eyes so thickly covered in fog that their irises and pupils weren't visible.

They began hissing like angry house cats, then issued the most awful battle cry any of their living prey had ever heard, filling the combat-hardened Marines with fear.

Then, betraying their earlier aimless march, the dead things began running after the six Marines as fast as their stiff legs would allow them. Some moved just as fast as they would have in life, others more slowly due to wounds received either during the fighting or from being killed by the reanimated dead.

"Open fire!" Lieutenant Huckmen ordered without looking back.

The Marines sent a torrent of lead streaming towards their reanimated foes. Many of the bullets missed their marks and sent small plumes of dirt clouds into the air behind the animated corpses, but others scored direct hits and sent chunks of dead flesh and congealed blood flying everywhere.

A few of the attackers fell to the ground and stayed still, however most of them got back to their feet, or due to new injuries, crawled and continued their assault.

Losing ground to the reanimated dead, the six Marines began to fall back. Suddenly single shots were heard amidst the gunfire. With each single shot fired, an attacker's head blew apart in an explosion of bone and brain matter, causing the corpse to fall and remain motionless.

It wasn't long until the six Marines stood alone on the road, looking with complete and utter confusion at the prone corpses before them, each one with a head wound.

"How did that happen?" Private Victor Koy asked, rubbing his bandaged hand.

The relatively minor wound had been caused after the fighting when one of the undead had come at Koy from out of the jungle and bit him. Since receiving the bite, he'd been feeling increasingly ill, vomiting regularly, had aches all over his body, was running a dangerously high temperature, which caused him to sweat profusely, and occasionally shake involuntarily, among other symptoms.

He ignored his discomfort and pushed on along with everyone else in true Marine Corps fashion.

Sgt. Suust was completely dumbfounded. "I don't know."

Then they heard rustling from the jungle foliage and the six Marines turned their weapons towards the sound. They were relieved to see a man wearing Marine Corps-issued OD green fatigues come out into the open. He was holding a Japanese-made Type 99 Long Rifle, with its bayonet still attached, over his head.

"Don't shoot, I'm one of you. I'm alive," the man said.

"Who are you? What's your unit?" Lt. Huckmen asked as he removed his camouflaged combat helmet.

"Corporal Ron Tellson, sir. I'm with the 54th but got separated. I'm a sniper." He snapped a crisp salute to the officer.

In awe, Private Isleman asked, "How did you kill them? We weren't having much luck with it."

"It's all in where you shoot them. If you shoot them anywhere besides the head, they'll get back up. If you shoot them in the head, they stay down for good," Tellson explained.

"Well, Tellson, you seem to be a fine shot. I think I'm gonna be happy to have a sniper in our merry little band. Thanks," Lt. Huckmen said, returning the salute.

Tellson looked around at the assembled Marines and noticed that their faces looked exhausted and haggard. They had two days worth of facial hair growth, and their uniforms were caked with dirt, mud and in some cases, blood.

He wondered if he looked as bad as they did.

"So, where are you all headed?" the sniper asked no one in particular as he pulled a pack of cigarettes out of his breast pocket and lit one.

Noticing that Suust hadn't made the new arrival put out his cigarette, Tiin spit out the chewing tobacco the sergeant had given him and lit a cigarette.

Taking a drag, he looked at Suust and smiled. Suust just groaned, rolled his eyes in disgust, and shrugged his shoulders in surrender.

"The Japs had a fortified communications compound somewhere to the north of us that one of our squads captured before all of this happened. We thought we'd go there and wait this thing out. This has to end sometime," Corporal Billy Desido said.

Tellson took another drag from his cigarette and exhaled the smoke. "Don't you think we'd be better off making our way back to the beach and finding a way to get back to the ships? The Navy isn't on the land so those ships have to be a lot safer than it is here."

Sgt. Suust shook his head. "No dice. We must have lost close to a thousand Marines on that beach. All of which aren't dead any more. First we'd have to fight our way through all of them, and I don't know about you, but one thousand to seven doesn't sound like very good odds to me."

Tellson nodded his head in agreement and Suust continued. "Not to mention that many of those wounded on the beach had been evacuated to the ships. I know for a fact that some of the wounded had life-threatening injuries, and some of those would have died on board the ships. So, even if the ships are still there, they'd have the same problems we have, and we'd be in tight quarters there. We're better off here on the island at the fortified installation and digging in until the blowhards in Washington get us some help."

"I agree with Sgt. Suust," Lt. Huckmen said as he scanned their surroundings. "There's simply no way we can make it back to the Squids. But I don't like just standing here. It makes us too much of a buffet line, so let's keep moving."

Without another word, the Marines fell back into their column and began walking along the dirt road.

They walked for hours, but it seemed like more to the weary soldiers. Disappointment filled them as they discovered the road they were following came to a dead end at an inland lake.

Lt. Huckmen took off his helmet and threw it into the lake "No! No! No! This wasn't on the map! No!"

Sgt. Suust quickly moved next to him. "Sir, get a grip. All of us are at the breaking point and you and I need to make the others believe we've got everything under control. They see one of us lose it and they'll all lose it too."

Feeling humiliated by his own actions, Lt. Huckmen hung his head in shame. "You're right, Sergeant. I shouldn't have acted like that," he said in a voice, so low it was almost a whisper.

"Nothing you can do about it now, sir. You just need to fix any damage you might have started with it," Suust said with a slight rumble in his voice.

Lt. Huckmen straightened his posture and turned around. "Okay, men. It's starting to get dark and we don't want to stumble into a pack of those things, or run into an intact unit of Japs in the jungle once the sun's gone down. We'll camp here tonight. Now I know I made everyone drop most of their gear before and I'm glad I did. If something happens, we'll be much better off sleeping on the ground than we would have been in tents and with sleeping bags around us." He paused as he looked each of his Marines in the eye. "We'll bed down here for the night. Two of you will be on sentry duty at all times, for three-hour shifts. Sgt. Suust and I will be out of the rotation. Isleman, Desido and Tellson, I want the three of you to go out there and kill us something to eat for dinner." He tossed Desido a silencer for his rifle. "Here, use this."

Desido caught it and the three men prepared to go hunting.

"And men?" Lt. Huckmen called, the three soldiers stopping to face him.

"Don't get yourselves killed out there."

"Yes sir," they said at the same time, then hurried off into the jungle to quickly disappear from sight.

The three soldiers returned a little over an hour later with various species of small game. It wasn't enough to fill the men's stomachs, but more than enough to keep them alive and healthy for another day. A small fire was built to cook the meat and the lower ranking Marines made small talk like they would have had they been on a camping trip back in the States.

Sgt. Suust finished his dinner, stood, walked behind Lt. Huckmen, and tapped him on the shoulder. When the lieutenant turned his head, Suust motioned that he would like to speak to him in private.

Lt. Huckmen stood and attempted in vain to brush the dirt off his uniform pants. After a few moments, he gave up and followed Suust down the road enough that the men wouldn't be able to hear them.

As soon as they were out of earshot, Suust turned to Huckmen. "So what's the plan, sir? Do you have one?"

Huckmen nodded. "Tomorrow we'll enter the jungle, skirt the lake and get back on track towards the communications compound."

"Are you positive you know where it is and that we still have control of it? After all, we couldn't raise them on the radio."

"All I know is that it was reported as captured and secured by our forces. Anything else I'm taking on faith."

"Okay. That's all I wanted to know. Thanks, sir."

Suust began to walk off, but Huckmen halted him by saying, "Sergeant, wait." Suust turned to look at him. "Thank you for correcting me earlier. You're right, the men are looking to the two of us for guidance and I could have damned them all with the fit I threw. Thank you for bringing me back in line."

Suust smiled. "Anytime, sir." He walked back to his fellow Marines and joined them in their chatter around the fire.

Lt. Huckmen and Sgt. Suust were both looking forward to a good night's sleep when they laid down on their bed of dirt, closing their eyes. However, that wasn't to be.

Suust knew his snoring was obnoxiously loud, so he opted to sleep down the road as far as he could and still remain under the protective umbrella provided by their sentries. At 0200 hours, well before sunrise, which was when Lt. Huckmen had ordered that the two of them be woken up, Private John Isleman shook him awake.

"Sarge, sorry to wake you, but we're having issues with Koy," Isleman said as soon as Suust's eyes were open.

The sergeant began to sit up. "What's going on?"

"He's sick."

"Sick? I know that, he's been sick all day. Why bother me with it now?"

"No, I mean real sick. Scary sick. Tellson and I don't like the way he looks. I think he's dying."

Hearing that, the sergeant hurried to his feet and moved off with Isleman.

As soon as he was back to where the other Marines were bedded down, he didn't waste time getting on his knees next to the stricken Marine. As much as he would have preferred not to, Suust had no choice but to kneel in blood since it coated the ground all around Private Koy.

He looked at Isleman. "Were did all of this blood come from?"

Isleman shrugged. "He threw it up. He's been throwing up all night. First it was dinner, then it was this yellowish green stuff, then he was throwing up without anything coming out, and after that, blood."

Nodding his head, Suust put his hand on Koy's wrist to check for a pulse and noticed the private's flesh was burning hot even though the man was shivering. He noticed Koy's mouth was so dry his lips had cracked to the point of bleeding, and he was sweating profusely. But his eyes were the strangest of all. They had lost their natural color and had taken an odd milky look with a hint of cataracts.

"What's wrong with him, Sarge?" Isleman asked.

Suust looked at Isleman and shook his head sadly. "I don't know." Then, looking back down at the sick Marine, he said, "This isn't anything I've ever seen before. And look at his eyes. I've never been briefed on any kind of illness that causes that. Go and wake the lieutenant."

Nodding, Isleman quickly disappeared into the mass of sleeping bodies.

With his eyes fixed on Koy, Suust saw the private's eyes flutter and heard his breathing take on an almost gurgling sound.

Suddenly, Koy's shivers turned into violent convulsions. He flopped around on the ground, like a fish out of water, and animal-like grunting sounds escaped his mouth. As much as he wanted to help his fellow Marine, all he could do was back away so Koy didn't accidentally hurt him with his flailing.

As suddenly as Koy's convulsions began, they ended. Once they'd subsided, Koy went still, his limbs bent at awkward and almost impossible angles. His eyes stared lifelessly at the star-filled sky above as they rapidly fogged over. He was obviously dead.

As Lt. Huckmen approached, he'd seen Private Koy's convulsions and then saw him come to his final rest. When he was standing next to Suust, he asked, "Sergeant, what happened here?"

The confusion on Suust's face said it all when he looked up at Lt. Huckmen, but he answered anyway. "Sir, I don't know."

Before anything else could be said, Koy began moving his head from side to side, apparently looking with his now fully glazed eyes. In reality, he was looking at his prey through a new and inhuman sense that only the dead possess.

Suust and Huckmen failed to notice the recently deceased Marine's movements. Before anyone realized anything was wrong, Koy was back on his feet, hissing at first, which was then followed by the same inhuman battle cry they had heard the dead make before.

There wasn't any question in any of their minds what had happened. This was no longer a Semper Fi situation. Koy was now one of the walking dead and no longer a Marine.

Sgt. Suust's mind didn't have time to process what was happening before Koy had a hold of his shirt and was trying to bite his face.

Suust considered it a Marine's duty to train outside of his life as a soldier in as many combat skills as he could. One of the skills he'd trained in over the years was Judo and he instinctively grabbed hold of Koy's shirt, fell to the ground and rolled onto his back, placed his feet on Koy's stomach, and launched the dead man over him.

Koy landed on the road, kicking up a lot of dirt in the process. By this time, the noise had awoken the rest of the Marines and they were all on their feet watching. Koy recovered quickly and looked around, as if choosing which potential meal he would go for first.

As quick as he would have in life, Koy ran straight for Corporal Desido, who leveled his weapon at the reanimated Marine, but not fast enough.

Koy took Desido off his feet as he plowed into him, like a linebacker sacking a quarterback. Desido's weapon hit the ground too far out of reach for him to have a glimmer of a hope of recovering it.

All the other Marines pointed their weapons at the two combatants, but none of them fired, knowing they would hit Desido as well as Koy.

As Desido fought for his life, Private Tiin sprang into action by rushing to them, grabbing Koy and pulling him off Desido.

Koy broke free of the private, and ignoring Tiin entirely, continued his assault on Desido, who screamed in pain as Koy's teeth sank into his cheek. Koy pulled his head back and removed a moderate-sized chunk of flesh.

A single shot rang out and Koy's dead weight slumped on Desido's back. Desido rolled to the side, removing the now truly dead corpse from him as he stood up. He cradled his face with his hand as blood seeped between his fingers. Tears filled his eyes as he dealt with the pain.

Taking in the scene around him, Corporal Desido saw Tellson standing with his Japanese-made rifle still up to his shoulder a few feet away, the muzzle still smoking from the single gunshot.

With the danger over, the men got to work dealing with the aftermath of Koy's transformation.

Desido's cheek was bandaged, Koy's corpse was dragged off into the jungle and given a shallow grave, the dog tags taken from the body; Isleman stripped down, bathed and washed his uniform in the water of the lake to remove any blood, and after a great amount of justifiable confusion, the Marines once again bedded down, although none of them slept any more that night.

Even if Private Isleman's nerves hadn't been as tied up in knots as they were, the nauseous feeling he had from accidentally swallowing some of Koy's blood would have kept him from sleeping.

Daybreak was very somber after the events of the hours preceding it. The Marines didn't need time to become alert again. None of their alertness levels had dropped in the slightest since the Koy incident.

Throughout the night, every little noise they heard brought all weapons up in the direction it had come from. Although shared tribulations had made this band of men closer than brothers, no one dared mention Koy's name, or what they had all witnessed the night before, as if doing so would invoke a long-forgotten ancient curse.

After hours of walking through the jungles of Tarawa, a voice came over the radio on Private Tiin's back, which had been silent since shortly after the dead began to walk. Each of the Marines halted their progress to hear whatever was being said.

"I hope someone can hear me out there. My ability to receive messages has been damaged so I don't know if I can send them or not. My name is James Mattering and I'm a cook aboard the aircraft carrier U.S.S. Essex. As far as I know, I'm the last person alive aboard. We took on some of the injured from the initial invasion, many of which died shortly afterward. Then they came back to life and began killing and eating the living. Now they run the ship," the voice trailed off briefly and the sounds of the battle cries of the dead were clearly heard in the background.

"I don't think I have very long left," the voice said. "Whatever's happening here is worldwide. We've been receiving calls of distress from U.S. Navy vessels throughout the world and others have relayed news to us that whatever is happening is occurring at home, in England, China, Russia, Germany, France and every other country that you can think of. Don't expect help. Repeat, don't expect help. We're on our own. Please...." The voice trailed off and was replaced by the sound of something crashing. The next sound the Marines heard were screams of terror and agony as the man was ripped limb from limb. Then the faint gurgling sounds of sloppy mastication.

The Marines stood and stared at each other in stunned silence. The jubilant, even playful mood that had steadily grown after the events of the night before was now back in ashes. The talking and joking Sgt. Suust grudgingly permitted would not be returning to their trek any time soon.

While he was just as shocked as the rest of his men, Lt. Huckmen silently congratulated himself on his decision to head for the communications compound, instead of returning to the beach, in hopes of making it back to the perceived safety of the Naval ships.

"Well, Devil Dogs, there's nothing we can do for that man, he's dead now...or worse. If we don't want to join him, we have to push on for the communications compound," Lt. Huckmen said. He began walking onward, the six soldiers following behind him.

They moved in a mournful silence for many more miles, the tropical heat causing them to sweat heavily. Because of this, no one paid any attention to how profusely Private Isleman and Corporal Desido were perspiring.

Isleman was by far the sicker of the two men. His head felt like it was being bounced around on the waves of a typhoon. Finally, his equilibrium had had enough and decided that it needed a rest. In a wave of dizziness, he collapsed to his knees.

Sgt. Suust had been bringing up the rear of the column and was directly behind him. Suust stopped, knelt next to the private, and placed a hand on his shoulder. "You okay?"

A single shot cracked the air and Suust looked up to see Lt. Huckmen, who now had a fist-sized hole in the back of his head, collapse slowly, almost theatrically, to the ground.

"Take cover! Take cover now!" Suust shouted.

No one needed the order. As soon as the shot was heard, the Marines dove behind the biggest trees they could find. Each of them had their weapons ready to return fire as soon as whoever was sniping them made the mistake of shooting again and revealing his position by the muzzle flash.

When that didn't happen, Tellson crawled over to Suust. "He's smart, Sarge. He won't fire from the same position again and has probably already moved to a different one."

"What do you suggest?" Suust asked.

"That's easy. We need someone to be bait to get him to fire again."

"That's risky. I won't lose another Marine to this guy."

"Sergeant, if he fires again, we'll be able to tear him apart. Everyone but me has automatic weapons. He fires, one of us sees his muzzle flash and opens up right at him. It's that or we sit here and wait to be picked off one by one."

"Fine," Suust sighed. "But I'll be the target. I won't order any of the others to do it."

Minutes later, each of the Marines had been made aware of the plan and all of them were looking for the telltale muzzle flash. Suust stood up, waited a second, then dropped back down. He heard the bullet that was meant for him hit a tree behind him.

He brought his Reising Model 50 around as soon as his men started returning fire and joined in. After thirty seconds of continuous firing into a tree a hundred yards off, Suust started waving his hand and ordering, "Cease fire! Cease fire!"

Once all the weapons fell silent, the sergeant, now the highest-ranking Marine in the group, said, "Tellson, go and see if we got him."

"You got it, Sarge," the sniper replied as he disappeared through the trees.

Five minutes later, Corporal Tellson returned carrying a brown steel helmet. "You guys got him, a Nip sniper." He smiled. "You tore him up pretty badly, too. Probably was dead before he fell out of the tree. When I found him, his eyes were all messed up, like Koy's were, and though he was too messed up from being shot up so badly and from falling out of the tree to move, he did his best to bite me."

"We didn't hear you shoot him," Corporal Desido said.

Tellson shrugged. "Didn't see the need to waste the bullet. He couldn't walk, he couldn't crawl, hell, he could barely move his head. He's no more of a danger to us now than he would have been if he was dead and gone and I've got one more bullet to use on one of those things if need be."

Sgt. Suust removed his combat helmet, then scratched his head as he put the helmet back. "See, I told you guys we can't trust the Nips. You made the right call, Tellson. If it was one of our men I'd say use the bullet and put him out of his misery, but one of them yellow bastards can stay like that for all I care. Okay, boys, let's keep movin'."

Private Tiin gave Suust a confused look. "Sarge, what about the lieutenant?"

Suust looked at the motionless corpse of his superior officer. "Leave him. There's nothing we can do for him. Just drag him off into the treeline. There's no time for a grave, we need to keep moving."

Two soldiers did as Suust instructed, taking an extra second to cover the body with some large leaves as a makeshift shroud. After taking the man's dog tags, they joined the others.

Suust began walking again, his Marines following close behind, including Private Isleman, who had recovered enough of his equilibrium to walk again.

Three hours later, the surviving Marines came upon the wreckage of a crashed Grumman F6F Hellcat. Its left wing was ripped completely off, its right wing crumpled up under the plane, and its fuselage, while still intact, was bent almost in half, making it look like a lopsided U.

The cockpit glass, while severely cracked, was sufficient enough to restrain the pilot, whose helmet had come off at some point. He was pounding on the cockpit, trying to escape, but none of the Marines were inclined to lend a helping hand. They could tell by looking at him that the pilot was one of the living dead.

The column of Marines moved past the downed fighter, each of them casting it a sad and forlorn glance as they walked by.

Only Tiin was curious enough to stop and take a closer look at the plane. "Hey, hold up. I've always loved these babies, but I've never been this close to one before," he said as he dragged his hand along the blue fuselage, walking around the downed fighter plane.

"Keep moving, Tiin, Don't make me tell you again," Suust ordered.

Tiin looked back towards Suust, but before he could reply, one of the reanimated dead, who was dressed like an island native, came around the crashed aircraft. The native grabbed Tiin by the back of his head, knocked his helmet off, and pulled his head backwards to then bite down on the front of Tiin's neck

Tiin began to scream.

Knowing Tiin was already dead, Suust began to fire at the private and the native, the other Marines joining in. Both were hit by bullets so rapidly they were reduced to nothing more than gory chunks of meat in less than a minute.

Sergeant Suust turned towards the few remaining Marines still alive. "You men see? That's why you listen and do as you're told. My job is to get us to the communications compound safe and sound. I can't do that if you don't listen to me. If Tiin had listened, he would be alive now and we would be a few feet closer to safety. Remember that the next time one of you gets a hankering to disobey one of my orders." He walked over to Tiin's corpse and pulled the bloody dog tags from the pile of meat. "Let's move out, we're burnin' daylight." He turned his back on the others and began walking off.

With one last glance at the mangled mass of blood and gore that was Private Tiin, the men followed.

They walked until it began to get dark, which was when they found a clearing and decided it was the safest place to bed down for the night.

Since both Isleman and Desido were obviously sick and growing worse with each passing second, Suust decided he and Tellson would take sentry duty for most of the night. Since there were only four of them left, and they would arrive at the communications compound the next day, Suust decided against sending out a hunting party, as they had done the night before.

Desido and Isleman were so physically worn out that it didn't take long for the two ill Marines to drift off into a very sound sleep.

Looking at their sleeping comrades, Tellson lit a cigarette, inhaled and exhaled. "You know they're turnin' into those things, don't you?" he asked without looking at Suust.

Frowning, the sergeant nodded his head. "Yeah, I'm afraid so, but I want to give them the benefit of the doubt. I won't let them turn, but I won't kill them till I know for sure."

"Come on, Sarge. Koy bit Desido and Isleman must have accidentally swallowed some of his blood, or he got bit and hasn't told us. Now, look. I don't know how you can catch this walking dead disease, or whatever it is, but they're showing the same symptoms that Koy did. I'm a Marine too, and the thought of killing one of my own turns my stomach the same as you, but these aren't ordinary circumstances. We have to protect ourselves, and if it means putting a fellow jarhead out of his misery, then we do it."

Suust was about to continue his argument against the execution of the two Marines when Isleman started vomiting. Instead, the sergeant just lowered his eyes and looked at the ground for a minute "Yeah, you're right."

"Hell yeah, I'm right. Look, you've known them longer than I have and you're closer to them than me. I'll do it for you if you want," Tellson offered with a combination of compassion and sadness in his voice.

Suust nodded his agreement slowly. A long moment passed in silence. "I know it probably isn't very wise, but I think we should keep traveling through the night once it's been done. I won't be able to stay here with their bodies."

"Whatever you think is best, Sarge. Why don't you start walking out of the clearing so that you don't have to see me do it. I'll catch up."

Suust turned his back and began walking off without acknowledging what the man said.

With his cigarette hanging out of his mouth, Tellson walked over to Private Isleman, who after vomiting, had passed out with the left side of his head laying in the vomit. Tellson placed the barrel of his weapon against Isleman's left ear and pulled the trigger. The top half of the man's head separated from the rest of his body in a shower of gore that coated the ground as well as Tellson's boots and the lower half of his legs.

The sniper then walked over to Corporal Desido, who was sleeping on his back. He placed the barrel of his weapon between the sleeping Marine's eyes and pulled the trigger. While Desido's head didn't separate into two pieces like Isleman's had, the eruption of gore and the resulting mess made the sniper confident that the man would be staying dead.

He grabbed the dog tags off of both Marines, slung his weapon over his shoulder, and ran to catch up with the sergeant.

Night became day, the two Marines walking in silence, occasionally running into more of the reanimated dead, which they gave true death quickly. After having had five of their companions die in the last few days, neither was in a cheerful state of mind and the hours they walked felt more like days.

They arrived on a hilltop above the valley in which the communications compound was located a little before 1200 hours. Sgt. Suust observed the compound through a pair of binoculars, while Tellson examined the compound through his rifle's scope.

"Well, what do you think?" Suust asked.

"I don't see anyone moving inside the compound, living or dead, but there sure are a lot of American and Nip dead moving around outside of it. Something about this gives me a bad feeling, but it's what we've come for and we have nowhere else to go. Might as well check it out."

The sergeant lowered the binoculars and held his rifle ready for immediate use. "Let's do this," he said and began walking down the hill slowly and cautiously, Tellson right behind him.

Fifteen minutes later they came upon an empty Japanese machine gun emplacement; it was covered in dried blood and bits of gore. They assumed the mess came from when their brother Marines had fought their way through this area to take the compound. Neither of them had any doubt that the Japanese soldiers that had manned the emplacement were still around somewhere, and still a danger to them.

They moved on and came to the gates of the compound, which were wide open—by the invading Americans or by the living dead, neither could tell who was last inside.

Once they were through the gate, Suust leaned toward Tellson. "I think it would be best if we split up. There's too much ground for two of us to cover if we stay together. We can always respond to the sound of gunfire if the other one gets into trouble."

Tellson motioned that he would take the left side of the compound and began moving off with his rifle raised.

Suust went the other way, and after five minutes of walking, came upon one of the undead eating a deer that had been unlucky enough to enter the compound. Strewn across the ground were inanimate bodies of Marines leftover from the battle that had raged here.

He placed the sights of his weapon on the back of the undead Marine's head, and was about to pull the trigger, when he felt a sharp pain above his right knee. Looking down, he discovered another undead Marine with no legs had crawled over to him and had bitten a large chunk out of his leg. Warm blood was already filling his boot.

Fighting the urge to vomit and cursing himself for assuming that every body on the ground was truly dead, he struggled to keep himself steady on his wounded leg.

He brought his weapon around to fire at the legless soldier, but paused when he heard the one eating the deer issue a scream. He looked just in time to see it lunge at him, tackling him and forcing Suust to the ground. He felt flesh rip off his face as the soldier bit into him, then more searing pain on his leg as the second corpse came back for seconds.

Knowing he was in a hopeless situation, Suust still fought against his attackers. Every time he knocked one of them away from him, it was quickly attacking again, biting him wherever the most convenient mouthful happened to be. Finally, the legless soldier bit into the front of his neck, opening a wide chasm that bubbled blood.

Sergeant Suust's eyes went wide with panic as he felt his life-blood pour down his neck and chest. In a matter of seconds, a numbing sensation overtook his body and he no longer felt any pain. Slowly, his vision faded to darkness.

Minutes later he rose up; he felt no pain, and the undead were no longer the enemy.

And he was hungry.

While Sgt. Suust went to his death, Tellson continued his inspection of the objective.

His first encounter with the dead came when he opened the door to one of the many buildings. Inside, he found over one hundred reanimated Japanese soldiers.

Even though he knew he was in danger, a part of his mind was rational enough to assume that this had been where his fellow

Marines had placed the bodies of the enemy soldiers they had killed during the assault.

They knew he was there in an instant and the collective hiss and battle cry they raised was enough to cause Tellson to urinate in his pants out of fear.

He turned around and ran from the building, leaving the door wide open. Soon, the undead occupants followed him as fast as they could.

He ran, unaware of the compound's layout; just wanting to escape, but his ignorance would prove to be his undoing.

His flight took him around several buildings as he attempted to lose his pursuers and soon found himself in a dead end.

Tellson turned to run again, but found his path blocked by a legion of the walking dead.

He knew there was no way for him to escape and he didn't have any desire to become one of the undead as they closed on him.

Instead of being eaten alive, Tellson placed the barrel of his weapon into his mouth, said a silent prayer for God to save his soul, and pulled the trigger, creating a crater where the back of his skull had been.

The wall behind him was covered in pieces of brain, blood and bone fragments.

OSIRIS

ADAM P. LEWIS

Josh couldn't close his eyelids. The muscles in his face were weakening. His heartbeat and breathing started to labor within his tightening chest. He fought to catch his breath but couldn't control his diaphragm.

The shirt he wore heaved up and down a little less with each drawn breath. His body was suffocating itself. Although he couldn't move or control his breathing, he could still smell, hear, feel and see.

He could feel the coldness of the hardwood floor seeping through his clothes and onto his skin. He could see the florescent bulb hanging from the ceiling and hear its electric hum. The constant staring into the bright core of the bulb burnt his eyes.

The burning sensation radiated from the back of eyeballs into his frontal lobe, creating a jabbing headache. He wanted to blink or at least look off to the side, but couldn't.

Whatever was happening to him became severe enough to hinder any movement no matter how slight.

The bittersweet scent of roses perfumed the room. On top of the roof, he could hear the pouring of rain splashing on the shingles. The noninvasive scents and sounds were pleasurable to him. They relaxed his mind, taking his worries away from the condition he'd awoken to.

From the corner of his left eye, he saw a vase filled with the roses. The vase was colored brown and decorated in red and green hieroglyphics. The walls were painted green and he saw two black and white photographs hanging above the vase.

One was of the Pyramids of Giza and the other the Sphinx. To his right he saw a coat rack standing next to a closed door. Behind the door, he heard muffled footsteps approaching on the opposite side. The footsteps grew louder with each step. They sounded as though they were headed towards the room where he was lying defenselessly on the floor.

All Josh could do in his vulnerable state was wait and hope that whoever was walking in his direction would open the door, find him, and get him the help he so desperately needed.

The doorknob turned and the door was pushed open. A person entered. Josh was unable to recognize who it was at the angle he was laying on the floor. All he could tell was that by the wide shoulders, musky cologne, and clothes the person wore, it was a man.

The man wore a gray overcoat with the collar flipped up. The coat was covered in dark speckles from the falling rain. A fedora crowned his head and was pulled down over his eyebrows that blocked any recognizable facial features. He wore dark-colored slacks and matching dress shoes with mud clinging to the soles.

The man turned his back to Josh, took off the fedora, and hung it on the coat rack. Next, he took off the coat and snapped it downwards. Drops of rain whipped off the coat and onto the floor. He hung the coat on the rack over the fedora.

"Help me, please," Josh begged. Only the words didn't come out of his mouth. The words were only a thought. His condition had turned him mute.

The man rifled through his coat and pulled out a large serrated knife from an inside pocket. Josh's heart skipped a beat when he saw the knife. He feared he was about to be stabbed to death. His weakened heart began to pound faster as what little adrenaline his body produced fought through his building weakness.

The man turned and bent over Josh with the knife raised over his head. His head and shoulders blocked the light. Only his silhouette was in Josh's view. Still, Josh couldn't make out who the man was until he said, "Hello, Josh."

It was Dr. Manning, the head of the archeology department at S.U.N.Y. Albany. "How is my favorite graduate student doing this term?" he asked with a smile, then lowered the knife and placed it next to Josh on the floor.

Unable to speak, moan, or grunt, Josh was silent. He cursed Dr. Manning to Hell.

"I'll translate that silence as you being stressed and underappreciated. Don't worry, Josh, you'll get the respect you deserve in due time. The undergrads just haven't warmed up to you yet. They will soon. They have to. You're going to be helping me teach them next semester," Dr Manning said.

Josh quickly took back his curse to Hell thought. Only high-spirited thoughts filled his mind. He was going to get the help he needed. He wasn't going to die on the floor. The close relationship with Dr. Manning that over the past few years had turned father-and-son-like was working to his advantage not just inside the walls of the college but outside them as well.

Dr. Manning held up his index finger and said, "Excuse me a minute. I have to go get something for you."

Dr. Manning exited the room, leaving the door open. Josh could hear the doctor's footsteps go in the opposite direction he'd arrived from. The footsteps stopped and seconds later were hammering the floor again. This time, they were barely audible as the sounds of squeaky wheels rumbled across the floor as well.

Dr. Manning pushed a metal gurney into the room and positioned it parallel to Josh's body. He then wedged his hands under

Josh's shoulders and lifted him onto the gurney. The metal was colder upon Josh's back than the hardwood floor. Josh's body couldn't form goosebumps from the cold shock because of the paralysis. However, he could feel a slow, cold shiver trickle down his spine and dissolve before it reached the middle of his back. His sense of touch was starting to cease.

Dr. Manning threw a blanket over Josh and pushed the gurney out of the room. As he wheeled Josh down the hallway, he said, "I suppose you're wondering how you got here in such a state. Well, to be frank about it, I poisoned your coffee this morning. It wasn't a strong dose, just enough to keep you alive for the time being."

Josh recalled the morning. He'd arrived on campus a few minutes after nine in the morning and had gone to Dr. Manning's office. There, fresh coffee was steaming in a pot. The doctor hadn't poured himself a cup. Josh found this odd as Dr. Manning drank coffee on a regular basis and consumed numerous cupfuls throughout the morning and well into the afternoon. The doctor ran on coffee as cars run on gas.

Sitting next to the pot, out of its normal resting area on the shelf below the coffeemaker, Josh's 'Howe Caverns' coffee mug rested, cleaned and ready for coffee to be poured into it. Normally the mug had a coffee stain from where the evaporated remnants of yesterday's coffee were.

He'd shrugged off the cleaned mug as something that one of the janitors may have done, and poured the coffee into it. He offered to pour a cup for the doctor but he'd refused by waving off the cup with his hand. Josh thought this was odd but didn't think much of it at the time.

After allowing the coffee to cool for a few minutes, Josh had taken a long sip and let out a long, exaggerated *ahhhh*. Minutes later, he'd felt ill and remembered asking Dr. Manning if he could leave early. Dr. Manning took the cup from Josh's hand, opened the office window, and dumped out the coffee. The last thing Josh remembered was losing total control over his body and passing out.

"Like I was saying, Josh, it's just enough to make you feel ill and ask if you could leave class early. I said yes and you accepted my ride to see your physician but you can tell we never went there. You recognize my house don't you?" Dr. Manning asked.

Josh wasn't paying attention to the hallway, he was now thinking about his live-in girlfriend, Claire, who he'd met during their freshmen year. She too was an archeology graduate student. Her course of study wasn't focused on Egyptian studies, it was focused on general archeology.

Josh was worried. Not just for himself but for Claire. She'd be a nervous wreck by now, not knowing where he was. She'd lost her father when she was ten-years-old to an automobile accident. Just the sound of screeching tires or a car horn made her clutch anything in sight in a death grip. Every day she worried that Josh wouldn't come home and she'd be asked to identify him at the hospital after he'd died in a car crash. Josh knew that was exactly what she was doing at the moment, worrying. If only she was thinking of something else.

Josh lost his train of thought and focused on listening to Dr. Manning. "The poison works slowly," he explained. "You'll soon drift into a coma and die. You won't feel a thing. The poison works similar to lethal injections that death row inmates receive. Though I can't promise you'll die soon after you become comatose like other students I've poisoned in the past. They got larger doses, you see. You remember them, don't you? You should. You studied their mummified bodies."

Disgust swept over Josh. He remembered x-raying, measuring, and documenting the mummies in past years. He knew they weren't actual Egyptian mummies. He thought those mummies were produced by those who gave their bodies to science upon their deaths. But now he knew the truth.

"As I was saying, you're lucky, unlike the past students. You can still see, feel, and hear everything that's going to happen to you. The others I just killed quickly. Do you know what's going to happen to you next?"

Dr. Manning stopped pushing the gurney and looked down into Josh's eyes and said, "You're going to be mummified, my boy. I bet you're just as excited as I am. The students who'll be studying you will be excited, too. I remember when you studied Steven Williams. You never knew that was a student of mine five years prior to your arrival on campus, did you. That information is irrelevant to you now though. As is recalling Osiris, the Egyptian deity of death and resurrection. He won't bring you back from the dead I'm sorry to say. Osiris is only a myth to explain how the world works when we don't understand its meanings."

Dr. Manning slapped Josh's shoulders and laughed, "I tricked you. I've got to admit though, Josh, I thought you would've figured it out. You're the smartest student I've ever had. Where'd I go wrong with you? I'm not sure, but that's neither here nor there. What is here and there is that as a student of mine, you know I wrote my thesis on mummification. I've touted my Egyptian expertise in vain during my lectures. Lucky for you, you're one of the few students who'll get to experience the process first hand and help your fellow alumni learn. Consider yourself lucky, my boy, many other students would die for you to get this opportunity." He laughed. "Other students would die for you. That's a nice play on words, isn't it?"

The gurney rolled from the warm and dry confines of Dr. Manning's house out into the cold and rainy outdoors. Raindrops fell into Josh's face and not once did his body produce an involuntary movement to keep the raindrops from hitting his open eyes. The raindrops pooled within his eyeballs and dripped down from the corners and over his cheeks as if he were crying.

Dr. Manning pushed Josh down the driveway and into a garage, where he opened and closed the garage door, turned on a light, and wheeled Josh under it. He then used sheers to cut into Josh's clothes and strip him naked.

"Now, my dear student," he said in a devilish tone, "the lesson begins. And I do hope you're taking mental notes. I wouldn't want you to forget anything you're about to learn tonight."

Josh's eyesight became hazy and grayed. Not from the raindrops that had washed over his eyes but from the paralysis. He could still see but only a few inches in front of his face. His thought process diminished to the extent that he could no longer think of Claire, Dr. Manning, or anyone else.

He could only perceive sounds, touches, and smells. And what he could smell was the dirt that covered the garage floor. He could hear the doctor shuffling across the dirt as he moved, and he could smell the sweet scent of roses lingering in the air.

"First, the Egyptians would bring the body to a tent they called an 'ibu', or 'place of purification.' They did so to begin the purification process of the body. Since I don't have a tent, my garage will work just fine," he said, dipping a sponge into a bucket of water.

He lifted the sponge, rang out the excess liquid, and began to clean Josh's body. Josh could barely feel the warmth of the water on his skin. He couldn't feel it at all on his legs, but as Dr. Manning moved the sponge closer to his chest, the more warmth he could feel. It was a welcomed feeling compared to the cold rain that had pelted his face and the metal table he was lying on.

"In case you're wondering, and you shouldn't because I know you're smarter than that. I'm not giving you a bath. You should already know that I'm cleansing your body," Dr. Manning said, ringing out the dirty water. "You should recall from my lectures that the embalmers would wash the body in palm wine and use a rinse from the Nile. Being that the river Nile is thousands of miles from here, I'm using water from the Hudson River. Oh, I'm not using palm wine either, I'm using Ivory soap because its 99.44% pure!"

He began to laugh, his eyes becoming teary from his horrid joke. "Sorry, Josh, Hudson River waters the best I could do on such short notice. I wasn't expecting to mummify one of my students so soon. I had another student in mind for mummification. Do you know Sara? She's that blonde dimwit who is barely passing my class. It should've been her lying here instead of you, but you decided to backstab me. I selected you for the graduate course and what did you do? After one year, you decided to transfer to another college because of Claire. She decided to take another graduate study program in Vermont and you both just couldn't be apart for months at a time."

After cleansing Josh's body, Dr. Manning picked up the serrated knife off the gurney. He held it under the light and checked the blade for nicks.

"Next the embalmer makes an incision on the left side of the corpse's body."

He pressed the blade into Josh's chest, making a horizontal incision leading from the ribcage to the pelvis.

Blood cascaded down Josh's torso and dripped off the table. He could *feel* the incision. It didn't feel like he was cut open, it felt more like a bee sting that quickly faded. Even the warm blood oozing from his side and pooling under the arch of his back was unnoticeable.

Dr. Manning stopped cutting and placed the knife on the gurney. "I want you to pay close attention to the next step, which is the removal of your organs. This is done because the organs are usually the first to decompose. I'll start with the intestines."

He inserted his hands into the cavity he'd created, grabbed the intestines, and before pulling them out, he paused. "You know what? I think I'll skip this step and do it later. Removing the brain is the most difficult. If I remove your organs first, you'll die before I can move on to the next step. I want you alive while I pick at your brain. Just like all those times you picked at my brain in and after class, asking questions about Egypt."

A long, thin metal prod came into Josh's view and inched towards his face. The tip was crimped into a V-shaped hook.

"Sorry, but I had to make this hook out of one of those metal coat hangers. Backstreet hookers use them for abortions I hear, so I figured I can use it to abort your brain." He chuckled again.

The prod inched closer and closer to his face until he felt the coldness of the hook insert into his right nostril. The hook expanded the nostril and crept up and between his eyes. Every centimeter the prod moved created an odd discomfort that took his mind off Claire and his demise. He felt the urge to sneeze or at least want to pick at the prod with his fingers. His body struggled to breathe and a sneeze was too much of an effort for his weakened body to create. There was no longer any feeling left in his arms; the tingling had stopped. Trying to raise his hand and pull the prod out would be his last daydream.

"The Egyptians had no concept of what the brain was capable of doing so they removed it. They thought the heart was the life source for the body," Dr. Manning said, giving the prod a hard push.

The prod jammed through Josh's front sinus cavity. Dr. Manning twisted the prod, pushing as he turned until a slight pop was heard, allowing the prod to continue into the brain. He moved the prod in an up and down sliding motion, in and out of Josh's brain.

"The embalmers mashed the brain like potatoes to make pulling out the brain through the nostrils easier. But those whose brains were removed were already dead, unlike you. If you weren't already paralyzed, you would be soon enough as I turn your brain into goop. Lucky for you, you'll be brain dead any second now. You'll never feel your brain oozing out from your nostrils and tickle your nose hairs. I'm sure that would be annoying and uncomfortable. That is, if it's anything like a long nose hair curling out from a nostril."

Josh's eyes glassed over and his chest stopped expanding as he died.

Dr. Manning removed the remainder of Josh's brain, followed by the organs. He then poured natron over the organs, wrapped them in cloth, and stuffed them back into Josh's body. Next, he buried Josh with natron to remove all remaining moisture.

Looking at the wooden box Josh was in, Dr. Manning stared down at his buried student, turned off the light and said, "I'll be right back; don't you go anywhere!" He laughed as he walked away.

A few minutes later, the garage door opened and the doctor wheeled in another gurney. This gurney had a woman lying on it. She was alive and paralyzed like Josh had been. He turned on the light and pushed the gurney underneath its pallid glow.

"Sorry, Claire, but I can't let you live," he said. "I have to mummify you, too. The police will be hanging around and asking questions about how Josh went missing and they'll ask me if I know anything about your disappearance as well. My response will be, 'Josh told me he was going to propose to Claire and elope. They must've done that. I know they went to Vegas last year for spring break. Maybe they went there to get hitched.' Does that sound convincing or should I work on it in a mirror? Maybe I shouldn't use the term 'hitched.' Who says that anymore? So, with the both of you missing, the cops will figure my story is legitimate. Your disappearances will be nothing more than two, love-crazed kids running away from life to get married. Ah, isn't love grand?"

Dr. Manning pressed the knife against Claire's skin. "Now don't move. You'll feel a slight prick."

After showering the blood from his body, Dr. Manning sat in his study and pulled up on the lever on the side of his Lay-Z-Boy. The footrest sprang out and hoisted his legs into the air.

He leaned back and took a sip of red wine, then let out a long sigh as he closed his eyes before taking another sip.

He opened his eyes and stared at his extensive collection of Egyptian decorations hanging on the walls. He began to think about his next class lecture, when his concentration was broken by a sound similar to a wet mop plopping onto tile flooring.

The sound traveled down the hallway leading to his study. A soft wet splash, followed by another, and then another, grew louder and more irregular as whatever was making the sound grew closer to the study.

He pushed his legs down on the footrest and locked it back into place inside the chair. He crept to the study door, pressed his ear against it, and listened to the splashing sounds.

They reminded him of footsteps. He focused longer on them and realized they were just that, wet footsteps not from one person but from two.

Underneath the wet footfalls, he began to hear voices. They were muffled, but as the people walking down his hallway got within ten feet off the study, he could decipher the voices just as he had over the years with Egyptian hieroglyphics.

"Dr. Manning—Dr. Manning," the voice repeated in a drawn out and gargled voice.

The doctor's eyes widened as he slowly stepped away from the door, "It can't be," he whispered, recognizing the voices.

His arm jerked in shock as a wet sounding *pop* smacked the study door. Wine spilt over the lip of the wine glass and trickled down his forearm.

"What do you want?" he asked, stuttering.

"Dr. Manning," the voices gurgled and the hinges on the door rattled with each wet smack against it, until the voice suddenly stopped calling his name.

He stepped forward, reached for the doorknob, squeezed it, and turned. He then gasped and jerked his hand back from the doorknob as he felt it turn in the opposite direction in his palm.

The door opened and the wine glass Dr. Manning held in his hands tipped over and spilt the remaining wine onto the floor. The glass followed after tumbling from between his fingers, shattering on the floor.

To the doctor's horror, standing in the doorway was the re-animated remains of Josh and Claire. Their bodies were caked with blood-stained natron that clung to their naked bodies.

The incisions on their torsos stretched with each step. The organs he'd removed, wrapped up and replaced wiggled free and fell to the floor.

He backed up and stumbled onto his Lay-Z-Boy ass first, "Osiris, why have your forsaken me?" he muttered.

He then raised his hands and held them in the 'stop' position, waving them back and forth. He wanted to beg and plead with Josh and Claire to stop but his vocal cords wouldn't work.

His hands then stopped waving as he froze in fright. All he could do was hear, see and smell.

He could hear Josh and Claire moan. They sounded starved and angry. He could see their pale skin and the lifeless expressions on their faces.

They were more disturbing than any mummy he'd come face to face with.

He could smell the rot perfuming from their wounds. It gagged him unlike it had in the garage. There he had roses near the gurneys and a fan to blow the stench in the opposite direction.

Josh and Claire lumbered forward. Their heavy footfalls smacked the flooring and their arms reached out for the doctor. When he was within reach, Josh and Claire grabbed his clothing and began ripping through his shirt.

Their fingernails scraped at the top layers of skin until it began to peel away. Blood seeped from the scraps and raw skin was exposed.

Dr. Manning, unlike Josh and Claire hours ago, was able to break through his frozen fear, and he screamed as the hands of the undead couple clawed at his body. Within seconds of his evisceration, his heart stopped.

Claire and Josh's fingers disappeared into Dr. Manning's abdomen until they were wrist deep into his gut. Josh yanked on the doctor's intestines and pulled pieces of them from the gaping wound as Claire tore open the torso.

The skin pulled apart like Velcro from the belly button to the neck.

Claire then chewed around the stomach, pulled it free and ate it. Bile dripped from her mouth and partially digested food plopped out to splash on the floor.

Josh raised his hands to his mouth and sucked his fingers clean, then reached into the doctor's torso and tugged free more sections of intestines.

Claire pried her fingers through the muscles and fat between the ribs until she was able to grab hold of the ribs and crack them free.

She raised a bloody rib to her mouth and wrapped her lips around the end, sucking the marrow from within.

Josh continued feeding on the lower organs. He ate through the intestines to the rectum where he fed on Dr. Manning's body waste until he reached the pelvis.

Once there, he scraped his fingernails along the bone and sucked his fingers clean before sinking his teeth into the thigh meat.

Josh and Claire continued feeding until all that remained of Dr. Manning's body was bone, hair and small flaps of skin.

WAKE THE DEAD

ANTHONY GIANGREGORIO

The dead man slept the slumber of oblivion.

Interred in his grave more than twenty years ago, he was lost to the ages, forgotten in the passage of time.

No one visited his grave as he lay rotting in the earth. His tombstone was covered with moss and lichen, the grass so high it nearly hid the crumbling marker.

The entire graveyard was a shambles, a dilapidated junkyard of discarded humans.

More than five years ago, the owner of the cemetery had gone under due to financial concerns and once the bank retained ownership, the land quickly fell into disrepair.

One year ago, a small housing development purchased the adjoining acres, and within six months new houses had sprouted up around the graveyard. There had been talk in the back hallways of City Hall of disinterring the bodies of the old cemetery so that even more homes could be built.

The bank wasn't complaining, for they wanted the money the land would provide and this was a world for the living after all, the dead were merely in the way of what many called 'progress.'

As the machinations of the living conducted themselves above ground, below in the cool soil, the dead man slept, cradled in Death's embrace.

His casket had given way to the animals and insects that thrived around him many years before. Worms crawled across his legs, some burrowing into his withered flesh. Rats clawed their way through the soft wood to then feed on bits of skin, nibblets of muscle and tendons.

Maggots were no more, as the flesh was now dry, but beetles still clung to the desiccated skin. The eyes were withered and dry, two dull orbs that for some miraculous reason had never been touched by the vermin seeking sustenance. The tongue also remained, shriveled and small but still lying within two layers of yellow teeth.

As the dead man lay rotting, a vibration began to seep into his casket. Similar to the drums of Africa, the cadence began to infect the cadaver, filling it with energy. Slowly, as the hours passed, the body began to become stronger. Flesh began to mend itself and muscles filled with strength.

The music never stopped, the steady cadence hitting the perfect frequency, as if some voodoo master was aspiring to some unholy ritual.

Slowly, ever so slowly, the zombie's eyes opened, the dry orbs now filled with dead-life. The irises were pure white, and almost seemed to glow in the darkness of his small tomb.

With what seemed like Herculean effort, the zombie raised his hands and began to explore his prison. Fingernails, now long from recessed skin, began to scratch at the moldy wood of the coffin, weakened from years of water damage. As time passed yet again, progress was made. An inch at a time, but slowly, the zombie began to free himself.

Sometimes the savage drums would stop. When that happened, the zombie would fall still, just another corpse in a graveyard of putrid remains, but soon the music would begin anew and the newly wakened zombie would once more begin his quest for freedom.

As the coffin was torn apart, wet soil cascaded into it, covering the zombie's chest, stifling it. But the dead don't need to breathe and once more the zombie would scratch and claw, making the hole wider, then digging a tunnel in the soft earth.

When enough of a hole was created, the ghoul began his upward climb. Halfway there, an infinite time having passed, the music stopped yet again.

With no drums to further the zombie's animation, the corpse stopped in mid-climb, sagging into the casket where it ended up half-in and half-out of his tomb.

The dead man didn't know how much time passed, but eventually the drums began again, and it was woken from his oblivion dream to start his journey to the surface once more.

How long it truly took was unknown. Weeks, months, perhaps years, but finally, like an earthworm waking in the early morning before even the bird is up, a withered, pale and cracked hand of dried flesh broke through the surface of the soil and into the air.

The hand slowly flexed and then slapped the hard-packed dirt. As it snaked along the ground, an arm began to appear, then the top of the head.

Blinking dirt from eyes that could barely see, the head popped free of the cold earth and then a shoulder. With both arms now free, the lower torso and legs were easy to pull loose of the sucking dirt that seemed to fight to hold onto its charge.

The dead man lay prone on the ground, staring up at the dark sky. Stars twinkled here and there, tiny jewels in the darkness. It was possible the zombie would have stayed there forever, content to gaze up at the stars, but the drums called him, forcing him to rise, to seek out their origin.

Standing was awkward, his legs unused for more than two decades, his feet bare. When the dead man had been interred, shoes weren't placed on his feet.

And why should they?

He was dead and the viewers at his wake were not able to see his footwear, and what dead man would need to go for a walk in the afterlife? Even socks were spared this dead man, for they were not needed either.

His toes curled back and forth, the soil squeezing between the digits. But it was reflex, for the dead man felt nothing such as pleasure…or pain.

But there was something deep inside him that filled him to the core. Hunger? Anguish? Perhaps even annoyance?

Deep within his fugue-filled mind, the drums beat, calling him ever onward.

His glazed eyes looked around him. The graveyard was silent, the moonlight casting it in a pallid glow. Only he had risen, the others all still slept the never-ending sleep.

A beetle crawled out of the animated corpse's nose and fell to the dirt to scurry off, while nightcrawlers slid from cracks in his skin.

Taking a halting step forward, the zombie began to walk. The first few steps were trepiditious, like a toddler taking those first hesitant steps into a new world of motion, but with each step, the dead man grew more confident.

He began to walk across the graveyard, passing tombstones much older than his own. A few pieces of dried flesh fell off his body to fall in his backtrail, but the zombie paid it no mind.

It took over an hour for the ghoul to reach the perimeter of the cemetery and stop at the gate to peer out at the outside world.

Only one house surrounding the graveyard was lit up, the moon high in the sky, denoting how late it was by human standards of time.

Grabbing the rusty wrought-iron gate, the bars cold within his even colder flesh, the zombie pushed the gate open.

There was no lock for it had disappeared years ago. There was no reason to lock the gate anyway, for many places in the wrought-iron fence surrounding the grounds had missing bars, so an adventurous spirit could easily gain access if they so choose.

This had happened on many occasions, evident by the cigarette butts, fast food wrappers and beer bottles littering the graveyard like fallen leaves. There was no caretaker either, for there was no money to pay for one.

The gates opened on equally rusty hinges, the creaking lost in the night.

The zombie took his first step out of his home and entered the world of living man, leaving the death and despair behind.

Moving faster now, the dead man headed straight for the house with the lights. Shadows could be seen moving past the windows, and as the living corpse grew closer, the drums never ceasing, the sounds of people laughing and talking came to his ears.

Upon crossing the street, headlights lit up the night as the dead man turned to face an oncoming car. The driver leaned on the horn and drove around the figure standing in the road, yelling as he passed the lone zombie.

Passing so fast, the driver never got a good look at the living dead man and was soon gone, brake lights fading into the night.

The dead man continued on his short journey until he reached the front door of the house. He could feel the bass of the drums right through his bare feet and it filled him with anger and rage.

The steady staccato was an abomination to music, and with rage filling his desiccated muscles, he reached out and pushed on the door.

With the strength of the grave, the door was pushed in, torn from its hinges, as if made of paper.

The dead man stood in the doorway, his glazed eyes taking in the party before him and registering that not one of the revelers had noticed him yet. None had seen or heard the door fall in, for all were drunk, high and the music too loud, thus masking the crash of wood connecting with the floor.

Pot smoke hung heavy in the air and one side of the room had a table filled with an assortment of alcohol. On another table, a large glass dish was filled to the brim with narcotics and barbiturates. On a table off to the side, three men and a woman did lines of cocaine on a mirror using a rolled-up hundred dollar bill.

The dead man entered the dwelling and gazed about.

A young white girl with half a shaved head, covered in tattoos, as well as wearing more earrings on one ear than any woman had a right to, walked by the dead man, a drink in her hand, her midriff showing thanks to the shirt she wore cut raggedly with scissors. Her bellybutton ring and the tramp stamp above her ass were in clear view also.

The dead man reached out and grabbed her head between his hands.

With one mighty yank, he tore her head off her shoulders, the rip of flesh and muscle slicing through the cacophony of bass and heavy music.

Holding the head in his hands, the body slumped over to land heavily, the jagged stump spitting blood that slathered the floor in crimson.

A partygoer, not yet knowing mayhem had happened behind him, stepped back and slipped on the blood. He went falling on his ass, the world turning upside down.

Then he looked up and saw the dead man and the severed head in his hands.

He screamed.

But only for a moment, for as he opened his mouth and yelled, a skeletal hand thrust itself into the open orifice, grasped his flailing yet pierced tongue, and tore it out. As the man began to choke on his own blood, his eyes went wide, nearly popping out of his head.

All revelry stopped then and each partygoer turned to face the walking dead man. Only the steady bass of the music continued to pound and fill the air with its annoyance.

The dead man hissed angrily, and before anyone could move, he dropped the severed head and reached for another reveler. A black man with a thick cornrow and gold teeth, his arms heavily tattooed, found himself the next victim.

Grasping the cornrow in one hand, the zombie pulled as hard as he could, tearing the scalp and half the black man's face off in one mighty heave.

A rictus of a smile was the man's new appearance, thanks to half his face being torn off. As he reached up and felt his missing skin, he ran off screaming.

Pandemonium ensued as everyone began screaming and tried to escape. But the zombie stood before the door, and as each one attempted to run by him, he took them down, one at a time.

Eyes were pulled from sockets and abdomens were sliced open with long fingernails that appeared to have grown after death.

Eviscerated bodies with viscera strewn about and limbs torn clean off screaming victims, became the theme of the party as one by one the guests were slaughtered. Limbs were used as bludgeons and intestines as garrotes.

By the time the zombie was through, not one person remained alive. Internal organs covered the floor, making a soggy, splashing sound as it settled.

The aroma of offal, blood and bile filled the air with its heady scent as the zombie stood and surveyed the carnage it had wrought.

A charnel house of corpses was now the decorations for this home, blood an inch deep from wall to wall.

The zombie hissed angrily as it turned to face the stereo lining the far wall. It was a massive machine with speakers towering to the ceiling.

The bass still filled the home and surrounding night with its insistence, and as the zombie went to it, his feet splashed in the still warm gore.

Three times the zombie slipped and fell on the slippery floor, and by the time the dead man reached the stereo, he was crawling on his hands and knees.

Coming to his feet once more, he reached out and grasped the stereo in his blood-covered hands. Picking up the main housing, he raised it over his head and smashed it to the floor, wanting to silence the infernal racket for good.

But the dead man wasn't done yet. He tore down the speakers, the wooden shells cracking and breaking as they hit the hardwood floor.

He tore out the speaker wires, tossing them away where they landed to be lost in the gore and blood covering the floor like a carpet.

When the last speaker was smashed, the drumbeat finally ceasing forever, all became silent once more.

Without so much as a backward glanced at the carnage, the dead man walked out the front door and back to the graveyard. Bloody footprints followed him for more than halfway before the blood simply ran out and the trail stopped completely.

The dead man even took a moment to close the wrought-iron gate behind him as he entered his home of more than twenty years.

Crossing the cemetery, the moon waxing down on his blood-covered form, he finally reached his final resting place and carefully climbed back into his hole.

He slid down inside, and began to cover up the hole with as much dirt as possible, wanting to reclaim what he'd lost.

As the last handful of dirt was dragged across the hole by the skeletal hand, the dead man opened his mouth to speak.

With withered vocal cords and a tongue that was nothing more than a dry muscle, the words were difficult to make out and were more than a hiss than true words.

"Damn rap music, loud enough to wake the dead."

If any ever came to visit the grave of this man, they would still be able to make out the inscription on the marker.

JOHN STILLMAN
1954-1991
FATHER
HUSBAND
COUNTRY MUSIC SINGER
HE MAY BE DEAD BUT HIS MUSIC LIVES ON

The hand was withdrawn into the earth. With the hole refilled, the dead man returned to the sleep of oblivion, the silence of the grave restored once more.

JESSI'S AWAKENING

SCOTT SHOYER

Run, just fucking run! she kept telling herself. *Don't look behind you; just run!*

She had no idea how long they were being chased. It felt like hours.

She looked to her right and could see him running next to her; the same look of panic and terror filled his eyes. How had things gotten this out of control? How had things gone so wrong? They were only trying to find some place safe to hole themselves up in until this...this what? 'Epidemic' was over.

But now they were running for their lives.

They could hear the footsteps behind them, and the moans. These *things* were determined and wouldn't give up until they either caught up to them or found new survivors to chase down.

How the hell are they so fast? she wondered.

Losing momentum, the desperate woman looked to her partner with pleading eyes. His mouth moved but the blood pounding in her ears made it impossible to make out his words.

Push goddamn it, push! she screamed inside her head. But physically she couldn't keep this pace up much longer.

She saw him turning towards a house and followed. Those things were getting closer.

Just a few more feet ... you can make it.

She pushed on harder.

The door to the house opened and she saw some figures waving them towards the house. More survivors.

Thank God, she thought as hope welled up inside her.

She could feel some distance growing between the things following her. Seeing that open door and the survivors gave her strength and re-energized her. As she ran past an abandoned car, she saw something move out of the corner of her eye. She tried to veer away but it was too late as the thing jumped towards her with extended arms.

She heard the others yelling her name and urging her on to get to the house.

The house was so close.

Without looking she knew that thing was behind her, wanting her. She could feel it's hot, sickly breath on her back and did the only thing she could—run.

She ran up the driveway and felt the thing's cold fingers on her. Approaching the house, she slowed down, as she dodged small shrubs and avoided loose stones.

The front door was so close.

She ran up the pathway to the door and saw the survivors' horrified looks. Her smile faded as she felt that thing's hand grab her shirt.

Her eyes opened in a primordial darkness. She wanted to move her body but was having trouble lifting her head. There was a dampness under her left hand.

Where the hell am I? she wondered. Confusion clouded her mind. She was having trouble focusing on any one thought.

My name…I can't remember, and this room. Why does my body hurt? Questions flooded her head but came and went as fast as the pain shooting through her body. A thought flashed through her mind like lightening in a dark sky.

Bolting upright into a sitting position, the blood rushed from her head, making her dizzy as she sat there trying to piece together how she wound up in this room. A familiar room, but she couldn't place it.

I was running away from something...they were chasing me. Her thoughts were as sluggish and slow in her mind as her tongue was in her mouth.

It was hard to focus on anything with the pain shooting through her body. She leaned back against the wall to keep from fainting and took a mental inventory of her body. Everything felt numb and hurt at the same time.

She panicked when she realized she couldn't feel her legs. Her hands found her knees and she was relieved to feel her legs moving around. They were moving but she couldn't feel them move.

She felt like she should be panicking but was just relieved her body was responding.

Her thoughts returned to being chased. She remembered running with other people. *Being chased...by a gang? Why were they chasing me...us? Where's the other person I was running with?*

She tried to call out in the dark room but couldn't find her voice. Her tongue was thick and heavy and her mouth was void of any moisture. She croaked out a few monosyllabic sounds, but even in the darkness she could feel that there was no one with her.

It was just her, the darkness, and her failed memory.

She placed her hands on the floor to get some leverage and felt something between her fingers. It took a lot of focus but her fingers finally wrapped around the object. Bringing it up to her eyes, it felt like it weighed a hundred pounds. It shifted in her hands and she thought she'd dropped it but felt it brush against her wrist.

It was a pendant hanging from a chain.

Deep in her numb and stagnant brain, something flickered. The pendant was a catalyst and a memory began to flash to the surface.

This is mine, she thought, not even realizing that her eyes were becoming more accustomed to the darkness. She realized the pendant was open. With fumbling fingers she found a picture inside. Two smiling faces looked back at her, happy and holding each other in a loving embrace. She ran her finger down the picture.

"Is that me?" she asked out loud, finding her voice raspy and faint? She winced as the words left her mouth. It felt like she'd swallowed a handful of razor blades.

The more she stared at the picture in the pendant the more she was convinced the woman staring back was her.

Is that my husband, she thought, deciding not to talk again? She searched for some moisture in her mouth to sooth her throat but was met with more razor blades.

Then, like a sliver of light that grows in the darkness, a memory flooded her mind. In it the woman in the picture (*that's me, right?*) was watching the television with a concerned look on her face. The man in the picture was there, too. He walked in from another room and sat down besides her (*me?*). They were intently watching some news show. Violence was erupting all around the city as roving gangs of...of...thugs? They were rioting in the streets. They weren't shattering windows and stealing things. They were attacking other people.

In a flash the memory faded and she was alone with her pain back in the dark room. The pain was fading into a warm pulsating feeling ebbing throughout her entire body. It almost felt...nice. She remembered that sticky dampness on her hand.

She brought her hand up to her face but the surrounding darkness prevented her from seeing anything.

But I saw the pendant.

She blinked hard to try and clear the fog in her head. She brought her hand closer to her nose and inhaled.

Blood.

Her mind raced as she tried to figure out if the blood was hers or...what? Someone else's? Maybe it belonged to the man in the picture? Her mind searched for answers and found none.

Her mind was not helping so she decided to eliminate other possibilities. She ran her hands over her body, searching for an injury. Her arms and legs felt bruised and sore, but there were no wounds. Her fingers ran through her tangled hair and found nothing. She sighed with relief, eliminating herself as the source of the blood.

But the question remained...

She leaned back against the wall and closed her eyes. She was tired but knew she couldn't sleep. Her mind raced but still couldn't settle upon any one thought. She felt the pressure of the wall on her back and tried to focus her mind on that. It seemed to work. The thousand thoughts racing through her mind slowly disappeared as the light of that faint memory slowly returned.

She remembered watching television with that man...her husband...again. Now they were huddled close together, holding each other as they watched the news program. They were both scared.

But I'm not scared now. Why were we scared? What was on the television? Where the hell is my husband?

An eerie calmness blanketed her body and when she opened her eyes she noticed she could see better. Her eyes were getting used to the darkness and faint shapes began to emerge from within it. She knew she wasn't in a large room, and now could feel just how small it was.

A loud noise erupted in the silence. It was followed by three more quick bangs. "Are you in there, Jessi?" a voice yelled through the door.

Jessi, she wondered. *Is that my name?* She was about to shout something back but a voice deep inside warned her that it was better to stay silent.

"Come on, Jessi," the voice repeated, this time sounding angry. "Just let us know if you're in there."

Us...he said 'us,' she thought.

She closed her eyes and more memories slowly flooded her mind. She was with that man again but this time they weren't watching television. They were in the bedroom throwing clothes into bags. The man went to the dresser and groped around the top. He pulled something down wrapped in a towel and laid it on the bed and unwrapped it. It was a shotgun. He found two boxes of shells, loaded the gun and put the remaining shells into the bag with the clothes.

Her eyes shot open. *We were running away...we were in danger. There was...*

But her thoughts faded away. Her foggy mind was trying to put all th*e pieces together. The pendant; her and that man* (my husband?) watching the riots on the news, packing duffle bags and taking a gun, the banging on the door. The dots were there but she couldn't connect them.

She attempted to stand and found her legs to be knotted up in tight cramps. Stretching them out sent excruciating pain shooting through her body.

Pressing her back against the wall, she used her legs to push herself up into a standing position. It felt like all the blood rushed out of her limbs and settled into her feet. She became dizzy again and inhaled deeply. Nausea swept through her body as she threw up. She leaned over as bile and other fluids left her body. There wasn't much in her stomach and she was soon dry heaving.

"I think she's in there," she heard someone say on the other side of the wall. Then there was more banging on the door.

"Damn it, Jessi, are you in there?" the original voice from before yelled out.

"Just break down the fucking door," the second male voice said.

"Calm down, Tommy. We might be in this house for a while," the first voice said. "Last thing we need to do is start breaking it apart. We need all the protection we can get."

Tommy shook his head in agreement. Then the first man turned his attention back to the door: "If you're in there, Jessi, just give me some kind of signal. Are you hurt? We can help you."

Jessi stood in complete silence. *But what if I'm not Jessi? What if they were the people I was running away from? Why can't I remember anything,* she wondered, growing more frustrated.

With the pain ebbing out of her stiff limbs and nausea fading away, she could once again re-focus her attention to her surroundings. Looming in front of her was a car. She realized she was in a garage and tried to force her mind to remember how she got there.

She took a hesitant step forward to test her legs. They were still numb but were at least listening to the impulses coming from her brain. After walking a few feet to the car, she rested her palms on its hood. She could feel the pressure of the car under her palms, but couldn't feel if it was hot or cold.

Do I have some kind of brain damage? But she disregarded the thought, remembering that her hands had found no head injuries during her body search.

She shuffled her feet to the door. The men on the other side weren't there anymore. Reaching up to rub her throat, she realized the pendant was still wrapped around her hand. She stared at it, the pendant evoking another memory.

They were running now. She and...her husband...were running down the street. The memory was fuzzy but she remembered being chased. They left the house and were getting into a car in the driveway (*my car?*) when they were attacked. A group of people, seemingly coming out of nowhere, were reaching and groping for them. Her husband panicked and dropped the keys. His fight or flight instinct kicked in and he grabbed her hand and started running.

"Where are we going?" she cried out in her memory. But her husband (*yes, I'm positive that's my husband*) just looked at her.

"We need to find some shelter!" he yelled to her.

That voice...that's the same voice. Her mind was slowly putting the pieces together. *My husband's on the other side of that door.* She walked to the door leading into the house, but something inside stopped her. Something urged her to stop; something was telling her there was danger on the other side of the door.

She stood still in the middle of the garage, just listening. The darkness embraced her like a lover. A strange sensation began in her nose as she realized she could actually smell her husband and the others in the house.

They were all huddled together in one room, no doubt trying to figure out what was going on just like she was.

On occasion one of the group members would either walk away from the larger group or join them from another part of the house.

How the hell can I know this? she asked herself. But she wasn't scared anymore; she felt...good...strong.

Her body still had no feeling but she was regaining control over her movements. Plus she was starting to feel hungry. She tried to remember the last time she'd ate but gave up on trying to recall such a small thought, only the same urge that stopped her from going to the door was also telling her that some food would make her feel better.

Food, in fact, would make everything better.

Maybe it's time to rejoin the others, she thought.

She began walking to the door but stopped walking as the voice inside told her that was a bad idea.

Six hours earlier.

Jessi and Rick were stunned as they watched the news coverage. Reporters were calling it the worst riots the city had ever seen. When the news started getting out about the rioting and looting, Rick had called Jessi at work and told her to get home immediately.

"...All over the streets as the police attempt to end this wave of violence," the reporter on the news said. "The disturbance started about an hour and a half ago and very quickly escalated into a full blown riot... "

They could hear the fear in his voice. Jessi and Rick looked at each other suspiciously. The screen changed to a picture of downtown and none of the store fronts looked vandalized in any way. The rioters weren't looking for inanimate things.

The cameraman pointed his camera down the littered road as policemen in full riot gear stormed past, telling him to get out of the way and get to a safe place.

Jessi and Rick were sitting close on the couch, holding each other's hands.

The cameraman found something off in the distance and tried to focus on it. Jessi and Rick squinted and moved closer to the television set as they tried to focus their eyes on the blurry figures in the background.

The figures were getting closer to the cameraman, who stood his ground.

"What the fu..." Rick started to say but was cut off by Jessi screaming and burying her head in his shoulder.

The blurry figures came into view. They were walking funny; not really limping, but almost like they were shuffling their feet. They were also moving pretty damn fast. It was a large pack of rioters and the four up front had a determined look in their eyes. They were focused on reaching the cameraman. They had an almost dead-like stare as they looked straight into the camera.

The cameraman didn't move.

As they got closer, Jessi raised her head from Rick's shoulder and everything seemed to flash into slow motion. The four rioters approaching the cameraman were bloody. Not some streaks of blood here and there; they were covered in blood and had what looked like pieces of flesh dangling from their hands and stuck in their teeth.

They got closer to the cameraman and he stuck his hand out from behind the camera to push the lead rioter away. The rioter violently grabbed the cameraman's hand and bit off three fingers. Screams filled the screen as the other rioters pulled him down to the ground. The TV went black but the screams echoed through the speakers.

The feed switched back to the newscaster in the studio.

"Folks," the newscaster said, "I'm not sure what we just saw, but the police have declared Martial Law and are requiring everyone to stay inside their homes. The National Guard has been called in..."

Rick grabbed Jessi by the shoulders. "Those aren't fucking rioters, Jessi," he said trying to remain calm.

Jessi's eyes were wide as she turned to Rick. "What's going on?" she asked.

"I think it's that virus, Jessi. I think the virus that's been making all those people sick is causing this."

It seemed as if Rick was trying to convince himself as much as her.

"Come on, honey," he said as he suddenly stood up, grabbing her hand. "We're getting the fuck out of here."

The present.

Oh my God, Jessi thought. *They're infected. I need to figure out how the hell to get out of this garage.*

But she knew the only way out was either going through the house, where she'd be seen, or to open the garage door, which would make a lot of noise.

She was stuck—trapped.

Standing with her hands still on the hood of the car, she remained unusually calm.

Think damn it, she told herself. Out of frustration and fear she balled up both her fists and slammed them on the hood of the car. The noise echoed all around the empty garage. Pounding on the hood of the car two more times she heard something crack in her left hand. 'Heard,' but didn't feel it.

Looking at the car, she saw two deep dents in the hood. She stood wide-eyed, staring at the damage and wondering why she hadn't felt anything. Rubbing her left hand she knew something wasn't right. She winced, seeing that she'd broken two bones in her hand.

"I'm telling you that I fucking heard something in the garage, Rick," Tommy said as the two approached the door.

"We've banged on the door twice," Rick reasoned, "and no one answered. If she was in there she would've said something."

Jessi moved the broken bones around in her left hand and could see where a portion of the bone was pressed up against her flesh. She picked at the spot with her right index finger until the flesh opened.

There was a slight trickle of blood that ran down and off her left palm. She scratched at the spot more aggressively.

She ran so hard to reach that front door. It wasn't fair. Rick reached the door and there were several other survivors in the house...six, if she wasn't mistaken. What had happened?

She fingered the small bone that protruded from the growing wound on her hand. Staring at the small bone, it looked foreign, as though it didn't belong inside her. It also didn't hurt.

She grasped a small flap of skin and slowly peeled it back, exposing more of the bone. Blood pooled up like molasses and dripped away from the wound.

Shouldn't there be more blood? she thought, staring at the gaping wound.

Pressing down, she attempted to reconnect the snapped bone in her hand. She continued to tear away pieces of skin, peeling them back away from the wound as if she were peeling some grotesque banana. One strip of flesh tore midway up her forearm.

But there still wasn't any pain.

The looks of the people standing in the doorway should have been different. They should have been happy she'd made it; happy to welcome her into the house of survivors. But instead they looked sad...horrified even...

Her entire hand was stripped of flesh. Torn pieces of skin dangled as she continued to play with the broken bone. She had laser-like focus on the snapped bone and didn't even jump when the banging at the door started up again.

"Jessi! Jessi! We...I know you're in there. Please open the door and let me in," pleaded the familiar voice on the other side of the door.

Jessi looked at the door. To prove that the bone couldn't possibly be hers (*I'd be in tremendous pain right now, right?*), she gripped it between the fingers of her other hand and yanked it. There was a small snap as she tore the bone out of her hand. There was still no pain.

As her hand reached for the survivors standing in the doorway, she could feel the tug on her shirt. That thing had gotten a hold of her!

"Damn it, Jessi," the voice behind the door was getting angry. "Don't make us break down the door. We only want to help you and see if you're okay." The voice softened a little. "I love you, Jessi, and only want to help you."

She heard the others mumbling incoherently. They were arguing with Rick.

She let the snapped bone slip from her fingers and heard the faint click as it hit the cement floor. She walked to the side of the car and adjusted the side view mirror so it faced upwards.

She glanced in the mirror.

She twisted as the thing grabbed her shirt but there was no shaking it. The thing's desire to have her was obviously stronger than her desire to be rid of it. Everything seemed to be in slow motion as she watched the others retract their hands. It seemed that the more firm the thing's grip on her got, the survivor's hands moved further away from her.

She then felt the thing's other hand grip her shirt and start to pull her down. She started to lose her balance...

Jessi looked hesitantly into the side view mirror. The banging and screaming on the door seemed to fade into the background. Her torn apart hand had stopped oozing blood already. Flaps of pale skin dangled from the hand and she caught a whiff of what smelled like rotten flesh.

The banging on the garage door was louder and more violent. They were using something other than their fists; they were tearing down the door.

She was falling to the ground. Panic filled her eyes. She knew that if she lost her balance, it was all over. But it was too late.

She could feel the weight of the thing...the undead thing, on her back. She fell face first onto the ground, feeling the cool grass against her scalp.

The undead thing landed on top of her. A white hot pain shot through her entire body as it sank its teeth into her...

Jessi stared at the black circles under her eyes and her pale skin. She didn't recognize the face staring back and turned around to see if someone was standing behind her.

Two more loud bangs came from the garage door, two more violent sounds of the doorframe cracking.

She lifted up her shirt and found more pale, lifeless skin. She slowly turned around. Black-looking veins and bruises traveled all around her body like a twisted road map. Her hand brushed against something on the back of her left shoulder. She removed her shirt and slowly leaned down to try and see what it was in the mirror.

Her head was swimming in a fog as she felt the undead thing rip away a chunk of flesh from her shoulder. She looked up to see the survivors retreating into the house. They were just going to leave her out there. She knew if she didn't make it into the house before they closed the door she'd be trapped outside with that thing.

She fought back a wave of unconsciousness and pushed herself up, knocking the undead thing off her back. Her attacker was caught off guard and rolled away.

She ran towards the quickly closing front door. The undead thing seemed happy enough chewing on the chunk of flesh it had torn from her left shoulder...

Jessi saw the large chunk of flesh torn out of her left shoulder. Something deep inside of her wanted to scream, but she knew it was pointless.

She threw herself at the closing front door head first and managed to squeeze her way into the house. She didn't know if the undead bite or crashing head first into the door made her dizzy but she knew she was going to pass out.

She stood up quickly before unconsciousness took her and looked frantically around the house. The others were frozen in place with terrified looks in their eyes. She started running through the house, looking for sanctuary from both the undead and the survivors.

No one was following her. Not even Rick.

'They'll expect me to run upstairs...' she remembered thinking.

She found a door in the back of the house through the kitchen. She opened it as quietly as she could, expecting it to lead back outside, but found the darkness of the garage.

Closing the door behind her, Jessi thought she'd rest for a second, maybe take a little nap, then rejoin the others after they had a chance to calm down.

She found a large flattened down cardboard box and laid down.

'I'm just gonna rest my head and take a quick little nap.'

Her eyes closed.

She was fingering the deep gash on her left shoulder when the garage door splintered one last time and flew off its hinges. Rick and the others came barging into the garage, flicking the lights on.

Jessi winced as the light penetrated her eyes, feeling like a million little needles.

Rick quickly turned his head in disgust.

Standing there shirtless and fingering a deep gash on her left shoulder, he barely recognized the thing as his wife, Jessi. He looked down to see her other hand was completely devoid of flesh.

Jessi looked at him through dead eyes, feeling she should recognize the man, but the only thing she felt was hunger. She dropped her hand from her shoulder and lunged forward.

A shot rang out and Jessi felt herself hit the ground. There was a burning sensation that started between her eyes and slowly engulfed her entire head in a searing white hot pain.

Her brain felt like it was on fire as the bullet searched for an exit and found one. She lay on the garage floor and watched as everything around her slowly faded away into a primordial darkness.

She smiled, happy that the last thing she'd experience would be to feel something again.

ABOUT THE WRITERS

Jeremiah Coe lives in Portage, Michigan. His novels are The Dead of Space Book One: Brave New World and Book Two: Journey's End and Here Comes Santa. He has also authored several short stories and has created and written a vampire web series that can be watched for free.

Go to www.transitionstheseries.com.

Contact him at facebook.com/jeremiah.coe or you can email him at jeremiah_coe@yahoo.com.

Michael C. Dick was born in Buffalo, New York and currently lives in Northern Virginia with his Wife, Michele and two children, Marissa and Michael Jr. along with an assortment of animals. His stories have been published in several anthologies and if you wish to read more please visit him on his blog at michaelcdick.blogspot.com and become one of his followers.

P. A. Douglas is a nationally touring singer-song writer, and author living in Texas. His debut novel "The End: A Zombie Novel" was published in 2011 by Living dead Press. To hear music and learn more about the author, visit www.indie-inside.com

Anthony Giangregorio is the author of 38 novels, almost all of them about zombies and has edited over 25 anthologies.

His work has appeared in Dead Science by Coscomentertainment, Dead Worlds: Undead Stories Volumes 1-7, and Wolves of War by Library of the Living Dead Press. He also has stories in End of Days: An Apocalyptic Anthology Vol. 1-5, the Book of the Dead series Vol. 1-6 by LDP, Zombie Zoology by Severed Press, and two anthologies with Pill Hill Press.

He is also the creator of the popular action/zombie series titled Deadwater and his action/ horror novel Dead Rage is being optioned for a movie. Check out his website at www.undeadpress.com.

Aaron Gudmunson was born in Belize while his parents volunteered for the Peace Corps. He lives and writes in the Chicago area. He has had fiction and essays published in numerous outlets including Apex Horror and Science Fiction, Doorways Magazine, Withersin, and Theatre of Decay. He has been writing since able to hold a pen.

Dane T. Hatchell lives in Baton Rouge, LA. He has stories appearing in over fifteen different anthologies from Living Dead Press. You can contact Dane at Enadious@gmail.com.

Kelly M. Hudson was born in Kentucky and currently resides in California. He loves horror and has over a dozen stories published in various anthologies, as well as a novel called The Turning published by Living Dead Press and available on Amazon.com and other places. If you wish to know more about Kelly, please visit his website www.kellymhudson.com for links to other stories and news.

Adam P. Lewis is an author within the horror genre. He has written numerous short stories, essays, and reviews published by Wicked East Press, Pill Hill Press, Living Dead Press, Static Movement, Dark Quest Books, and Ambrotos Press. For more information follow Adam P. Lewis at http://www.facebook.com/adamlewis518.

Darren WJ Mills resides in the UK and discovered his passion for horror and the written word at a very young age. His zombie novel, "The Unnatural Dead" is published by Living Dead Press. He's the creator of www.theworldofhorror.com, where he has a homepage as an author, and writes horror articles and reviews as one fifth of a handpicked team. He can also be found on Facebook under the website name, under Unnatural Dead and himself. Look for the sequel to The Unnatural Dead coming soon.

Bennie L. Newsome was born and raised in Birmingham, Alabama where he currently resides. He considers himself to be a humorous and unique person; therefore, he strives to instill those traits in his work. Bennie's first publication, a short story entitled Summer Assignment (anthology: Chivalry is Dead), appeared in June 2011 making him a relatively new author. More of his publications and their sources can be found at www.bnewsome.yolasite.com

Suzanne Robb's debut novel Z-Boat will be released by Twisted Library Press, under their Lbrary of the Living Dead Imprint. Her stories are in current and upcoming anthologies with Coscom Entertainment, Pill Hill Press, Wicked East Press, Rymfire eBooks, Library of the Living Dead, Library of Fantasy, Norgus Press, May December Publications, Living Dead Press, Panic Press, Hidden Thoughts Press, and Static Movement. In her free time she reads, watches movies, plays with her dog, and enjoys chocolate and Legos.

Scott Shoyer is a long time horror fan ever since seeing The Last House on the Left and Cannibal Ferox at the tender age of nine.

He runs the popular website http://www.anythinghorror.com and has short stories published in various horror anthologies and is editing his first zombie novel for publication. He lives in Austin, TX and can be contacted at the following address: anythinghorrorscott@gmail.com

Rebecca Snow lives in Virginia with her husband and a small herd of inherited cats for inspiration. Her fiction can be found in various anthologies from Books of the Dead Press, May December Publications, Library of the Living Dead, Static Press, and Pill Hill Press. She has a Bigfoot lure in the backyard and plans to teach him how to do yard work and brush cats. You can find her on Facebook (look for the bloody hand print) and Twitter @cemeteryflower and at cemeteryflower.blog.com

Alan Spencer is a horror author from Kansas City. His novels include "The Body Cartel," "Ashes in Her Eyes," "Inside the Perimeter: Scavengers of the Dead," and "Zombies and Power Tools"—The last two published by Living Dead Press. Keep an eye out for his forthcoming book "Cider Mill Vampires." Seek him on Facebook or e-mail him at: alanspencer26@hotmail.com

ZOMBIES, MONSTERS, CREATURES OF THE NIGHT

OPEN CASKET PRESS

OPEN CASKET PRESS.COM

THE NEW NAME IN HORROR